PAGEPICKUP

MW01104246

DANCING ON GLASS

Susan Taylor Chehak

Dancing on GLASS

TICKNOR & FIELDS

NEW YORK   1993

For information about permission to reproduce selections from this book,
write to Permissions, Ticknor & Fields, 215 Park Avenue South, New York,
New York 10003.

Library of Congress Cataloging-in-Publication Data
Chehak, Susan Taylor.
Dancing on glass / Susan Taylor Chehak.
p.   cm.
ISBN 0-395-60198-3
I. Title.
PS3553.H34875D34   1993   92-21185
813'.54 — dc20   CIP

BP 10 9 8 7 6 5 4 3 2 1

Book design by Melodie Wertelet

For Parker and Jesse

ONE

I N THE SODDEN HEAT AND THE HEAVY SWELTER OF
the warmest evening of the hottest summer, in Iowa, in
the middle of July — a semiformal dinner dance, at the
country club, in Cedar Hill. Outside, past the shimmer
of window glass, a glowing hover of low-hanging haze. A
ribbon of flat green fairway rolling down toward the darker
gash of a running creek. A throng of trees shot with the sparkle of fireflies. Inside, a crowded ballroom, the press of
dancers and diners and drinkers, round tables draped in cloths
of white damask, the heads of thick-petaled flowers nodding
on stems in crystal vases, heavy-handled silverware, gilt-
edged china, the glass-and-flame cascade of a chandelier.

A waiter's black hair, glossy with brilliantine and sweat; a
woman in a silvery dress rolling her hips and snapping her
fingers behind the microphone on the carpeted platform of a
makeshift stage. Head lolling back, throat exposed. Behind
her, a bald man in a green tuxedo bending over a piano. Girls
in strapless dresses dancing, rolling their bare shoulders,

swinging their full skirts below their pinched waists. A zipper running straight up the long slope of a woman's back to twine between the angled rise of her shoulder blades. A pearl necklace nestled against the dip and swell of a collarbone. A pair of silk shoes with bows on the toes — their fabric dyed to match the fragile green stems of the flowers that bloom within the shadowy folds and pleats of a long print dress. Men in shirts so white they seem to glow, their collars stiff with starch, their cuffs hard and straight as cardboard at their wrists. The rich curl and turn of a paisley tie. A madras plaid jacket. Square shoulders, navy blazers, bright brass buttons, the pale blue ripple and crease of a seersucker suit.

Loud laughter rolls from a table in the corner, where three young men are leaning in closer to an older woman whose hair has been packed like a yellowy gauze against her skull. A fist is slammed down on another table — goblets shudder, water is sloshed.

And Katherine Von Vechten is reaching out to curl her hand around her husband's arm. She nuzzles Bader's shoulder, moves her cheek against its roll, and he tenses under the pressure of her touch. His face is shining. Out in the crush of the dance floor, he holds her, lining the hard length of his body up to the softer stretch of hers. He is her husband, and she reveals their intimacy through the placement of her hands.

She slips away from Bader, moving through a pause in the music, through a crowd that opens up a path in its midst for her. At the table, he sits close to her. Katherine's skin is as silky and white as the damask napkin that she's unfolded in her lap. He reaches out and yanks the diamond-studded gold barrette from the nest of her hair, and he watches its brown cascade, rippling like a river down her back.

Katherine Von Vechten, laughing. Katherine sipping vodka through a thin green straw. Bader fidgeting. His face florid, painfully red. He's unbuttoned his collar, and, stretching his neck, he tugs at the knot of his tie. When he spreads his hands against the tablecloth, they look to him to be as coarse and raw and heavy as slabs of meat laid out on a fold of butcher paper. The vodka in the tiny fluted cavity of Katherine's crystal goblet is cold and sharp and clear; a sunken olive swims near the stem.

Katherine tapping her long fingernails. Her laughter holds the hollow sound of ice cubes rattled against glass. She fiddles with the platinum chain that's looped in the hollow of her throat. The diamonds in her earrings glint in the candlelight, bright and cold and sharp as stars.

But Bader's own restlessness is turning in his stomach; it squirms in his throat, and he's afraid that it might begin to strangle him. What's wrong? Well, for one thing, the heat.

"I can't stand this anymore," Katherine is saying. He looks at her with lowered chin and hooded eyes, and he wants to ask her, What? She can't stand what anymore? The heat? The noise? Her life? Him?

"It's killing me," she sighs, and he wonders whether he's heard her right. "You're killing me." Is that what she's said? Music and movement roar in his ears.

He dips his fingers into her drink. He dabbles at her temples with the melting chips of ice. He fans her face with the sweep of his hand.

Katherine is standing, and she's pulling on Bader's arm. They've separated themselves from the swelter of the crowd, moving out of its tumult and its din — so many bodies writhing into the beat of the music, turning on the glassy surface of the ballroom floor. Katherine leads the way, and Bader winds behind her, following along the opening she's made for him, through the dancing throng. She threads a tunnel toward the exit; her arm is stretched out behind her, with Bader's hand clasped over hers. Her hand is like a fluttering, soft spirit that he's somehow managed to capture, for the moment, in the pocket of his palm.

Katherine has brought Bader out of the crowd, through the arched doorway and into the hushed formality of the club's front room. And then he's seated on the velvet cushion of a reading chair. His feet have been planted side by side on the deep pile of the carpet as he leans forward toward his wife with his elbows on his knees, his hands hanging, long thin fingers curled into fists. When he says to her, "I love you," she looks at him and asks, "Do you?" Her eyes are solemn, steady, openly regarding him, waiting for him to answer. He returns her look, and he smiles, and he shakes his head. He reaches across the space between them to touch her shoulder, to take her hands, to pull her body over onto his. He brushes away a strand of her hair with the flange of his thumb. Her dress is a shimmery blue, deep as midnight, held up over the billow of her breasts by thin straps that wrap her shoulders and squeeze her flesh. Her skin shines, white and smooth as glazed snow.

Katherine is drunk. She wavers, perched on the ledge of Bader's knee, so slight that she seems to be almost weightless there. When she lets her head fall back, her long hair purls. She closes her eyes, wags her head to the music, dim, swings her leg. The single stone on the platinum chain around her neck, an opal, flames.

"Let's go," he whispers, his lips brushing the hard curved folds of her ear.

She smiles, ducks her head. "This way," she says.

And then Katherine is ahead of him, with her hands clutched and folded, prayerlike, against her throat, under her chin. Bader's knuckles prod her from behind. His fist is a hard ball that rolls in the small of her back.

The sharp points of Katherine's heels peck at the cream-colored carpet and leave a serpentine trail of dime-sized circles in its pile. To a stairway, half hidden, in the corner, leading off and up into some strange darkness beyond. The wall on one side of the staircase is lined with framed botanical

prints — halved apples and apricots, cherry blossoms, fir
trees, water lilies, pomegranates, and palms.

Bader follows Katherine. Her laughter bubbles upward.
He stops her, turns her toward him, presses her back against
the wall, and kisses her. A picture has come off its nail; it
slides down behind her and crashes on the stairs. The glass is
cracked, shattered, scattered over the carpeting like cold,
bright chips of ice. Startled, Katherine has tripped away from
him.

The corridor at the landing is narrow and long, brightened
by a moonstruck bank of paned glass windows, laced with
the leaves and curled stems of ivy that struggle up the brick
walls and burrow for a foothold in the wood of the ledges
outside. Katherine staggers, puts out a hand, pecks at the
window glass with her nails.

At the end of the hall, a door. Bader has stopped, but
Katherine insists, she drags him on. She pulls at him, wob-
bling on her high heels. This is her idea, then, not his. That's
an important point, one that he'll remember, later, to make.

"It wasn't my idea," he'll hear himself say, his voice rising. "It was hers."

She's tugging at the hem of her dress. She's curled her
hand around the glass knob, and she's turning it, and at
her urging, the door swings away and opens silently, in-
wardly, in.

"Katherine, I don't think . . . ," Bader has begun, or has
he? Does he try to stop her? Does he try to talk her out of it?
Does he reach to pull her back? He won't remember. He
won't know. His voice trails off, words drifting, drowned
out by the roaring in his ears and the faint music that's playing, muffled, far away and dim. She's stepped away from
him, over the threshold into the empty room. Her laughter
echoes ahead of her, and then it comes rushing back to him.
At her feet, the floor is like a glowing stage, lit from below.
And in it, shadows, dancing.

The sputter of Katherine's high heels is a hollow sound, like the tap of a fingernail on slate, or the gentle tinkle of silver on glass, and Bader's hand, sweeping the wall inside the door, finds a light switch. He nudges it upward, and flips it on.

And then he understands where they've come.

There, outside that closet, at the top of those stairs, at the end of that hall. In a room that had been safely sealed off during the first remodeling of the Cedar Hill Country Club, when the roof was raised over the ballroom and a third story built up on top. Money saved, pennies pinched — instead of boarding over the old skylights above the dance floor, the carpenters simply enclosed them in closets, behind what were supposed to be closed and locked and bolted doors.

But this one was not closed. And it was not locked. It was not bolted. It yawned. It gaped. It was a trick. It was a trap set to catch Mr. and Mrs. Bader Von Vechten, to ensnare the two of them, in different ways, but both at once.

Bader lurched forward to grab hold of Katherine and snatch her back to him, but, too late, already she'd tripped nimbly beyond his grasp. Slight and quick, she turned, and she spun. She was walking on the surface of a mirror. She was dancing on a skylight; she was turning on a floor that was made out of glass.

Bader's fingers tangled briefly in the smoky mist of her hair as Katherine, blinded by the glare of the overhead bulb, slipped farther from his reach — her long legs, her high heels, her tippytoes, as dainty as a water spider stepping gingerly across the sticky, taut surface of a pond. And then, abruptly aware of where she was, her impossible position, she stopped. She froze.

"Hush, Katherine," Bader whispered. As if sound were weight. "Don't move," he said. "Don't breathe."

He stretched his hands out toward her, his palms up, his fingers spread to prop the void around her and contain her in that vacuum of empty space, levitate and hold her there before him, weightless, suspended in thin air.

Her dress hissed against her body as she lifted up one foot, daintily. She spread her arms and raised her hands. Her skin seemed so white it would burn his eyes and blind him, like a hillside glare of sun-reflected snow. She dropped her chin and eyed the pointed toe of her shoe against the plane of frosted glass that shimmered with shadows and light from the swirl of movement on the crowded dance floor below. She raised her eyes, and she smiled at Bader. She lifted first one foot and then the other. She twirled, wobbled, regained her balance, spun. He could hear the maddening click and clack of her heels against the glass as she attempted an awkward, drunken pirouette, like a music box ballerina, broken, bent, on a perfect circle of mirror. She stumbled, and she stopped herself, hands out.

"Oh!"

And then he could see her fear, as it rose up like a blush into her cheeks. It constricted the muscles of her face, knotted her mouth, crumpled her brow — in a minute she might start to scream, and he guessed that once she started, she might not be able to stop.

"Shh," Bader whispered, "shh," and then, "You'll have to lie down, Katherine, slowly, that's it, okay, just spread your weight."

And so Katherine was stooping then, she knelt and her hands groped for balance, her palms slid away, her arms spread, like wings. Her dress was hitched up around her hips. She flattened her belly and her breasts against the floor, turned her head to the side and pressed her cheek to the cool, slick surface of the glass. The music, louder, a distant thrumming sound. One fingernail, tapping. And then there was only the gentlest murmur, as a chink took root, and it splintered, and there was the cruelest crackle of shattering glass, greedy fingers, a myriad of slivers, glittery cracks, eagerly branching, multiplying, radiating away in every direction, like intricate lace, a spider's web, and an explosion of crystal, smashed.

Bader saw the flame of Katherine's necklace, her earrings, her hair like a huge dark wave surging upward as she fell, hands and feet waving helplessly, her dress taut across her hips; she was floating downward, a petal in a downdraft breeze. She landed with a thunk and a moan on top of a table — glasses shattered, china smashed, flowers crushed, a spreading seep of spilled water and the splatter of red wine — then bounced and rolled, and sprawling, she fell farther, to the floor.

Bader leaned in through the open closet doorway with his hands braced against its frame, and he craned forward, and he peered down through the jagged hole in the frosted glass, and what he saw there below him was Katherine's body — so far away, so small, like a moth with its wings outspread and pinned, face up, her arms outstretched, one leg twisted back awkwardly, impossibly bent, her hair like a dark lace settled on the milky surface of her skin. And the deep red blossom of Katherine's blood, unfolding its velvety petals against the gleaming polished wood of the dance floor in the ballroom at the country club in Cedar Hill.

*   *   *

Bader Von Vechten is asleep and dreaming. Drowning in his slumber, he floats off on the flow of his blankets and his sheets with his long arms raised up over his head and his legs stretched out and his bare feet wide-flung. He drifts and rolls with the current of his dream until he's slammed up hard against a nightmare jut of rocks — Katherine dancing, music, shadows, Katherine falling, Katherine fallen, bleeding, sprawled — and brought thrashing into consciousness, painfully aware and brutally awake.

He flails his legs, kicking off the bedsheets, and, groaning, his head throbbing, he hoists himself up into a sitting position against a bank of pillows. He shakes his head from side to side. He runs his fingers over his hair, smoothing down its thick, pepper-colored tufts. He sucks on his teeth and smacks his lips. He coughs and feels the rattle of phlegm in his chest, the last remnant of a recent bout with the flu. He rubs his burning eyes with the balls of his thumbs and then turns to peer at the digital clock that sits on the table by the bed. The blur of its glowing numbers seems as green as what he can recall of the shine in Katherine's bright eyes. Bader's hand trembles as he gropes to turn on the lamp. He squeezes his eyes shut against the sharp stab of its light. His hand finds the bottle of scotch that he knows, by way of habit, he's left standing on the floor beside his bed. He brings it up to his mouth and sucks on it, gasping. And when he lets his head sink back into the pillows, he opens one eye, just a crack, to see the gray envelope on the dark tabletop nearby.

"Dear Mr. Von Vechten," the letter says, "I am returning herewith your check. I hope you won't take offense, but I honestly had no idea that my father has been accepting money from you all these years, and I was shocked when I found out that this was so. We have appreciated your generosity, I'm sure, but can't possibly continue to accept it, under the circumstances, which I'm sure you will understand. I hope this letter reaches you. Sincerely yours, Darcy Kimbel Mackin."

His check, for five hundred dollars, returned. And, then, one thin paragraph of redemption, clipped from the local paper, swimming before his eyes.

Roy Gary Kimbel, 63, of Bell Road in Empire, died Friday in his home. He was born January 15, 1930, at Cedar Hill, and married his wife, Margaret Kimbel, nee Butler, of Empire, June 21, 1951. Survivors include his wife, a daughter, and one grandson.

And so, now, with those few words Bader has been, finally, set free. It's just as simple and as stupid as that: the
scrawl of Darcy's handwriting on a piece of plain white paper, a smudged black framework of sentences on a ragged-
edged bit of newspaper, torn out and folded over so that the
crease cuts straight across the center of the vague smear of a
man's flat face, then slipped into the pocket of a business-size
envelope, with a postmark from three months ago and a return address stamped in the upper left-hand corner — Bell
Road, Empire, Iowa — splattered with the yellow stickers
that have forwarded it to him from hotel to boarding house
to post office box to here.

Bader Von Vechten lies sprawled out on top of his tangle
of sheets and blankets and pillows, on the sagging mattress
of a double bed in a single room at the back of the Skyway
Motel, off the interstate somewhere in the middle of Ne-
braska, and, comfortable in the very squalor of it, he wallows
with a carelessness and ease that he has otherwise forgotten
how to have. He takes another swallow of scotch and feels
the familiar comfort of its gold flame glowing in his throat
and then his chest. He lights a cigarette and, exhaling a billow
of harsh gray smoke, he pushes off the last lingering traces of
that same familiar dream — Katherine laughing, Katherine
dancing, Katherine lying, broken, bleeding, limp and pale
and still. He allows himself to sink back down, to doze again,
afloat in a warm pool of health and well-being, rocked and
cradled on the waves of good luck that seem to be lapping
over him, for the first time in what he knows has been too
long. So, he thinks, Roy Kimbel is dead.

He squints against the smoke. His hand moves up to his
shoulder, and he fingers a round raised nub of scar tissue
there on the surface of his skin. He thinks of Roy's son, Lee,
Darcy's brother, a youth standing barefoot in a patch of dirt
behind the limestone cottage where Bader lived, tossing a
pocketknife at the ground. Bader sees again the hard snap of

Lee's wrist, the arc and plunge of the blade, bright in the sunlight, the shiver of the wooden handle when it caught the ground and stuck. Lee's hair falling into his face as he bent to retrieve it, then stood to wipe the blade clean against his pant leg. His white T-shirt, torn on one side. His dimpled smile when he looked back over his shoulder and saw that Bader was behind him, standing there on the porch, leaning on the iron railing, watching him. How quickly Lee had spun then, and in one graceful fluid motion he'd raised his arm and brought his hand back behind his head and he'd thrown the knife again, toward Bader this time, so fast and hard that Bader, caught off guard, had tried to duck away and was nicked by the sharp bite of the blade. It would have hit the porch post beside him, Lee insisted, later, as blood spread on the fabric of Bader's shirt. It would have hit and stuck there. It was just a trick. If Bader hadn't flinched and moved. If only he'd trusted Lee enough to keep still.

By the time Katherine saw the wound and told him that he should have gone for stitches, it was too late. That night, she'd pulled off his shirt, and cupping his shoulders with her hands, she'd heard Bader gasp and felt him draw away. Her hair was hanging in her face. She reached over and turned the light on beside the bed. The thin strap of her nightgown had fallen off her own shoulder. She'd been angry with him. Jesus! What if he'd hit you in the face? she'd exclaimed. But he didn't, Bader had answered her. Or what if it had gone into his eye? It hadn't. She could feel it in her belly, she told him. His pain. It was an aching that came up from deep down inside of her. "Here," she said, taking his hand and pressing his fingertips into her soft belly, just above the hard mound of her pubic bone.

Untreated, the cut had healed badly and scarred. Bader rolls his fingertip over the raised flesh, and he thinks of how, over the years, he's allowed the blame for what happened to Lee and to Katherine, too, to become a part of him, like this scar. How it's attached itself to him, like an extra organ, or a tumor, not growing and taking on shape inside him, but around which he himself has grown and molded the contour of his life. So that over the years it's his guilt that has come to define him. It's there in the lines on his face and the graying of his hair. In the sag of his belly and the softening of his chin. It has informed Bader Von Vechten; it has told him, This is who you are, and this is what you have become. He has taken his substance and his form, his way of being, his reason for being, from the shape and the size of his negligence, from the cast and the structure of his crime. As if it might be the only one real true thing that he has ever done.

But now all of that has been simply, elegantly changed. Because, now, Roy Kimbel is dead. Now there is nothing left to stop Bader. There is no one who will stand up against him and hold him away. He has nobody to hide from, nothing to be afraid of. Now Bader Von Vechten can, finally, come back home.

*　*　*

Beyond the windshield of Bader's car, the early springtime landscape seems a drab patchwork of brown fields, black soil, sooty snow, and gray trees. The murky loop of a river, the straight white line of a road. The dark splash of a lake, the rough-edged cluster of a huddled town. The cold air, screaming in through the open windows of his car, sucks his breath away and leaves him gasping. The trees that curl toward him from the edges of the highway are brown and bare, their trunks blackened and wet. The sky is steely gray, bruising over into night.

And yet, for all its bleakness and chill, the sight of the familiar farmland warms Bader. As he slows on the main streets of the small towns that crowd up against the meandering line of the highway, he sees people working in their yards, walking the sidewalks, and driving in their cars, and among them are faces that seem as familiar to him as if he might be able to call out to them by name — wide-hipped girls in leather shoes and long skirts and their rangy boy-friends in hats and jeans and hooded sweatshirts that bulge out under their quilted vests. Girls in dingy white or pink nylon parkas with fluffy, fur-lined hoods. Men in overalls and raveled sweaters and steel-toed boots. Women with bulky purses and zippered snow boots, their hair flattened by scarves or bristling with plastic curlers and copper pins.

For years he's avoided this place, drifting from one part of the country to another, dodging its center, circumventing its heart, and his only contact has been the canceled checks that came back to him with the angry scrawl of Roy's endorse-ment on their backs.

From the interstate, Cedar Hill is at first only a glow in the distance. It shines on the horizon, its lights seeming to draw Bader near, and as he approaches its outskirts, he begins to feel a shimmer of recognition and a sense of wellness and of welcome. He follows the sweep of highway along the outer edge of the city, past the bright new lights of the car lots and movie houses and discount stores, and he can see now how much things here have changed while he's been away. Shop-ping malls and quick-stop stores are wrapped around certain corners that he can remember at one time had sidewalks and houses and fences and driveways and yards. Some streets seem to have been altered altogether, rerouted to cut through a neighborhood where he can recall another building, a fence, an alley, or a dead end. The white bungalows beside the river look bright and newly painted, and the whole city has ex-panded, ballooned outward, branched farther off onto the flat disk of farmland that surrounds it all the way to the horizon on every side.

By the time he's crossed the old Third Avenue Bridge, past the thick columns of the courthouse and the broad post office steps, the gray walls of the banks and office buildings, the lighted signs and windows of businesses and restaurants and department stores and shops, Bader has begun to feel as lost as if he's a stranger here, in the tangled knot of streets in downtown Cedar Hill. He cruises blocks that he thinks should be familiar to him, past storefronts that he knows he ought to recognize and office buildings that he's been expecting himself to know. He parks his car against the curb and gets out and walks, roaming up one avenue and down another, as aimless as a bum, looking at the boarded-over windows of stores that have gone under in the economic decline of the past few years, stepping over the debris that fills the gutters and blows up against the curbs, amazed at the spread of decay that seems to have attacked the heart of what he has held in his memory as having been a pretty town.

The whole place looks to him as if it has been drastically changed and yet at the same time has somehow managed to stay vaguely the same, an intriguing shadow of itself, like a withered old woman whose face has been altered by the markings of her age, framed by hair that has paled, but whose eyes are still full of fondness and curiosity and intelligence and life. Except that in the case of Cedar Hill, it seems to be the outer shell that has grown younger, while its center relentlessly deteriorates, becomes feeble and aged, neglected, shabby, and dull.

The effect is one of leafing backward through the pages of a photo album and watching the people inside the pictures shift and change, shed the weight and worry of the years, become younger and fresher and newer. He might recognize himself and Katherine, too, somewhere within the limbs of those youthful bodies. They walked together on these sidewalks, once, hand in hand. They drove up and down these streets. They shopped in these stores and ate in these restaurants, alone and with friends.

For twenty-five years, Bader has been gone from this place, and he's missed it; he's longed for it, and he's worked to bring it back. He's lain on his back in hotel and motel room beds, and he's gazed at the stained planes of the ceilings looming over him, and he's summoned up all his memories of the life that he lived once, here in Cedar Hill. He's worked to make the whole of the city rise up from a bright swamp of neon light, cast upward from the shops and the bars that line the sidewalks beyond his room. To bring Cedar Hill, in all its manifestations, back to life again, like a paper flower blooming in a glass of water, solid and real, and fundamentally unchanged.

But now that he's here, he can see that it's not the same. And he's not sure whether it's time, or his own imagination that has altered its face. He remembers wider roads, longer lawns, cleaner sidewalks, smaller trees, the bright blue dome of a clearer sky. Where he has recalled fields, now there is a sprawl of houses and a snarl of streets. Where he has remembered neighborhoods, there is instead the loom of lofty office buildings, labyrinthian shopping centers, vandalized warehouses, grim back alleys, a network of chain link fences and high, blinding cinder block walls.

Bader gets back into his car again and rolls out of this unfamiliar squalor of downtown, turning east to follow First Avenue toward the parts of the city that are the places of his past here, through the neighborhoods and along the streets that at one time in his life seemed so familiar and ordinary and safe. He cruises the rise of Linden Lane, past the big brick house that was built by his grandfather, Heinrich Von Vechten. He sees the pair of station wagons that are parked under the shade of the porte cochere and the spill of bicycles and wheeled toys scattered on the drive beyond the rails of the black iron fence, and he understands that there is a family living here now. The arch above the front gate is long gone, and with it, of course, the scroll of iron letters that once spelled out the Von Vechten name. The firs alongside the driveway look as if they've grown up more than twice as high as Bader remembers they had been. An elm tree that used to shade one corner of the sweeping yard has been cut down. Every spring the lilac bush outside the dining room window was ornamented with its fragrant clusters of purple flowers. Now it, too, is gone.

Bader parks his car in the empty lot at the Cedar Hill Country Club, and he climbs the steps past the barren flower gardens, to the clubhouse at the top. He looks down at the empty swimming pool where a murk of melted snow and soggy debris has settled at its bottom, near the drain. The screened porch, where parties of men and women used to sit together on a Sunday afternoon, drinking martinis and playing hands of bridge, has been closed up for the winter, boarded over against the ravages of wind and blown snow.

He climbs a wooded rise at the edge of the golf course, and as his soft leather shoes slip in the dirt and gravel and grass, he stretches his hands out for balance and stumbles, tearing a hole in the knee of his pants. He scrabbles on until finally he's made it to the top, where he stands for a moment to catch his breath, with the palm of one hand resting flat against the rough bark of a tree. Here is where Katherine brought him once, in the beginning. He pressed her down onto her back in the grass, and she lay still beneath him while he touched her, put his hands up inside her blouse, spread his palms against the glassy cool surface of her skin. Her eyes were dark and glittery, a pair of polished green stones.

Bader buys a bundle of fresh flowers, and he takes them out to the Cedar Hill Memorial Cemetery. He walks in through the graveyard gates off the back side of Edgewood Road. He stoops in under the clumsy filigree of the wrought iron archway, following the path that leads up beyond the duck pond, frozen over, and the chapel, boarded up. He stops halfway across a rickety bridge to lean over its railing and cough and spit into the meager trickle of the runoff stream.

Bader follows the path along to its end, to a rolling slope of grassy ground where the air seems colder, darkened as it is by the tangled edging of wild raspberry and the umbrella shade of a venerable wall of tall birch trees, their trunks as stark and white as sun-bleached bones. The hillside here is littered with the entombed remains of several generations of deceased Von Vechtens, their graves marked by somber monuments and carved stones, winged statues, columned porticoes, scrolled inscriptions, some glorious, others humble, many softened with age, their edges crumbled, their faces weathered, their etchings eroded and water-stained and worn. There lies Karl, and beside him is Juniper Von Vechten. Over to one side is Bader's mother, Eleanor Von Vechten, and his father, Tom, and then rows and rows of others whose names he can recall now only vaguely — Beloved Anna and Dearest Lissi and Our Cherished Walter and Treasured Eugene.

But at the top, closer to the corner where the east wall meets the north, beside the writhe and twist of a juniper bush, apart from all the others and cast off from all the rest, is the one plain limestone marker, planted askew amid an overgrown tangle of dried weeds, its soft surface pockmarked and scratched, its rough edges rounded and broken and chipped. To Bader's faltering touch, it feels soft, grainy, dusty as ash, powdery as chalk:

WOLFGANG VON VECHTEN
1904–1919
WAS GESCHEHEN IST, IST GESCHEHEN.

Turning away, Bader has lifted his gaze upward, past the twine of the graveyard path, over the crest of the hill, beyond the buried Von Vechtens. He squints into the failing sun, toward the far opposite slope, and his eye is caught by the gleaming, soaring white marble obelisk that still marks the remains of the man that young Wolfgang murdered, Horace Archibald Craig.

He knows that Katherine's grave is there in its shadow somewhere, too, but he doesn't climb the slope to find it. Instead, he turns, and he walks up the rise in the other direction, to a more recently sodded plot, its mound marked by a simple black granite rectangle that's been embedded there in the ground. Bader stoops, and with his bare hand he brushes the cold crust of dirt and debris from its face, to read the name that's been cut into it in plain hard letters:

ROY GARY KIMBEL
1930–1993

No "Loving Husband." No "Treasured Father." Just that, the name and the dates. There is no other inscription, no comment, no summing up of the man, no expression of love for him or of loss or of grief, in fact, no epitaph of any kind at all. Only the solemn reassurance that Roy is really dead.

Bader stands again, and he turns again, toward a genuflecting marble angel. She's barefoot in the cold grass, and her smooth white face is uplifted, as if in ecstasy. Her lips are slightly parted, as if in prayer, and her eyes closed, as if in swoon. Her hands are folded in supplication, and the thick feathery arches of her outspread wings cast their cold shadows over the ground. At her feet is another inscription:

LELAND BUTLER KIMBEL
1952–1968

When Bader nestles his bundle of flowers in the bent crook of the angel's arm, the bouquet that seemed an extravagance to him when he bought it — pink and green peppermint carnations, yellow roses, purple irises, golden glads — there in the vastness of the Cedar Hill Memorial Cemetery, in the

midst of its green lawns and budding trees, is hardly enough,
no more than an insubstantial splash of color and an insuffi-
cient flash of fading hue.

*   *   *

Since her husband's death, it has become Mudd Kimbel's
habit to stand here in this room that she shared with him for
over forty years and take the time to consider again the pros-
pect and the promise of its empty bed. By now the storm of
Roy's final emergency has blown over, and her house and her
life here have been pulled back into what she can begin to
look at as some kind of a state of normality again. Like a
woman fanning the hectic flush in her cheeks, patting the
windblown muss of her hair, smoothing the careless rumple
of her skirts — the property has regained for Mudd its more
familiar aura of solitude and serenity and dignity and calm.
In fact, there has begun to seem to be such a stillness in it,
sometimes, that she can get an uneasy sense now and then of
how it might feel to be cut off from the world, wholly separate and self-contained, afloat in a hollow of cold, bleak
space.

When Mudd splays her fingers out on the solid shelf of her
hips, her hands are fat, short-fingered and thick-wristed, so
puffy by now that Roy's gold wedding band seems to have
become embedded in her flesh, like a strand of barbed wire
that gets wrapped around a tree limb so tightly, squeezing
into it so hard, that it cuts a deep, mean crease into the swollen bark. Weight has gathered in her buttocks and her belly;
her breasts have softened, they droop and sag. Her hair is
thick, gray and brown. She's used to wearing it short now,
cropped up close to the doughy wrinkles and creases in her
neck.

Mudd. This is not the name that she was born with, but it
is the one that she was given, and it is the one that she has
kept. It was the single, sturdy syllable that the boys at school

extracted from her real name, Margaret Butler. Mudd Butt, they used to call her, to her hot indignation and deep shame. But now she can imagine that over the years she's grown into it, she's become herself like mud, thick and heavy, solid and unforgiving, slow-flowing and dull.

Because that's exactly how she's felt — like sludge amid the clearer, faster flow of the rest of the world around her — since she buried Roy.

He died after Christmas, early in January this year, and right from the first, to tell the truth of it, Mudd has in a way been enjoying her widowhood. Alone, for once, for what seems to her like the first time in her whole life, away from all the urgent clamor of a husband and a family and neighbors and friends. Although — and she does understand that this is true — she isn't alone for long, not really, and never likely will be, either. Because, even with Roy gone, there still remains for Mudd Kimbel the obligation of her daughter, Darcy, and her grandson, Cort, those two whose lives will always be intermingled with hers. Cort, who at fifteen has his own life all laid out ahead of him and waiting, and he's carrying on with it, in the same old way, as if nothing is very much different, as if little has been much changed. And yet it has begun to occur to Mudd that perhaps everything is different now and perhaps everything has been changed.

Mudd tries to remember, what were Lee's words for death, when he saw it, as a child? The neighbor's dog, run over by the snowplow, lying on its side in a pothole, its fur matted with blood and its ears frozen stiff with cold. Old man Garver, cleaning out the leaves in the gutters on his roof, who had lost his balance and fallen over backward, cracking his head open like a melon on the cement sidewalk twelve feet down. Johnny Kanaly — they said that all that was left to identify him by was his teeth — a boy incinerated with his car after it flew off the highway, slammed into a tree, and exploded in an angry billow of smoke and flame. A squirrel,

squashed flat in traffic, spread like butter on the blacktop.
The limp body of a baby sparrow, slammed down out of its
nest in the tall fir tree, gray slime in the grass after a hard
summer rain.

Fodder for the worm farm.

Leland Kimbel, watching his sister Darcy pull a rusty
wagon along behind her over the grass, its bed piled up high
with a tumbling cascade of rich black garden dirt. Darcy with
that smudge of freckles on the bridge of her nose, grimy
knuckles and filthy fingernails, torn sneakers and scraped elbows and scabbed knees. When Mudd asked her what she
was planning to do with all that dirt, she told her that it
wasn't only plain dirt that she had piled up there in the back
of her wagon. It was more, plenty more. It was also minerals
— calcium and phosphorus and potassium — and it was bac-
teria and fungi, microbes and germs and water and air.

"It's alive," Darcy said. "It's a farm."

It was a worm farm. Just because you maybe can't see
something clearly, well, that doesn't mean that it's not there.
You might have to dig your fingers into the dirt and find
them, but they were there, all right. Earthworms and blood-
worms, night crawlers and grubs.

Dirt, soil, loam, sludge, mud — the famous Iowa topsoil
was many-layered and inches deep, deposited by the melting
glacial ice, blown by winds, piled up along the rivers, a blanket that cloaked the prairies and was spread out over the limestone ridges and hills like skin on bones, the blackest, richest
earth in the world. A person could drive down any back road
in the springtime and smell the raw, wet grit of the upturned
soil, see the springy clods of it, black as ink on the flat breadth
of a plowed field.

As Darcy dragged the wagon full of dirt along after her,
through the mat and tangle of the rain-soaked grass, its four
wheels had wobbled and squeaked, snagged in the mud, left
a sinuous double-grooved trail.

How she loved that dirt then. She wore it on her body and in the fibers of her clothes; she collected it in the back of her wagon; she carried it in her creases and her dimples and in her pockets and in the bottoms of her shoes. She even ate it sometimes, Mudd remembers. She made a mix of watery mud in a mason jar, and she sipped at it, smiling to show the film of gray grit that splattered her lips and coated her tongue and filmed her teeth. Darcy had dared her brother to take a taste of it once, too — "Go on ahead now, Lee," she'd whispered, "I'll give you five dollars if you do." And he knew she had it, because Darcy always had money, she saved it, squirreled it away. So Lee had dipped his finger in and touched it to the tip of his tongue, then spat it out again, gagging on the smell and the taste and the feel of it against his teeth. He'd bounded off toward the house, crashing into the kitchen through the back screen door. Then Mudd had smacked Darcy for that, too, while Lee was sitting at the table, huddled down into himself, with the back of his fist pressed against his mouth. To Darcy, the earth was life, but to Lee it had borne an aftertaste of death and decay. Maybe, Mudd thinks, because he already knew that he'd be the one to die young.

Shirtless, Lee's shoulders were knobbed, his bones sharp and muscles stringy, his belly flat. His trousers hung on his narrow hips, below the bright white elastic waistband of his underwear. His bristly buzzed hair was shiny; sweat beaded on his lip. Mudd could hold her son close to her and smell him, feel him wriggle away from her, twisting himself out of her arms, wrenching his body from the strain of her fierce embrace.

After Lee was killed, it was this single memory of him that Mudd kept locked up in her mind. It is her one favorite image, a picture that she's come to treasure over the years, like the feathery white snowball of a dandelion that's encased in a solid plastic cube — timeless, unchanging, trapped, and kept.

She took Darcy aside during Roy's funeral and tried to explain this thought to her. But she could tell by the skitter of her eyes that Darcy didn't believe a word of it, that she wasn't able to see that the idea Mudd was passing on to her was an important one — how the same kind of thinking might hold true for her and James Mackin, too. If only she could be made to see it, she could maybe find her own kind of consolation in the fact that Cort's father had left them when he did, before he was worn out and crabby and old, when he was still a young man, still handsome, in his way, still reckless, and still wild.

Because, hasn't Darcy been able to keep her memory of James just that way? And doesn't she have a vision — as safe and as sure as a photograph, one that she may never grow out of or beyond, one that she will not lose track of, become numb to, or forget — of how James talked and how he felt and how he looked, without any of it being blurred over and blacked out, or obscured by the layers and layers of tiny changes and trivial details from the present, the moment, right now, today?

Standing in her bedroom, looking past her bed at the window and through the window at the landscape that's spread out beyond, Mudd's feelings are disturbed by the fact that she still, after all these weeks since Roy's death, can't seem to find a way to reproduce even one important feeling from her own past, from her life together with him and before, when she was Mudd Butt Butler, when she got pregnant with Lee and when Roy married her and they moved out here, into this big old empty house on Bell Road, and when Darcy was born. Outside her window, the sun has begun to sink down behind the bluff, and gray fingers of twilight are blurring the outlines of the trees and the outbuildings around the house.

So slowly, so softly, the landscape of Empire, Iowa, loses its ragged, rough-edged form.

*   *   *

There was a time in her life when Darcy Mackin might have been the first to admit that there were some bad moments over the years when she wished her father ill, but now that Roy is dead, it's hard for her to remember anymore what her reasons were. What could he ever have done to her that made her feel so bad, mad enough to hate him, even for a minute, and to hope that something unlucky might happen to him, like an accident where he was hurt? Standing at the kitchen sink now, with her hands buried in warm, soapy dishwater, Darcy is having a hard time mustering up the strength for either affection or dislike for anybody anymore. She has begun to feel just as drab and as drained as that dishtowel, and she can't for the life of her recall ever having had the energy to feel any other way about her father.

She keeps thinking she hears some familiar sound of him moving through the house behind her back, and — in spite of herself, and what she knows in her head is true, that her father is dead, buried, and gone for good — when she turns off the water in the sink and stands completely still, holding her breath, what she's listening for is the noise of his cough, the rustle of his newspaper, the brush and the bump of his shoes as he steps off the carpet in the hallway and onto the hard tiled floor in the kitchen, shuffling up close behind her, where she can smell him and hear his breathing and feel his body's big warmth.

She can imagine the rough timbre of his damaged voice, grumbling. He'd be pouring himself another cup of coffee now, slapping his folded newspaper against the side of his leg, cursing the damned Arabs, or the Jews, or the Catholics, or the blacks, movie stars, criminals, athletes, homosexuals, politicians, women — anybody at all who's had the bad luck to make the news in the headlines today. She wouldn't be at all surprised to feel the weight of his hand on her shoulder. Or the brush of his fingers in her hair. Or to hear him shouting at her, or at her mother, or at Cort, grabbing the boy by the collar and smacking him, slamming outside to the garage, letting the door crash back closed after him again when he's gone.

But at Darcy's back the whole house yawns, quiet and empty-feeling, shadowy with dusk. Mudd is upstairs, and Cort has shut himself away in his room, alone. He told her that he had to study for a history test, but Darcy knows without having to stop and think about it that was a bald-faced lie, and that if she goes and stands outside his door what she'll be most likely to hear will be the hiss of his window sliding open. And if she takes the trouble to look, she'll see him climbing out onto the porch, just like Lee used to do when he was that age himself. And even though Cort earnestly promised her that he'd be staying home tonight, everybody, including Cort himself, understands that his word isn't any good anymore, now that Roy is gone and there's not a man around the house to make it stick.

Darcy understands, too, that in spite of all those times when she used to get so mad at Roy for the way he was always yelling and hollering about one thing or another in that huge, deep, terrible raging voice of his, it was still a fact that Roy's roaring temper seemed somehow to work to keep Cort from straying off and away too far, toward too much trouble and too much harm, and everybody knows that it's not easy for a single woman like Darcy Mackin to be raising up a son, with no husband for her, no dad for him, so maybe it was just as well, good even, that Roy bothered to put forth the effort to step in every now and then to enforce what he'd long ago laid down to be the rules.

Because her mother is useless for any of that, Darcy knows. She never was any good at telling anybody that she cared about what she thought they ought to do. She just loved them too much, she said. She ruined Leland that way, was what Roy always claimed. And Darcy has accepted that as fact. She used to believe that she could take that hard lesson and apply what she'd learned from it to Cort.

But now she's begun to wonder. She would like to know how her mother feels about the way her life has gone, her years with Roy and even before that. And Leland, too — what she didn't do for him that she maybe should have, what she did that she knows now to have been wrong. Sitting up there in her bed with all her books and her magazines piling up around her, staring at the television screen but seeing something else, another drama, another plot played out in her own memory, in her own mind.

"Best not to dwell too much on the past," Darcy has tried to tell her. "You really ought to do something, you know. Get out and have a little fun."

Because it seems to Darcy that what she could see in Mudd's face that morning after she went in and found Roy lying there in the bedroom dead had to have been, in some final way, relief. And this understanding of her mother has given Darcy a new idea of who Mudd really is, a woman who may not have been so much to blame, after all. Who did her best, really, and only moved through her life from one day to another, doing what she thought she was supposed to be doing in the best way she could see how.

Darcy stood there with her mother, with her knees pressed against the edge of the mattress, and she took a good long look at her father's body there on the bed, familiar in the position it had taken and yet so unfamiliar in its stillness as to seem to belong to some stranger — too quiet to be asleep maybe, too pale and gray to be alive, but anyway the same face and the same hands and the same big feet poking up under the blankets as the man she'd known to be her dad. She'd leaned in closer, to see him better, studying the grizzle of

Roy's chin and the soft folds of the flesh around his throat, trying to find some trace of her own self there beyond the barbs of the whiskers in his skin and the tufts of dark hair inside his nostrils and the stubborn angle of his nose.

Darcy could not remember ever having seen her father so tranquil and calm. In life there had been some kind of violence or anger that seethed just below the surface of him, churning there in the clenching of his jaw or in the rolling of his shoulders, a pressure that seemed to build up and up and was only vented every now and then, unpredictably, with the loud slam of his huge fist against a tabletop or the hard kick of his heavy boot against a door. Like the old teakettle on the back burner of the stove, hissing and rattling and finally exploding, with a screaming hard whistle of steam. One time Roy tore the iron heat register in the dining room right out of the wall with his bare hands. Another, he lobbed a hammer through the glass of the picture window downstairs.

And yet, Darcy also felt grateful to him, for the way he helped her raise up her son. With James Mackin long gone. There had been an argument one night — Would she go with him? No, she couldn't leave her parents, not after what had happened to Lee, how could she? — and then the next morning when she woke up, James had left. He just took off — went away to work with the highway crew across the state to the county line and then past that, on and on, he kept going and going, and he never came back — and she waited for him in their apartment for days, his baby kicking, lurching, fluttering in her belly like the beginnings of the panic that might all of a sudden flame out and consume her, eat her alive. So she'd moved back into this house then, and over the years Mudd and Roy had helped her bring up their grandson, her boy, and Roy had done what he thought was best to make sure that Cort grew right, that he learned to stay away from trouble and do what he was told. And James never even knew that he had a son.

It was after Leland was killed that Roy swore off drinking, and Darcy has come to understand that not having the alcohol to help him keep his anger down was what brought about in her father a terrible change. There began to be a meanness there that she could see — it was as if something inside him had cracked, and it was leaking a slow spill of sour bitterness and black bile over all his good feelings and turning them bad. He had the same body, and he wore the same clothes, and he looked pretty much the same as he always had, but his movements were stiffer, forced somehow, so that at the end, just before he died, it seemed to Darcy that if Roy stayed still for any time all that wrath would freeze him up altogether and turn him into a wall of solid stone. His voice changed from its hoarse baritone to an angry, dangerous, noisy roar; his hands were more likely to be breaking something into bits than to be putting anything back together, and his face looked like it really was made of rock, never changing, locked into one cold, hard glower of outrage and hatred and pain.

And maybe that was just what Mudd had been trying her best to explain to Darcy after Roy was buried, when the two of them were sitting together in the mortuary limousine on the long drive back from the Cedar Hill Cemetery into Empire again and home. About James, and about how after he left and Darcy never heard from him again, well, he stopped changing then, didn't he? Just because he was out of her sight, gone?

Mudd, in her black pillbox hat with the veil pulled down over her face, rubbing a pattern of waves into the pile of the velvet upholstery with a gloved fingertip, telling Darcy that she was thinking about how if she wanted to she could keep James sealed up that way, she could embed him in plastic, she could press him like a flower between the pages of a big, thick book. She could just remember him the way he was when she last saw him. Because that's how Mudd is going to have to spend the rest of her life now thinking about Roy. And the point that Mudd was trying to make was that Darcy could at least find something to feel fortunate about, that the last time she saw James he was still his same young self, not a sour old cranky man like Roy.

So, now, Darcy takes her memory of James Mackin, of how he looked just before he left — his sandy hair and his pale blue eyes, his fists plunged down into his coat pockets, because if he took them out he might have been tempted to use them, to punch her, pound her, and knock her down. He was toeing the gravel with his boot, looking at her and having to look away again, squinting up into the trees, his face squeezed shut, reddened with anger and twisted with frustration the same as she'd seen Cort's turn when he was unhappy or angry or disappointed or hurt. She rolls this picture of him over and over in her mind. She holds him up and turns him first this way and then that way; she studies the features of his face, the length of his arms and his legs, the size of his hands and his feet, the color of his eyes, the texture of his hair, the temperature of his skin.

After James left her, at first Darcy missed him in a way that felt to her as if his being gone wasn't in fact an absence of any kind at all, but sort of a negative presence, a ragged hole, an empty space, a cutout silhouette completely real and solid-seeming, its existence dependent upon its not being there, its shape defined by what had been omitted, the places that had been left out. And that way, then, for the longest time after he was gone, Darcy kept thinking she could feel James, she could sense him — her memory of him itched and tickled her, it ached and stung, like somebody's arm that's been chopped off, a missing finger, a phantom limb.

Five years ago, when Cort was ten, her father persuaded her to file the lawsuit that allowed for her divorce from James.

"Forget about him now, Darcy," Roy had told her. "For your own damned good."

So she'd put a notice in the papers, thinking to herself that maybe James was going to see it and that it might be the one final thing that would bring him back, but when he never answered, well then, that was the end of that. Over and done. The judge in Cedar Hill slammed his gavel down and said, Fine, it looks to me like the man's gone for good, then, and that was the be-all and the end-all of James and Darcy Mackin's married life. No property to divide. No squabbles. No hair-tearing, hell-raising, dish-shattering fights.

Darcy could just about picture James striding into a coffee shop somewhere — wherever he was, most likely building roads out West someplace, like California maybe, or Texas, even Alaska wouldn't have surprised her. Someplace where everybody knew him, because he was so likable and friendly all the time. Where they all said good morning to him, "Hiya, James, how's it hangin'?" The waitress would have known what he wanted for breakfast without even having to ask him, because he was a man of habit, predictable that way, comfortable with the simplicity of his needs. And Darcy could imagine him sliding onto a stool at the counter, picking up the folded newspaper that somebody else had left behind, and reading, while he slurped at his coffee or slopped a piece of toast around in his eggs, pausing, frozen stiff with recognition when he came to the terse announcement of his own divorce. So, he would have known. He would have seen it and read it and, probably, breathed a sigh of relief. Maybe he would even have gone out that night to celebrate — "Hey, sugar, looky this. I'm a single man again, can you beat it?"

Either that, or he's dead.

But then where in the world does that leave Cort? Cort Mackin spending his whole long childhood in a house with his mother and his grandparents, without a real father over all these years, and now Roy's gone, too. Cort, who's grown

up so much in the last year that already he's bigger than
Darcy, and stronger, besides. At fifteen years old he's so
much taller than his mother that when Darcy puts her hands
on his shoulders and tries to stand him back and look into his
eyes to guess what kind of a change she might be able to get
a glimpse of coming into them, she has to lean her head back
and look up. Their eyes are not on a level anymore, and that
is something that's amazing and confusing and pleasing to
them both, all at once.

It's begun to tire Darcy to have to do too much thinking
about what might become of her son. About all the things he
needs from her. About what she, all by herself, is expected to
be able to provide. She isn't sure anymore whether she can
do it without her father, whether she'll be able to see him
safely through the next, most difficult years. She still remembers Lee, and how it was with him — coming and going nobody ever asked where, smoking cigarettes, drinking whiskey, when he was only fifteen — and how she'd always
believed that it was her mother's fault, for not paying attention to what he was doing, for not understanding what he
was. The sudden sting of unexpected tears that well up into
her eyes takes Darcy by surprise. She lost her brother, she
thinks, but she will not lose her son. She will not follow in
her mother's footsteps. She will not make her same mistakes.

*   *   *

Cort Mackin is in his bedroom downstairs, with the door
closed and the TV on, the sound turned down, the stereo
playing. He's studying this way, lying on his rug on the
floor, on his back, with a history book held up over his head
and his feet angled upward, pressed side by side against the
wall, where they leave two dusty prints from the intricate
swirled soles of his tennis shoes. Posters are tacked up on the
walls and the ceiling of his room — the huge, straining,
fierce faces of Cort's favorite athletes and musicians loom on

all sides. Wads of dirty clothes have been left in one pile in the corner and another under the bed. Cort's desktop is littered with books and school papers as well as the comics and magazines that he's swiped from the rack at the gas station in town. On the table by his bed is a framed black and white photograph of himself and his grandfather, taken in the fall before the old man died, the two of them grinning and squinting, standing on a bridge with a string of fish held up between them.

Cort closes his book, and he rolls over onto his stomach and pushes himself up to his feet. His denim jacket is hanging on the back of the chair beside his desk. He rummages in its pockets and pulls out a cigarette from the pack that he's hidden there.

He opens the window before he lights up, cautious because he knows his mother would be angry if she knew how much he smokes and that his grandmother wouldn't want to think that he was lighting matches inside her house. Roy's back had been scored with scars, from a fire that burned his house down to the ground when he was a boy not very much older than Cort. Carelessness, he'd said. Flames catch if you let them, and they hold, and then before you know it they're whipped, brought up into a fire that, burning on its own, will soon be out of control. Roy's voice was gravelly and rough, damaged forever, he said, by the smoke that took his wind and lost him a track scholarship at Ames.

Cort leans his elbows on the windowsill and squints out across the yard toward the curve of Bell Road, and on upward to the shadowy rim of the bluffs beyond. He hears a train in the distance, roaring through Empire on its way across the state, and he thinks about traveling, about driving with his grandfather in the old truck, rolling along deserted back roads, following a meander of rivers and creeks and streams, looking out for the best place to stop for the afternoon to fish. He thinks about running, about taking off away from here the way his father did, about jogging along on a balmy summer afternoon, down an empty gravel road, with his heart pounding and his lungs aching, and his whole body drenched in a healthy slick glaze of sweat. His knees pumping like pistons, steadily, up and down and up and down. His feet pushing against the road, rolling it away, and sliding it out from under him, like a ribbon of skin that's sloughed off behind him as he runs, and is transformed.

The sky to the west through the high bare trees is smudged with darkening clouds, and a harsh chill has begun to seep into the shadows, sweeping off the last bit of warmth from a day of false summer at the end of April. A skin of ice clings to the twig ends of the smaller trees beside the house, and some humpy patches of dirty snow are cringing there in the gutter that runs down to the street alongside the narrow dirt drive.

The knock on his door startles Cort. Sorry for the waste, he flicks his half-smoked cigarette out onto the porch — its red ember skitters in the dark. When he turns, Darcy has opened the door and stepped into his room.

"Why's your window open?" she asks, although she thinks she knows.

"Fresh air," Cort says.

Darcy sniffs. "Were you smoking, Cort?"

He glares at her, defiant, and denies it. "No."

He knows she doesn't believe him. She's touring his room, circling, snooping, he thinks. She's always trying to pry into his business, because she doesn't trust him. Even when he's telling her the truth she thinks he's lying. So, he reasons, he might as well lie. Why not?

When she gets near his jacket, he moves, and he snatches it off the back of the chair and puts it on. She stops then, and looks at him.

"Where are you going?" she asks.

He's shoved his hands down into his pockets, and he's

clasping the pack of cigarettes there, squeezing it in his clenched fist. He shrugs.

"Out," he answers.

And then it's the old argument, the one they always have, about why he wants to do something, to go somewhere, to see someone, and why she thinks he should stay home.

"It's a school night, Cort."

"So what?"

She's put her hands on her hips. "Well, don't you have a history test tomorrow?"

He looks at the book on the bed and shrugs again.

"So what?" He steps toward the door, meaning to try and edge past his mother before she can keep him there and catch him in his lie — he only wants to get outside for a minute, he thinks, away from her, to stash the cigarettes in some place where she won't find them, and then get back to his school-work again. But Darcy, angered, and hurt, too, by what she thinks is his disregard and disrespect, is reaching out to stop him. Her hand moves toward him, and Cort's reaction is re-flexive and thoughtless and quick. He wraps his own hand around his mother's arm, and he twists her away from him, and then there is an awful moment when Darcy, wincing in pain, can see in his face that her son has come to the sudden understanding of what his strength is now, compared to hers. He lets go of Darcy, instantly, shocked by the knowledge that if he'd wanted to, he could have broken her arm. If he'd wanted to, he could have snapped it like a stick, right in two. Before she can find the words that will stop him and hold him, he's turned his back to her, he's climbed out his open window, and he's gone.

*   *   *

The sky has dimmed past twilight, and the air has turned suddenly cold and brisk, as Bader switches on his headlights and follows First Avenue out past Linden Lane, through the

park and down into the valley where the creek curls, then up
the long hill toward the broader curve of Edgewood Road.
Past what's left of the Craigs' original dairy farm. Alongside
the dark, rambling acres of Old Indian Woods. Over the
paved surfaces of what were at one time gravel roads, access
for the farmers to get from one field to another, oiled in the
summertime to keep the dust down. Rambling houses along
the road sprout illegal additions, a bedroom here, a family
room there, self-contracted and cheaply done. A long brick
wall rises up near the heap of a dilapidated barn; the oval
bowl of a satellite dish looms over a square garden plot; a
white, lozenge-shaped oil tank is hunkered up against a rambling fence. There are horse stables out here still, and stone
gateways, iron archways, landscaped hedgerows, picturesque
ponds. And then the road curves again to rise up toward the
massive stone monument at its end — a gray granite mono-
lith as ponderous and gloomy as a gravestone, and etched on
its polished face: CRAIG ESTATES.

Bader and Katherine used to ride her father's horses here
— Katherine bareback on a big silver mare, her own hips
spread, mimicking the high, rounded mounds of its freckled
rump; Bader bouncing awkwardly in his saddle, elbows
poked out, hair flopping up and down. They took picnics
into the meadow — fried chicken wrapped in waxed paper,
sticky brownies, cold beer. Katherine would stretch out on
the blanket with her straw hat over her face. She'd sleep for
an hour, with her head pillowed on Bader's stomach, wobbled by his breathing, jostled awake when he laughed.

Bader drives his car in through the open gates, along the
clean white streets that have been posted with bright green
corner cross signs — marked in white with names like Bram-
blewood Lane, Raspberry Hill, Breezy Way, Foxtail Drive
— past rows of new houses, some of them finished and some
not. In the houses that are vacant, undraped windows gape;
inside are empty rooms that yawn through wide doorways,

diminishing halls, curved staircases, and barren white walls. Every conceivable architectural style has flowered at the stem ends of these asphalt driveways — an English Tudor has been set down next to a Swiss chalet, a Georgian brick mansion rises up to overshadow the genial sprawl of an American ranch, white-washed colonial confronts Roman revival, Spanish stucco battles quaint Cape Cod.

"Open House" flags flutter on the corners, beyond stone fronts, brick walks, yards of hardened mud, and sodded lawns that are cluttered with swing sets and bicycles and sandboxes. Some sidewalks sidle up to empty lots, and dead end streets lead to huddles of abandoned equipment inside the press of gathered trees.

When Bader comes to the end of the last street and pulls his car up to the edge of the bluff, he can see — perched on its rim, crouched behind the farthest cluster of the bigger homes as if it has been cast off from their circle, its rough sides splattered with the hot white light from his headlights — the old Von Vechten cottage.

The place is abandoned, left to ruin, it seems. Its limestone walls have begun to crumble. Some of the windows are empty and open, some are broken, some have been boarded over. Shingles are missing from the roof. The old front door with its carved wooden knocker is swinging aslant on a broken hinge. A torn white curtain hangs in a narrow bedroom window, and it looks to Bader like a flag of surrender to the conquest of weather and time and neglect.

Cold fingers of wind ruffle his hair and brush his cheek, like a caress, and it's only now that he is struck, finally, with the full hammering force of what he's come to see clearly has been his loss. It shakes him hard, the realization that everything he ever had, and everything he ever was, is gone.

Shivering, he walks over to the edge of the bluff, and he looks down, and from where he's standing — as still and dark and thin and tall as if he's only another of the young trees that have been planted along the edges of the yard — he can just make out the slate roof of the Kimbel farmhouse deep in the woods below him. Its peaks jut up between the barren branches of the trees. There is some lamplight glowing in an upstairs window, and, as warm and yellow as butter, it spills out into the night like a leak, of coziness, it seems to him, and welcome and intimacy and warmth.

He pulls up the collar of his coat. A chill has come back into the air again, a last gasp of winter. Through swirls of falling snow, Bader begins to trudge back toward his car, and what brings him up short is a sound. The soft, quick snicker of a sneaker in mud. He stops, and he turns back again toward the cabin to see the shadowy figure of a boy materialize in the darkened doorway. A boy with a white face. A boy in a denim jacket. A boy, running. A boy with legs pumping, hair flying, fists clenched, arms bent up close to his sides. A boy.

There's an echo that's begun to ring in Bader's ears now. The deep growl of a man's angry shout. A boy's high, keening cry. The single, stupefying blow of a fist, the stunning crunch of cartilage, a rush of blood. The crack of a shotgun blast, thundering through the trees. And there is an image in his eyes, of Leland Kimbel's mangled body, sprawled out among the high weeds. Of Lee's eyes, as dusky gray as a roil of thunderclouds. Of fingers tugging at a flap of skin, nose and lip and chin, and arranging it over bloody muscle and bared bone, smoothing it back down, like fabric over flesh.

Bader calls out to the boy, and stepping forward, starts to follow him. "Wait!" he cries. But Cort has crossed the yard away from him, and he's climbed up onto the top railing of the fence. He stands balanced there for a moment, seesawing, and he turns to look back again at Bader coming toward him before he drops down to the ground on the other side, knees buckling, sneakers sliding in the muck, and he skids wildly down the hill — arms outstretched, through the high grass and the dry brush — and then he's disappeared from view.

The night has closed in over Bader. He stares at the darkened woods, squinting into the trees for another glimpse of the boy, and then he, too, begins to run. His coattails flap out after him. His breath is burning in his chest; it sears his throat. The bushy overgrowth of weeds and branches snags and swats at him. He scrambles onto the gravel bed of the railroad tracks and slips back into the dank cluster of trees before he's spat out again into the open near the edge of Bell Road. Bader hurdles the shallow ditch below the farmhouse, and then he comes skidding out into the yard.

Cort has scampered across the front lawn, onto the porch, through the open window, and into his room. Darcy looks up from the magazine that she's been leafing through when he comes into the living room. She notices the film of sweat that glistens on his face and the muck that cakes the sides of his shoes and the burrs that have burrowed into the sag of his socks and even the shortness of his breath, how his shoulders heave and his nostrils flare as he leans his head back and closes his eyes.

"What happened, Cort?" Darcy asks, afraid for him and for what she thinks he might have done.

Outside the house, Bader clatters over a lawn chair that's been left sprawled in the middle of the yard. He bounds up onto the porch, and as he bangs his fist against the door, he feels that burden of what he knows is still his guilt pressing in upon him. It's something soft and dark that tumbles through him like thunder, swelling like a storm in his chest, rolling in his blood like a cold, hard rain. He's gasping for breath, standing in a circle of light, on this familiar front porch, near the bay window that he recognizes, beside the creaky railing that he remembers, before the paneled door he knows.

But to Darcy, who has heard the bell and who is standing in the open doorway, Bader is no one she's ever met before. He might be a stranger for all she recognizes him at first, some handsome older man with deep blue eyes and graying dark hair, a black felt fedora, a gold watch that glints on his wrist, a clean, if rumpled, white shirt under his brown raincoat, creased trousers, torn in the knee, light leather shoes not meant for walking in mud or wet grass or snow. His face is pale, sickly-looking, slick with sweat. His hands tremble, his eyes are reddened, and he seems to be blinking back tears. He rubs his face with his hand and runs his fingers through his hair.

"What?" she's asking him, turning her head to the side for a look at the whole long length of him at once. She's keeping her hand curled firmly over the doorknob, prepared, just in case, to push it shut again, hard, in his face.

"I'm sorry," he says. He totters. He clenches his jaw and grinds his teeth together to keep them from rattling in his skull. He's begun to tremble and shake. He's a bag of bones inside his clothes, under his coat; he's a skeleton with no muscle and no fat and no skin to cover him and protect him from the gnawing cold. He hugs his coat around himself tightly, as if he's afraid it might blow open and then his whole bare being will be exposed.

He shakes his head. Puts up a hand, turns, staggers. When he takes a step back, his foot comes down too hard, and its weight and force seem to shake the whole house from the foundations up.

Snow swirls toward Darcy from the dusky shadows of the porch, sparking in the warm yellow light that spills out from behind her in the hall. A draft of bitter cold air comes gusting in through the door, and it whacks at her like a slap in the face. Her dress flaps up, exposing for a moment, while she struggles with it, the creamy, puckered flesh of her bare thigh.

"Darcy?" Bader is saying, and when he says her name, it comes to her, and she understands who he is.

He swoons, his eyes roll back in his head, and then there is the thud of Bader's body as he falls.

TWO

S NUGGLED UP NEXT TO A SLENDER SPREAD LEG OF the Illinois Central Railroad tracks to the west and sheltered by the shrug of bluffs that rose up from the river to the east, drowsing in the rolling folds of the prairie's lap and lashed by the winding filament of Bell Road as it ran its course northward, into the innermost urban center of the larger sprawled city of Cedar Hill — there lay the haggard business district of Empire, Iowa. Bell Road, the worn gray asphalt main street of the town, rolled up past a shaded block of stores and homes, before it sloped serenely down toward its dead end in the driveway of the Kimbels' big white farmhouse to the south.

At the farthest edging of their yard, a broad wire gate was closed and chained and locked across the grass-grown dirt access road that led up to an abandoned limestone cottage perched in a clearing at the edge of the bluff. From its porch, Lee Kimbel once sent off a bottle rocket that caught the dry brush and almost set fire to the whole of Indian Woods. His sister Darcy downed a whole bottle of warm beer one after-noon and then got so dizzy and sick from it that she bent over, with Lee's hand on her back, and threw up in the high weeds.

Lee had a dimple that winked in his cheek, gray eyes that could darken to deep blue, and blondish hair that he wore parted on one side and combed away from his face. He sat on the porch floor, leaning back against the bumpy wall and smoking a French cigarette from the pack that he'd stolen from a tobacco store in Cedar Hill. With his fingertip he traced the ugly dark blotch that stained the stones beside his leg. It was, he told his sister, the remains of a stunning act of violence — the splattering of Horace Craig's brains and blood when Wolfgang Von Vechten shot him in the head.

"No, it isn't," Darcy answered him, squinting. She was perched on the edge of the wrought iron railing, swinging her bare feet. Her toenails were polished pink. She was one year younger than her brother, with the same gray eyes, but softer, and the same blond hair, but longer, and a smudge of sandy freckles that were sprinkled out over her nose and cheeks. "Somebody would've cleaned that old mess up by this time, Lee."

He blew a billow of smoke, leaned his head back, closed his eyes. Sweat dampened the wisps of hair at his temples. The air felt heavy, wrapped around him, thick and hot and wet. "Maybe so," he said. "Or maybe not. Blood and brains and skin and bones might be harder to get rid of than that."

*   *   *

It was a story that everyone in Empire knew, about how Karl and Juniper Von Vechten came over together from Germany to Iowa, in the mid–eighteen hundreds, when it was early springtime and the trees along the banks of the creek had just that week begun to bud. Herr Von Vechten had hopped down from the train that had brought him here, and he'd

stood there on the platform with one fist at his wife's elbow
and the other wrapped firmly around the leather strap of the
black steamer trunk in which the two of them had packed up
everything they owned in the world — a family Bible, some
clothes and blankets and quilts, a pair of handmade lace curtains, a pewter pitcher and a silver tray, and the drawings for
the cream can that would one day make them rich.

Juniper and Karl dragged their trunk through the dust of
the train yard, over the tracks and into the woods and across
the creek to the east of what was soon to become the town of
Empire, and then the two of them together built themselves
a limestone cottage in the clearing up on the bluff.

Karl Von Vechten went to work as a butter maker at the
Craig Creamery in Cedar Hill. After he'd been there for a
few months, he unrolled his sheaf of drawings and showed
his employer his plans — for a cream can made of wood,
lined in tin, closed and insulated, with a float device in the
cap that was designed to keep the cream from churning in the
back of the wagons on the long, bumpy rides from the out-
lying farms into the creamery in town. James Craig had
squinted at the drawings with an instant understanding of
their worth. He'd stepped back and thoughtfully rubbed his
silky beard, and then he'd turned to Karl Von Vechten and
clapped him on the back. A deal was struck: James Craig
would invest in the production of the cans in return for an
equal share in whatever profits they eventually brought. Plain
and simple. A fifty-fifty split. He and Karl Von Vechten
formed their partnership on a handshake and began to man-
ufacture the cans in an empty shed behind the creamery.

Soon, word of the ingenious cream containers had spread
across the state, catching the fancy of dairy farmers and
creamery owners from as far away as Wisconsin and Illinois.
By the time the century turned, Karl and James both were
dead and buried, but the demand for the cans had grown so
great that Karl's son Heinrich moved the operation out of the

old shed and into a larger factory — a long wooden warehouse on the river, with a sign out front that read VON VECHTEN–CRAIG. Heinrich had married another German girl, Margot Muller, and the limestone cottage on the bluff in Empire was traded for the greater luxury of an imposing brick mansion at the end of Linden Lane in Cedar Hill. Two more Von Vechten boys, first Thomas and then Wolfgang, were born.

Meanwhile, the cream can business, under the watchful eyes of Horace Craig and Heinrich Von Vechten, continued to prosper and grow — by 1914, on the eve of the Great War, the Von Vechten–Craig Cream Can Company had expanded to include the production of sanitary ice cream containers, paddles, scoops, churners and whippers, egg crates, milk bottles, cream cartons, butter boxes, and ice trays.

But the Germans were the enemy then, and Heinrich agreed that he'd be wise to remove the Von Vechten name from the wooden sign that hung outside the factory, as well as from the invoices and the stationery and the product labels. Strictly business, Horace reasoned, desperate measures for desperate times. Nothing personal. The creamery and the factory couldn't expect to stay in business, much less prosper, as long as they could be connected to the kaiser's murdering heinie cabbageheads overseas.

In the fall of 1918, influenza took Heinrich Von Vechten and his third child, a girl, Lise, and the only way that Margot could think of to keep her foot in the door of the cream can company that no longer bore even a trace of her dead husband's name was to marry his business partner, the widower Horace Craig. But Wolfgang Von Vechten, only fourteen years old and the more devoted of Margot's two boys, was outraged by what he thought was his mother's disgusting betrayal of his father's honor and trust and good name.

"Leave it alone," Margot warned her younger son. "Was geschehen ist, ist geschehen!"

The boy turned his back on her. He left Cedar Hill and moved into the limestone cottage in the woods where his grandfather's life in America had begun. Wolfgang spent a week restoring the Von Vechten name. He nailed his homely hand-painted signs to trees and poles and fence posts all over Empire, claiming every nook and cranny for the memory and the honor of his father — Von Vechten Creek, Von Vechten Bridge, Von Vechten Hill, Von Vechten Clearing, Von Vechten Road, Von Vechten Woods. Even the sign that hung above the platform of the train depot was changed overnight to read VON VECHTEN'S EMPIRE.

Then that winter brought a series of increasingly violent accidents in — or acts of terrorism against — the Craig Creamery and Can Company of Cedar Hill, as it had come to be called. Milk turned up tainted. Guard dogs disappeared. Horses died. A bull was found slaughtered in its stable; the bodies of two dairy cows were discovered dismembered and mutilated in a field. Equipment was vandalized and sabotaged. Barns and sheds were torched; a house that Horace owned and rented out to tenants in Empire was burned halfway to the ground, and three people, including one infant, died.

The sheriff was sent out to arrest Wolfgang Von Vechten for murder and bring him back to Cedar Hill. But the boy was gone. Some guessed he'd given it up, that he'd lit out and left the state, took off to find himself another life in another county, in some bigger city, to the south, maybe, or the west, in a place where nobody had ever heard of him, where no one knew him or would recognize his name or his face. Others suggested that he was still in Empire, only hiding out, lying low, living off the land, sleeping in the woods or in the endless crazy maze of limestone caves out to the west of town.

Margot Von Vechten Craig talked Horace into going out to Empire to try to find the boy — he was just a boy, she argued, fifteen years old, only a child, after all — to talk to him, to bring him around to some understanding of the situation, some compassion for his mother, some sympathy for him. But when Horace finally found the boy, and talked to him, Wolfgang wouldn't be persuaded. He had a shotgun, and he pressed its muzzle up against the folds of flesh at the nape of Horace Craig's neck; he squeezed the trigger, and he blew off the old man's head.

*   *   *

That property up on the bluff was passed on to Bader Von Vechten when his grandmother, Margot, died. The cottage itself had been abandoned when age overcame her and she was moved into a convalescent home on the west side of Cedar Hill. There she had a room in the old school building that had been converted to a dormitory. She had a bed and two wooden chairs and a closet and a table with a drawer and a lamp and a window that overlooked a green pond, with deer in the woods, swans in the water, and geese on the grass.

"It's a relief," she told Bader, sighing. "You don't know what a relief."

What she meant, he guessed, was dying. Her life was almost over, she'd outlived everybody, her first and second husbands, her daughter, both her sons, and now there was nothing left for her to have to worry about for them, it was all out of her hands, she didn't have to be responsible, to look after anybody else's interests, or, even, take care of herself.

"You're on your own now, son, I'm afraid," she'd told him. "It's up to you. What's done is done."

Her head was as brown and bald and shriveled as an old potato, propped against the drift of pillows encased in their crisp white cotton slips. Her flesh had begun to collapse and fall through the framework of her bones. Her eyes, yellowy and bugged, had looked huge beside the chiseled wedge of her nose, and her lips were stretched and pulled apart to form a generous, blissful smile — or was it, Bader wondered, really the menace and fierce threat of a cornered animal's teeth, bared?

Bader sat in a chair at his grandmother's bedside, and he listened, as Margot's wooden fingers opened and closed, compulsively clutching at the blanket that had been pulled up over her chest and then folded neatly back. She caressed its satin edging — her coarsened skin rasped and snagged against its fabric as she rolled it in circles between her bent fingers and her thumb — taking comfort for herself from its unresisting softness, pliable and silky and smooth.

"See that?" she asked him, pointing. Hanging on the wall across from her bed, mounted on two brass hooks, was the shotgun that his uncle Wolfgang had used to murder Horace Craig.

"The next day, we found the body where he'd left it, under the trees," she said. Wolfgang had tried to hide it. He thought he'd drag it out into the woods and stash it in one of the long, deep limestone caves that riddled that area. But, she said, he was just a boy. And Horace was a man, a large man. Wolfgang had wrapped the body up in a blanket, and tried to drag it off across the lawn toward the trees. Maybe no one would find it, he thought. Maybe no one would know. When he got it into the woods, he couldn't budge it any farther. He was exhausted. He was covered with blood. And he knew he was in trouble. He was only a boy.

He thought that he'd be caught and tried, found guilty of murder and, most likely, sentenced to death. To save his mother the shame of that, he took his punishment into his own hands.

The note that he left behind echoed her own words.

"Was geschehen ist, ist geschehen."

What's done is done.

Inside the limestone cottage, hanging from the noose of a wrapped and knotted length of rope, the dead weight of the boy's body had circled and swung.

Margot's voice faltered, cracked. She wasn't able to remember it all anymore, she said. It was just like a row of kitchen cabinets, all of them slamming shut, one by one, inside her head — Bam! Bam! Bam! — with enough force to rattle the stacks of cups and saucers and quake the shelves of thick glass. And somewhere in that shudder of fine china and that quiver of cut crystal, words were lost.

"But if I can be patient. If I can stop thinking of things for a minute," she said, "if I stop trying, if I sneak up on myself, then it will always come to me, sometime. If I wait. If I look the other way and then I — pound. No, not pound. Bounce? Is that it, Bader?" But she knew it wasn't. She shook her head, clenched her fist, a flash of anger lit up her eyes, and she groaned. Her eyes roved back and forth over her grandson's face, as if she thought she might be able to read something there, to find the elusive word that she wanted, as if she believed that somehow what she meant to say might be printed in his familiar features, or outlined in his eyes. "What? Like a tiger does, you know, with his big feet? With his claws? When he jumps? Like a cat, it, not points, not pulls, what is it, Bader, do you know?"

"Pounce," he answered her, quietly. "It pounces."

Margot leaned back against the pillows, sighed, relaxed, and nodded at him.

"That's right," she said. "That's it. Pounce."

The mahogany bed that she lay in was as big as a boat, floating on a sea of the thick green rug that covered and gave warmth to the room's bare wood floor. The headboard was heavy, bolstered by tall shapely posts with fat pineapples impaled on dowels at their tops, and the shape of Margot's body seemed small and insubstantial underneath the white blanket. On a table nearby, an old plastic radio sat on a lace doily.

Beside the radio lay the book that the nurse had left off reading, before she went downstairs to prepare for Margot her
afternoon dosage of warm milk and cinnamon toast and the
paper cup of multicolored tablets and pills. And below the
book, a drawer, and in the drawer, a large leathery accordion
file, and inside the file, papers.

Margot told Bader, "Look at them. In the drawer, there,"
she'd said, her voice shaking, her hand trembling. Poking at
Bader's arm. "See that file there? Go on, take it. Pick it up."
Wagging her hand at Bader, impatient with him now. "Open
it, go ahead, look inside." The flap folded over the top was
tied with a flat ribbony string. Bader had fumbled at the knot,
struggling with it while Margot's fingers continued to rasp,
steadily, against the blanket trim. Her eyes, watching him.
Inside the file, several envelopes. Margot's will, giving over
all her property, such as it was. Two life insurance policies,
both of them payable to Bader in the event of Margot's death.
Some stock certificates, worth several hundred thousand dollars between them, she claimed, poking at Bader's arm with
her long finger again. His parents' marriage papers. Bader's
birth certificate. And, finally, the deed, entitlement to eighty
acres of woodland, a homestead, in the country, near Empire, Iowa, on the outskirts of Cedar Hill.

"That's your trust, Bader. All we've got. It's yours."

After Margot buried Wolfgang in the family plot with the
rest of the Von Vechtens — near his father and his little sister, on top of that one long low hill at the far back end of the
Memorial Cemetery in Cedar Hill — then she went to her
new family, the Craigs, and she asked them, was she going
to be thought of as a Von Vechten, or were they in agreement, had she become a Craig? Now that there was nothing
much else left to her anymore, did they plan to bring her into
the fold of their family and keep her there, in the shelter of
its wing? Would they open their arms to her, their murdered
father's widow? And, if not, if she wasn't going to be

thought of as one of them, if she was going to be looked at as a Von Vechten and not a Craig, were they at least going to restore that name to the title of the cream can company, where it belonged, and did they plan to share with her that which was by all rights already at least half hers?

No, they would not. No, they did not. Why should they, now, after all that had happened? The Craig family turned its back on Margot Von Vechten. They threw her out of their house. They closed their doors against her. They even tried to drive her out of town. She gave the house on Linden Lane to her one surviving son, Thomas, and she moved back into the cottage on the bluff.

She held her hand out toward Bader. "Picture this," she told him. And snapped her fingers sharply, a hard and solid-sounding plunk, plunk, plunk. "Picture this."

The sputtering sizzle and bright orange flare of a struck match. The hot flicker of a flame cupped in the soft white palm of a woman's hand. The warehouse that had been the factory, exploding into flame and burning, quickly, thoroughly, to the ground. The Craig Creamery and Can Company of Cedar Hill completely and utterly and perfectly destroyed.

"What was done," said Margot, "was done."

Everything that the Von Vechtens had ever had, everything that Karl and Juniper had given them, all that Heinrich and Margot had worked for and saved for and strived for, all that they had, finally, sacrificed their lives to, was gone. All, that is, but a limestone cottage and eighty unplanted acres up on top of a bluff above Empire.

She let her head fall back into the pillows again. She sighed, closed her eyes. And Bader sat there at her bedside, shuddering at what he saw now was the final despair of that room, and of his grandmother's life and of its end. It wasn't the steady rasping of the old woman's fingertips against the satin edging of the blanket trim that Bader heard then, but

only the swish and the whisper of the nurse's stockings, rubbing together where her heavy thighs overlapped beneath her
skirt as she walked into the room, after Margot Von Vechten
was dead.

*   *   *

As his black Mustang convertible swooped the long curl of
the parkway out of Cedar Hill into Empire, Bader was forced
to swerve to avoid the milk truck that swung out wide
around the curve toward him, just there where the road began to narrow again before the shrug of the wooden bridge
that arched over the creek. Both horns blared simultaneously
as the truck skidded, fishtailed, found its traction and then
trundled on, churning through the dust, up the slope and
away, diminishing until, finally, it dropped down out of
sight altogether behind the crest of the hill.

Then Bader — a college-educated young man in a convertible, a landed gentleman, with an inheritance and a future
full of promise and possibility, twenty-five years old, with
chestnut hair, gleaming brow, shadowy jaw, woolly wrists,
and Prussian blue eyes — Bader Von Vechten was alone,
rolling slowly along the deserted stretch of roadway, in the
middle of nowhere, he might have thought, if he hadn't
known better. Because this was somewhere, all right. It was
a halfway point, in fact, an equal distance either way from
Cedar Hill or from Empire, with a crowded dark acreage of
woods on the one side and a vast flat plain of farm fields on
the other, the populated neighborhoods of Cedar Hill behind
him and the sterner isolation of Empire up ahead.

The Mustang rattled onto the wooden bridge and crossed
the creek. It skidded through the intersection where the parkway stopped and it rounded the corner onto the pale gray
asphalt of Bell Road. Bader braked hard when he came to the
abrupt dead end, and he turned off just beyond the white
farmhouse, bouncing to a stop just short of the wire gate. He

got out of his car, and, cupping one hand over the top of the fence post, he looked up past the high gables of the house toward the soaring ridge of the bluff beyond it, where Old Indian Woods cast its huge dark shadow over the land as the park sprawled away to the north. He took off his jacket and his tie, and he tossed them into the back seat of the car. He rolled up his shirtsleeves, clambered up over the gate, and began on foot the long climb up the road to his cottage at the top of the bluff.

*   *   *

The Von Vechten cottage had a wide, high-ceilinged living room with a bedroom that jutted off at a right angle to one side and a bathroom that came poking out off its back. With the kitchen and the small dining room on the other side, the whole structure had the shape overall of a squat-legged T. The porch was littered with cigarette butts and a sprawl of empty brown beer bottles, their labels curled and torn. It was encircled by a filigree of black wrought iron railing, a solid entanglement of leaves and flowers and vines, and the yard was hemmed in by a straggle of split-rail fence. Two poles of a clothesline were planted in the ground on one side of the cottage, and the rope strung between them had stretched and rotted and been left to fall away slack. A crumbled, ivy-covered brick chimney rose up past the peak of the roof along the north wall. Three steps led to the wide stone porch. When Bader tried the old pump near the base of the steps, a spray of blood-colored warm water splattered in the dusty dry crabgrass at his feet.

The windows were cracked and broken, shattered by hurled stones and then halfheartedly boarded over again with scrap lumber and corrugated cardboard box ends. Inside, the rooms were dark, and the air was thick with dust. There were some odd pieces of furniture scattered around — a torn sofa and an overstuffed chair, an upturned ottoman and a glass-topped coffee table — all draped in dirty flowered sheets.

Bader could hear the scratch and scrabble of mice and insects under the floor and inside the walls. Cobwebs draped the beams of the ceiling and gathered in the corners of the room like fog.

The kitchen was equipped with a hobbled black iron stove, an old refrigerator, and a rust-stained sink. Cupboard doors hung open, their hinges broken and their shelves cracked. The hardwood floor was dirty, warped in places, and stained.

In the bedroom at the back of the cottage, Bader found a corrugated cardboard wardrobe box toppled over on its side. There was a stack of yellowed newspapers and a heap of blankets that looked like a huddled body in a corner, against the wall.

Bader stepped back out onto the front porch and pulled a cigarette and a lighter from his shirt pocket. Cupping his hand around the shuddering flame, he looked out past the scraggle of the narrow yard, toward the woods that were all overgrown with brush and thick with a tangle of sticky nettles and wildly flowering weeds. A sudden, subtle movement caught his eye, and he craned forward toward it, squinting to peer into the shadows of the trees, until — as in a child's trick drawing, where a single separate image is cleverly embedded in the lines and the shapes and the contours of an intricately detailed background — Bader was able to decipher the lean, leggy form of a youth, hidden in shadow and framed by a low arch of curled branches and flat green leaves.

His face was hard to make out, mottled as it was, with a leafy pattern of sunlight and scant shade. A thin white T-shirt, moist with sweat, was molded over the hard bones of his shoulders, and it clung to the smooth flat plane of his chest. He uncrossed his bare feet and combed his fingers through his hair. He swiped at his face with the back of his wrist. A swarm of black gnats hovered in the air near him, like a frail, thin wisp of soft, dark smoke.

The boy seemed to be aware now that he was being watched, and he brought one hand up to shade his eyes as he stepped out of the shadows into the sunshine. He tossed his head to throw his lank blond hair back from his face. He'd tied together the laces of his black sneakers, and he picked them up off the ground and slung them over his shoulder so that one bounced against his chest and the other bumped him in the back as he crossed the yard toward the cabin. Bader could see that his bare feet were long, flat-soled and fine-boned, smooth and white as china against the snarl of bright green grass.

The boy stopped below the porch where Bader stood.

"Hi," he said, smiling. "Got another one of those?" He nodded toward the cigarette that Bader was smoking, and his smile widened, aslant in his face, mocking and amused, teasing Bader, as if he were daring him to say no.

Bader reached into his shirt pocket and pulled out his cigarettes. The boy stepped up onto the porch next to him as Bader shook the pack at him. He took one and poked it between his lips; he gripped it in his teeth as Bader flicked his lighter and held it out toward him. Bader could see the flame, reflected then, a radiant warm flare that seemed to be burning in the deep ashy gray of the boy's eyes.

"You're too young to smoke," Bader said, pocketing his lighter again.

"I'm not." The boy squinted as he exhaled. "I'm fifteen."

Bader smiled. Well, he'd smoked at that age himself, hadn't he, upstairs in the attic of his aunt's house, with the window thrown open to blow away the smell?

"Lee Kimbel," the boy said, introducing himself. "I live in that white house down there." He turned, and pointed past the darkly tangled trees toward the farmhouse at the end of Bell Road.

Bader nodded and cleared his throat. "Bader Von Vechten," he said. He put his hand out toward Lee, but the boy
ignored it.

He was staring at Bader with gray eyes that were hard and
bright. "Von Vechten?" he asked. "Like Wolfgang Von
Vechten?"

Bader nodded.

Lee shook his head, looked at his feet, and coughed out a
hard laugh. "Shit," he said, turning to Bader, grinning.
"You related to him?"

"He was my uncle."

Lee crossed his arms over his narrow chest and cupped his
elbows in his hands, hugging himself. He lowered his chin
and looked at Bader. "This your land, then?"

"Well," Bader answered, nodding, "some part of it is, I
guess."

"You going to live here?"

"I might."

"What about the road?"

"You know who owns it?"

Lee looked at him again and smiled. "You don't want to
know," he said.

"Your father?"

Lee shook his head and pawed at the grass with his bare
foot. "Nah," he said, "he doesn't own anything much."

"Why don't I want to know, then? What is it that I don't
want to know?"

Lee took a long drag off his cigarette and exhaled. He
tapped ashes and then squinted again at Bader. "Well, sir, it's
Mr. Craig that owns the road. And the gate, too. Why, he's
got his name on just about every other bit of property around
here except this one, I'd say."

Bader looked at Lee, and then turned to the woods again.

Over the years since Margot had left, the Von Vechten
property had become encircled by Craig farmland on the one

side and an inviolable expanse of state parkland on the other. It was as remote as a foreign country, as isolated as an island. Only one road led up to it now, and that belonged to the Craigs.

"The truth is," Margot had told Bader, "our two families have always been" — and she brought her hands up, tangling her knotty fingers together to form one solid fist and then shaking it at him, just to show him what she meant — "impaled. Reviled. Divined." Entwined.

A knot of annoyance had begun to tighten in Bader's chest. The Craigs. Just the name itself sent a hot flame of sudden anger surging into his stomach. He kicked at an empty beer bottle, and it spun off, with a loud, hard clatter, over the stone floor.

Lee watched him, keeping still, with that same amused look still stirring in his face — as if he thought he could have expected just about that much, as if he understood just such a sudden violence, because it was exactly the kind of thing that he was used to, and exactly what he knew just how to handle, to tolerate, to watch over while it flared up, hot and strong, before it forgot itself again and cooled and, finally, died away. Lee's own calm manner was like a vortex that would draw Bader's anger into itself to quell.

Down on the road, a black pickup truck slowly trundled, kicking up a plume of dust after itself. Lee turned and studied it for a moment, then flicked his cigarette away.

"My mom," he said. "Home from church." He turned back to Bader. "If I were you, Mr. Von Vechten, you know what I'd do?"

Bader crushed his own cigarette out with the toe of his shoe. He shoved his hands down into his pockets and rocked on his heels. "No, Lee. What would you do?"

The boy smiled and ducked his chin. "Well, I guess I'd go and introduce myself to Mr. Craig. I'd find some way to be

his friend. Get him to give me the key. Make him want to let
me make some kind of good use of his road and my land.''

Lee took his shoes from around his neck, sat down, put
them on, and tied them. He stood up and dusted off his
hands. His hair had fallen into his face again, and he jerked
his head to one side to throw it back.

"Well, Mr. Von Vechten," he said, "thanks for the smoke,
I guess." And then he turned away and crossed the yard,
climbed over the fence rail and vanished into the shadows
between the huddled trees.

*   *   *

Mudd Kimbel's black pickup truck bounced off Bell Road
and up over the ditch into her driveway, where it stopped.
The air was still and hot, without the least whiffle of a breeze.
Sweat dribbled down Mudd's neck and dampened the collar
of her dress. Her body felt like a soft, moist mass inside her
clothes. It seemed that all morning long the sun had been
following her around, like some kind of a punishment, find-
ing out where she was and then beating on her with its re-
lentless heat.

She went around to the back of the truck and hauled out
two bags of groceries, hurrying now, to get them inside before the ice cream was melted and the milk spoiled. The pegs
of her pumps wobbled as she walked across the uneven
boards of the porch. When she pushed open the front door,
she was met by the exhilarating draft of damp chill that she'd
been hoping for. Even on a hot day, without any air condi-
tioning, the big old farmhouse could feel like this, as wet and
cold as a cellar sometimes. Its rooms were usually many de-
grees cooler than the weather outside made her think that
they ought to be. That was because the walls were thick, Roy
said, and well made. Mudd was glad then that she'd thought
to draw shut the curtains on the windows in the living room

and the dining room before she'd left that morning for church.

She could hear the gentle low burring of Roy's voice as it came to her from the kitchen, rising and falling, pausing, silent for a moment before it picked up again. He must be talking on the telephone, she thought, his voice a rumble that was so low she could just about feel it vibrating inside her own body, as gentle as a motor running, turning, humming, inside her own head. Drawn toward it, she walked down the hallway to the kitchen and then stopped, blocking the doorway like a boulder wedged in place.

Darcy was at the kitchen table, tipped back in a chair with her bare feet raised, reading the colored pages of the comic section of the Sunday *Gazette*. Her painted fingernails were chipped and chewed. She had on short shorts and a flowered blouse, its tails pulled up and tied into a knot at her waist.

Roy looked up at Mudd. "I'll meet you," he said, into the phone. He hung up and, with his eyes still locked on Mudd's face, he shook his head. "It's about time," he said.

Mudd sighed and stepped into the room. She moved past her husband and set the heavy grocery sacks down on the counter next to the sink. "I'm too hot to argue with you this morning, Roy," she said.

"Where've you been?" Roy asked.

Mudd could feel him looming behind her, powerful and large. She turned to face him, with her elbows bent and her hands gripping the edge of the counter. "Church," she said.

"Church let out an hour ago."

"I stopped at the store."

He mimicked her, raising his voice and wagging his head and pursing his lips. "I stopped at the store."

Mudd's face was hard. "Where is it you've got to go, Roy?" she asked him.

"Business," he said, avoiding her eyes. He turned away toward the back door.

"There's a couple more sacks out there in the truck," she called after him. "Bring them in before you go."

The back door slammed.

The kitchen sink was filled with dirty plates and glasses, from the eggs and toast that it looked like Darcy had cooked for Roy's breakfast. Mudd turned on the water in the sink and let it run for a minute, cold and clear over her bare wrists.

"Who was that he was talking to, Darcy?" she asked, trying to keep her voice calm. She touched her cooled hands to her throat. The newspaper rustled.

"Don't know," Darcy said. She looked at her mother, heavy and pale and plain-faced. "Somebody, I guess. How was church?"

Mudd turned off the water and began to shake her hands dry. She sighed. "Hot," she said. "It was hot."

Lee was standing outside the back door with a sack of groceries hanging from each hand. He smiled, and Mudd saw his dimple winking at her in the corner of his cheek. He'd got that when he was three and he was chasing a cat and he tripped and landed face first on the sharp corner of the front steps. Lee's dimple wasn't something he'd been born with. It was a part of his good looks that had come to him by luck, it had been a cut that had scabbed over and scarred, just like the mark of an angel's kiss, Mudd thought.

She opened the door for him. "Thank you, Lee," she said. She reached out and brushed the boy's hair off his face with her hand.

Time was, Mudd thought. Time was when she would have lain right down in the road and died for her children, for both of them, Darcy and Lee. But then after a while it came to seem to her that she just didn't have that kind of a power in the world. She wasn't going to be able to protect them, she could see that. Not even her own dying would be what saved either one of them, not from Roy, not from each other, not from herself. Not from anything or anyone at all.

She could remember a day that didn't seem so long ago, a morning just like this one, in the summertime, when Lee was still just a baby, and Darcy wasn't more than the softest small flutter in her belly, and they'd come home after church, and Lee was outside in the driveway, toddling around on the gravel, kicking at the stones. She'd stopped to tie his shoe before he tripped and fell and cracked his head. She'd stooped down, pressing one knee into the hard-packed dirt, not caring about herself at all, whether her dress got mussed and soiled or her stockings got snagged and torn, just fussing over her baby boy instead. She'd brushed her lips across Lee's forehead, tasting dust and sweat and salt.

Sometimes back then Mudd had felt like she could just about squash him, that was how much she'd loved that boy. And when she did hug him, when she squeezed his body up against her, she could feel his breath catching in his chest. She could just about hear Lee squeak.

She turned back to Darcy. She took a deep breath, working to control the tremble in her voice, trying her best to sound casual and unconcerned and nonchalant. "Well, was it a woman, Darcy? Could you tell?"

But Darcy didn't know, or if she did, she wasn't going to be the one to say.

The three of them stood there, looking at each other, not moving, only listening, waiting, it seemed, until they heard the pickup truck cough to life, shift into gear, and rattle away.

*　*　*

Mudd trudged up to her room at the top of the stairs. She kicked off her shoes and stepped out of her dress, letting it lie as it fell, a crumpled puddle of loose fabric on the rug in the middle of the floor. Her bare arms were soft and doughy, and almost the same dingy gray-white color as her slip. Her underwear was black and lacy, outlined like smoke against the

paler pouched surface of her skin. She rolled onto her back
into the bed. When she closed her eyes, she saw Roy's hands,
hovering over her body, like a blackbird's wings, whacking
the air and flapping through the dark.

*   *   *

The Craig family home was a large two-story house that had
been built up on a sloping mound of open green meadow
beyond a ramble of limestone wall that followed for miles
along the meandering curves of Edgewood Road. As Bader
pulled his car up into the drive, past the long, grassy lawn
under the heavy overhanging branches of a cluster of old
trees, he saw that all the garage doors to one side of the house
had been pulled shut. He was sure that Mr. Craig must be
expecting him, but when he got out of his car and closed the
door and listened, it was all so quiet, all around, that he began
to wonder whether it might be possible that maybe nobody
was home.

How long had it been since someone from his family had
spoken to anyone from theirs? Since Margot herself came to
ask for their help and forgiveness and support? They'd turned
her down cold, and in what way had anything since that time
been changed? What was there that was different now? What
would prevent them from doing the same to him?

He climbed the mossy stone steps that led up to the front
door. Dark green painted shutters were squared off around
the big windows whose glass was sparkling so clean that the
reflection of the sky and the leaves against them made it impossible to see inside. Bader stepped up to the front door and
reached forward to poke at the button of the bell, listening to
the descending tones of its chime fade off, muffled within the
puzzle of rooms inside the big house.

He waited, filled with doubt. Had the Craigs remembered
that he'd called, that he was coming by, that he had something he wanted to discuss with them, a favor to ask, in fact?

Or had they decided that he wasn't worth their trouble or
their time, they'd be better off to ignore him, to avoid him,
to be gone when he got there or at least to keep quiet inside
when he came, lie low until he gave up and went away and
left them alone? Or, if they were home, how would they
receive him? With animosity? With indifference? With scorn?
Just as he was working to decide whether he should reach out
his finger and press the bell again, or turn around and go
away, leave well enough alone for now, the door swung
open, and a tall, thin woman stood before him.

She looked to be in her midfifties, he guessed, with long
fingers that she held up to her mouth with the habit of curling
her index finger over her upper lip to hide what she must
have been told was the only serious flaw in the otherwise
pleasant features of her face, a mouthful of jagged, discolored
teeth. Her hair was gauzy-looking, tinted a golden blond,
and she was wearing it pulled into a twist at the back of her
neck, held in place there by copper pins. She glinted with
jewelry — a gold and silver watch, diamond earrings, an antique platinum wedding band set with a diamond encircled
by several small emeralds, a ring that must have been a family
heirloom, handed down through several generations of Craig
women, Bader's own grandmother Margot among them for
a while, perhaps.

"Mrs. Craig?" Bader said. "I'm Bader Von Vechten. I
called?"

She smiled at Bader, pressing her lips together still to hide
her teeth from him, and her face was suddenly lined with a
delicate pattern of creases and wrinkles, like a crumpled bit
of tissue paper that had been unfolded and then smoothed out
again, flat.

"Von Vechten," she said, nodding. "Yes. Please, come in.
I told my husband that you called and might be stopping by
here to see us today."

Even if Bader hadn't already known who Libbie Craig

was, and that she was a longstanding member of the Cedar Hill Country Club crowd, he'd have been able to tell just by looking at her that she was one of its ladies. They were, he knew, the wives of Cedar Hill's doctors and lawyers and bankers and businessmen, women whose fathers and grandfathers had been members there, too, whose great-grandfathers had been among the city's founders and had helped to build up its streets and its bridges, its post office and courthouse and schools and jail.

They were women who could all agree that their children were each of them precious and beautiful in some way, if not physically attractive or outstandingly talented or exceptionally smart, then at least polite and well dressed and well educated, thanks to their own involvement in their lives, healthy and well fed, without a care in the world, really, except to wonder whether to go into their fathers' businesses with them or to follow instead the trail of their own inclinations, secure in the sure knowledge that the lifestyle that had been their great-grandparents' and their grandparents' and was now their parents' would, when their own turns came around, naturally be passed along to them, as if it were genetic, as much a part of their overall makeup as the shape of their faces or the size of their bodies or the color of their hair. Mrs. Craig and her friends were the women who could be seen driving around certain neighborhoods of Cedar Hill, running their errands, diminished behind the wheels of their big, luxurious cars, who lived in houses like this one, well furnished and tastefully decorated and spanking clean. Women who had gone to college before the war — not to learn anything, really, but only to discover their husbands — who had married their childhood friends, who had had one or two or three children, sometimes four — only the Catholics had any more than that, because they couldn't help it, of course, they were under higher orders, they didn't have any choice — when their husbands came back home again after the war. Women who stayed home to take care of their families, who never worked for money, who never earned a penny, whose days were spent at volunteer jobs and ladies' luncheons, garden clubs and cooking classes, PTA meetings and bridge games, whose weekend evenings included cocktail parties with friends, dinner at the club, football games at the college on Saturdays, church on Sunday mornings, and champagne brunch at the club afterward, at noon. Women who were likely to survive their husbands by several years, who most often ended up living alone, widowed or divorced, with an inheritance or a settlement that gave them just enough money to finish up the last years of their lives in some comfort, in an apartment or a condominium, until they fell and broke a hip, became ill with cancer or pneumonia, were just too old and thoughtless and frail to be able to care for themselves anymore, who would be committed then by their children to a nursing home in a scenic country setting, while everybody waited patiently for them to die.

She turned, and Bader followed her through a wide arched doorway into the family room, where Archie Craig was sitting in a leather chair with his feet propped up on the matching ottoman, watching, over the tops of the half-glasses that he had perched on the end of his nose, a baseball game on TV. He held a tall, frosted glass in one hand and a cigarette in the other, and he was wearing a collared knit golf shirt and black plaid shorts beyond the hems of which his long bare legs were bruised-looking and white. He didn't stand up when Bader came in, or, for that matter, even look away from the game, but only put up the hand that held his cigarette and bared his teeth in a quick, broad smile.

"Archie," Libbie said, "this is Bader Von Vechten. The young man who called?"

A fan was slowly turning overhead, stirring the air that was otherwise stiflingly still, thick with the summer's humidity and heat. The doors and windows in the room had all been thrown open — they looked out from the back of the house, toward the blinding bright green shine of the grassy lawn and leafy trees at the edge of the nearby woods. The room was crowded with clusters of furniture, a variety of seating arrangements whose tables and chairs and footstools and lamps made the heat in the room seem even more stifling than it was.

At Mrs. Craig's invitation, Bader had a seat on a small, floral-patterned sofa near Mr. Craig's chair, and Archie turned away from the television screen for a moment to take a look at him. He nodded, pursed his lips, as if what he saw was just about as much as he'd expected to see, and then directed his attention back to the game again.

"It's Sunday afternoon, Von Vechten," he said. "As you can see, I'm watching baseball. I hope you don't mind." He brought his drink up to his lips and sipped at it. "Vodka tonic?" he asked. He tapped the end of his cigarette against the rim of the large, full ashtray beside him.

"Thank you," Bader answered, shaking his head. "No." He didn't plan to stay long enough to have a drink. He just wanted permission to use the road, that was all. A key to the man's gate, nothing else.

On the glass-topped coffee table before him was a plate with a wedge of softening yellow cheese on it, beside the carcass of a smoked duck. Soda crackers had been laid out on a white napkin in a basket, and red and green grapes were piled up in a glass bowl. Bader turned to look at Mrs. Craig. She was frowning at her husband, shaking her head, and finally she crossed the room to the television set, bending at the waist to peer at its buttons and knobs. When she'd found the one to turn it off, she pressed it with her fingertip. She stood in front of the darkened screen with her hands clasped before her and her back straight.

Archie glared at her for a moment. He turned to Bader and smiled.

"I'm sorry," he said. "Mrs. Craig is right, as usual. Very rude of me. So," he continued, eying Bader over the tops of his glasses, "you're a Von Vechten, eh?" Without waiting for Bader to answer, he nodded and went on. "The last one probably, too." He laughed. "Well, I would have known it. You look like a Von Vechten, do you know that?"

"I remember your father," Mrs. Craig said. "Tom Von Vechten?" She had curled her finger over her lips again and was regarding Bader as if maybe what she was seeing was his past, his whole entire heritage, all his ancestors, every Von Vechten back further even than the crowd of bodies huddled together in the hull of a boat on the open sea, gathered like some unruly mob that was struggling for recognition there in his bones, in the blue of his eyes, and the dark brown of his hair, and in the size and the shape of the features of his face. "Such a nice man. Very refined, as I recall. Didn't you used to see him out at the club a lot, Archie?" she asked, and Bader felt his face go hot, as he blushed. A warm pink flush crept up his neck to his ears; a rosy glow was shining in his cheeks. "Playing cards?"

Archie rattled the ice in his drink and frowned at his wife, nervously waggling his foot.

"What is it that you want from me, Von Vechten?" he asked.

Bader shifted uncomfortably on the couch. "Just a small favor, that's all."

Archie was smiling again. He nodded toward his wife, who nodded back and smiled, too, as if the two of them had been talking about him before he came and had predicted just about exactly this.

"Not money, I hope," Archie said.

Bader coughed, surprised, first by the man's bluntness and then by his presumption that a stranger might come here to his house to ask him for a loan. He wondered whether there

were people who did such a thing, and if there were, was he
in the habit of giving it to them when they asked?

"No," he said. "Just a key to the gate, that's all."

"The gate?" Archie crushed his cigarette out and lit another.

"Over the road."

"The road?"

"In Empire. It goes up to the cottage? My land?"

It seemed he'd caught, finally, Mr. Craig's interest. The
older man swung his feet down to the floor and sat up, scoot-
ing toward the edge of the cushion on his chair, leaning forward toward Bader. "What exactly is it that you want to do
up there?"

"Live," Bader answered. He shrugged. It was simple,
really. Not so much to ask, he thought.

"You're aware of the fact, I suppose, that the property's
become landlocked."

"I know that your road out there is the only way to get
into it or out of it anymore. I suspect that was done inten-
tionally. And I know, too, that you have your gate closed
and locked and posted, and before I start to use it, I thought
I'd better come here, and ask you if you'd mind."

Mrs. Craig was staring at him. "You're going to live in
that cottage?" she asked.

He nodded.

"But whatever for?"

Bader smiled. "Well, for one thing, it's mine."

"But that place must be a mess," Libbie said. "Nobody's
lived in it for years and years. Not since Margot moved out."

"Yes," said Bader, "well, in fact, I was just out there this
morning, and you're right, it is a mess. But I plan to fix it
up."

Archie sighed. He took off his glasses and slowly folded
them, deliberately setting them down on the table next to

him. He turned back to Bader again, looking at him squarely, as if he were trying to read some meaning in his eyes. He gave his head a little shake that wobbled in his jowls.

"Do you have a job, son?" he asked.

Bader reddened. "Not just now, sir, no, I don't."

"Then, why don't you just sell it, Von Vechten?"

"Sell it?"

"Take the money and run."

Bader smiled. "Sell it to who, Mr. Craig? To you?"

Archie shrugged. "Why not? It'd sure save you a lot of trouble. In fact, I made several offers for it to your father over the years, you know, but as even he would have been the first to admit, he wasn't much of a businessman. Didn't understand what I wanted with it. Told me it wasn't for sale."

"And he was right, Mr. Craig," Bader said. "It's not."

Archie leaned forward and cupped his knees in his hands. "I know you Von Vechtens think that holding on to that land has something to do with your honor," he said. "I've been hearing that for as far back as I can remember, about how your family was taken advantage of by mine. But I'm going to be frank with you now, Bader. What happened back then, it wasn't a swindle. Only some bad management, that's all. Bad management and bad luck. Sometimes it just happens. Things like that, they get out of hand. Everybody gets greedy. Everybody's trying to protect what's theirs. And my opinion about it now is that maybe if some of the people who were supposed to be in charge of your family's affairs would have realized the truth of that a little bit sooner, we'd have had some kind of a compromise, and you personally would be that much better off for it now. In fact, I don't think it would have been such a bad thing if our two families could have been kept together by old Horace and Margot's marriage back then. Not such a bad thing at all. But the fact is, that isn't what happened. The fact is, your uncle Wolfgang murdered my grandfather. In cold blood. And I'm not about to forgive anybody for that now." He leaned back again and lit another cigarette. "Take some advice from me now, all right, Von Vechten? You want to make a difference here? You want to change the way things have gone? Right some wrongs? Set a few things straight? That's fine. I don't blame you. Just try not to be as stupid about how you do it as your father was, that's all. Try not to make things any worse for yourself than they already are."

Bader heard the slur in Mr. Craig's words, the garbled consonants and the drawn-out vowels — speech that was slowed by vodka and tonic and summer heat and Sunday baseball — and he felt his anger beginning its familiar rolling in his chest again. "I just want the key," he said, fighting to stay calm. He took a deep breath. "That's all. Access."

Mr. Craig laughed. Smoke caught in his throat, and he coughed.

Bader stood up. "This is crazy," he said, stepping around the table toward the door. "I didn't come here to be laughed at, Mr. Craig. Or lectured to, either. If you'd rather not co-operate with me, I can understand that, and I'll find some other way. That's all."

Later, Katherine told him that his face had been burning up so hard then that even his ears had turned bright red, and his eyes were so dark with anger that they'd looked, to her, to be black.

She was standing in the doorway. She'd just come in, home after an afternoon of swimming in the pool at the club. Neither of them could remember, when they tried to recon-struct it for themselves later, exactly how it had gone. Mrs. Craig had introduced them, Katherine said. Then she'd gone to the small desk behind Mr. Craig's chair, and rummaged through the jumbled contents of its drawer until, finally, she'd found what she was looking for, and brought out a small bundle of keys. She'd reached over her husband's shoulder and dropped it in his lap. Grimacing, Mr. Craig had

crushed his cigarette out and then begun searching through
the keys, rolling them over his fingers, studying each one
closely before moving on to the next. When he'd found the
one he wanted, he'd opened the chain and removed it. He'd
held it up between his finger and his thumb, turning it in the
light, and then he'd tossed it to Bader, who caught it in one
hand.

Bader recalled that he'd been standing, dizzy with anger,
ready to walk out. That Katherine had put out her hand to
him, and he'd taken it. That her fingertips had been soft,
wrinkly, waterlogged. That she'd had a white towel with the
green Country Club logo on it folded over her arm. That her
hair had been wet, brushed back away from her face, hanging
down her back, dampening her shirt. That she'd smelled like
lemons and chlorine and coconut oil.

That when he saw her, that first time, he'd felt a door
opening up inside of him. And, he wondered later, was that
because he'd already begun to scheme? To make Katherine
the real key to her father's gate, and the only one true and
permanent access to the Von Vechten land?

*   *   *

In Darcy's room at the end of the hallway upstairs, Lee was
perched at the edge of the bed, watching his sister fiddle with
her hair. She'd comb it back away from her face and bring it
up into a bundle on top of her head, wrap a rubber band
around it, study the effect by tipping her head from one side
to the other, then take it out and brush it down and start all
over again.

"I think it makes me look older, Lee, wearing it up this
way, don't you?"

Lee's languid gray eyes followed the line of Darcy's reflected silhouette — the slope of her back, the arch of her bare
neck, the point of her chin, the curve of her cheekbone, and

the plane of her brow. He shrugged and scooted backward onto the bed, swinging his legs around and leaning back against the pile of her pillows at its head.

"I don't see any difference, Darcy," he said. "You look the same to me, either way. You just look like you."

The air in the room felt heavy, laden with the buildup of the long day's heat. The blades of the fan in the window turned and turned, but they were hardly able to make a stir. Lee closed his eyes. He was going to leave this place someday, he thought. He'd pack his bags and drive off out of here, heading where? Well, it didn't matter, just going away, that was all that mattered, going away in a black Mustang convertible, smoking a French cigarette, one hand on the wheel, the radio turned up loud, the wind in his hair, following the road, taking the curves tight, swallowing up the straightaways fast. At night he could park off to the side somewhere and build a fire. If it rained or got cold, he could put up the top on the car and sit inside, watching the lightning crack the sky, listening to the thunder shake the land. Without a care in the world.

Darcy was leaning forward, closer to the mirror, pouting her lips and dabbing at them with the tube of pinkish lipstick that she'd swiped from the drawer in Mudd's bathroom.

"I think maybe Dad has a girlfriend, Lee," she said, watching her mouth move. She licked her lips with the tip of her tongue. Her teeth were small, gleaming white and sharp. She looked away from her own face to get a glimpse of Lee's.

His eyes were open, but he was gazing at the ceiling, lost in thought, Darcy might have guessed, if she hadn't known her brother as well as she did. Most of the time if Darcy disturbed him, if she nudged him back into consciousness with her elbow and asked him what he was thinking about, what she was likely to get instead of an answer was a look of pure and honest surprise, because, she guessed, most of the time

Lee's mind was just an uncomplicated blank. Her brother was as empty and clear inside as the bright blue dome of the sky was outside.

"Did you hear what I'm telling you, Lee?" she asked.

He turned slowly to look at her, and his eyes seemed to cloud over before he recognized who she was, just like somebody who was waking up from a deep, hard sleep.

He smiled. "Yeah, Darcy," he said. "I heard."

"Well?"

"Well, what?"

"Aren't you shocked?"

Lee sat up, and he swung his legs around and stood, and then he moved up closer to Darcy, he came to stand behind her, looking at the wisps of hair that curled against her neck and smelling the warm fragrance of her flowery perfume. He touched her, feeling the warmth of her flushed skin against his cooler hand; he bent and brought his face down next to hers, and he studied their two reflections side by side in the mirror. Brother and sister, siblings — they looked so much alike, Darcy liked to say, they could, the two of them, be twins.

"Her name's Naomi," Lee told her. "She has red hair and freckles, and he met her in a bar."

Darcy turned and looked at her brother.

"How do you know all that, Lee?" she asked.

Lee was combing his fingers through his hair, pressing it back over his head, away from his face. He pointed to his head. "Brains," he said. "Now give me a cigarette, Darce. I need a smoke."

She frowned at him. "You smoke too much, you know that?"

"Don't start in on me."

"It's not good for you, Lee. You'll kill yourself. Look at Daddy, for Christ's sake."

"You sound just like Mudd, Darcy." His smile stung her, dimple winking.

"I do not," Darcy protested.

"You do," Lee said. "And when you make that face, you look just like her, too."

Darcy stood up and turned around and tried to grab him. "I'll kill you, Lee, you know I will."

He danced back away from her. "Same eyes," he said. "Same hair."

She swatted at him, hands fanning his face.

"Same shape."

She caught his wrist and clamped her hand around it. He struggled away from her, laughing. She held on tight, digging her fingernails into his skin, until he turned his back and flipped her over his shoulder onto the bed. She lay there, limp and breathless and flushed.

"Take it back, Lee," she said.

He put his hand out and touched her face.

"Hey, I was just teasing you, Darcy, you're a pretty girl, you know you are."

"You think so, Lee?" she asked. "Do you?"

He smiled. "Everybody does," he answered.

She looked at him, searching his face, trying to decide whether or not she should believe anything he said.

"You're bad, Lee," she said, finally. "You know that? Bad."

"Okay," he sighed, nodding, "good, that's all settled then — you're pretty, and I'm bad." He took her hand and pulled her up to her feet. "Now tell me, Darcy, where do you hide your smokes?"

*   *   *

Katherine Craig sat at the kitchen table, snapping the ends off the string beans her mother was planning to steam, with fresh dill, for dinner. Mrs. Craig was at the chopping block, slicing garden tomatoes and carrots and radishes for the salad.

Katherine had only the vaguest old memory of Bader Von Vechten, a thin, quiet boy, a few years older, with dark hair and pale skin and bright blue eyes. He'd lived beyond an iron fence then, in the big brick house at the top of the rise of Linden Lane. She'd passed by it a thousand times, at least. She'd even ventured up its driveway once, on a dare, at Halloween, with a gang of her girlfriends, and she'd been the bold one who stepped forward to ring the bell, but the house had seemed so quiet and dark and empty and still, without jack-o'-lanterns or lights or decorations of any kind, that everyone was afraid and they'd run off down to the street again before anybody had answered the door. Sometime around then, the house was bought by the Magruders, who lived there still, and Bader had moved away. When she thought about it now, that was all she knew.

"What happened between our families, Mother?" Katherine asked. "Why was he so angry?"

"It was an ugly business, dear."

"What did we do to them?" she persisted.

"*We* didn't do anything to them."

"Then why did they all hate us so much?"

Mrs. Craig sighed. She turned the knife over in her hand and let the light catch in its blade. "Well, Katherine, if you must know, they blamed us," she said. "Bader's father, Tom Von Vechten, he tried, but he was never as successful in Cedar Hill as he wanted to be."

Katherine laughed. "Who is?" she asked, rolling her eyes.

Libbie turned and looked over her shoulder at her daughter. She smiled. Katherine was such a pretty girl, she thought, so tanned and healthy-looking, with her fresh complexion and her deep green eyes. Her body was slim from swimming every day.

"Well, but Tom kept trying to blame your father for his own failures, dear. He accused him of sabotaging his business interests whenever he got the chance."

"Did he?"

Mrs. Craig shook her head and went back to her chopping again. "Of course not. The Von Vechtens, Tom and Eleanor, both of them, they were just not responsible people."

Katherine scoffed. "Maybe they were just unlucky," she said.

"No, really, they were an unconventional pair, those two."

"How?"

"Well, he was twice her age, for one thing, and the two of them were always acting like a couple of children, really, playing and partying all the time. Buying clothes and cars. Drawing attention to themselves. Spending more money than they had."

Bader's father Thomas was Wolfgang Von Vechten's older brother, and after the murder, even before he met Eleanor, he'd been living his life in Cedar Hill as if he thought the rest of them all owed him something. He was always trying to set things right with the Craigs again, trying to get them to give up some of their assets, to admit to some kind of wrong-doing, hoping for some compensation for himself when they did.

When he was almost fifty, he married Bader's mother. Eleanor was barely twenty, and she wasn't from here; her family came from Omaha, and she thought that she was marrying into a prominent family and some wealth. It wasn't until after she came to Cedar Hill that she understood the truth, and by that time it was too late, because she was pregnant already, with Bader. Tom blamed her "frailties" on her not quite upper-class upbringing, but she blamed him, and said he'd tricked her. She drank too much. She was beautiful. She loved parties and pretty dresses and good food.

Mrs. Craig put down her knife and turned to face her daughter. "If you must know, Katherine," she continued, wiping her hands on a towel, "they were very attracted to each other physically."

Katherine grinned at her mother. "What is that supposed to mean?" she asked.

Mrs. Craig sat down at the table and began to break in half the beans that Katherine had already cleaned. "Well," she said, "your father used to say it was a sort of a heat between them. Everybody knew about it. You could practically see it there steaming up between those two when they were together, the way they looked at each other and touched each other, especially the way they danced. Some people thought it was obscene, because he was so much older than her."

Under any other circumstances, Tom and Eleanor Von Vechten might have been an unusually happy pair, however. It wasn't that Tom didn't try, because he did. He took the money that was left from his family's fortune, and he used it to support one business enterprise and then another, from real estate investments to marketing schemes, never making any money, but not losing much of it, either, except in the card games that he kept getting into at the club. He didn't have a head for business is what people said later, and neither did she.

"What happened to them?" Katherine asked.

Tom had lost a lot of cash at the gin table at the club, and he and Eleanor had made plans to drive to Chicago for the weekend. Just to get away, they said. Tom had promised his friends that he was going to pay off all his debts with them just as soon as he got back. They left Bader at home with a maid and took off early in the morning, but they didn't even get past the city limits of Cedar Hill. The accident happened out on the Old Post Road, which had only just that summer been paved. It had been gravel before, and the going on it then was slow. But once the road was asphalt its sharp curves became deadly, without any barriers or markers or shoulders. Tom was probably driving too fast. He missed a turn. There was some question afterward whether he'd done it on purpose, but the official report called it an accident.

"Slammed into an embankment," Libbie said. "The car caught on fire, and they both of them were trapped inside and killed. Bader was sent off to live with his mother's sister in Omaha. Margot didn't die until just last year, I don't think. And she must have left Bader some money, because it looks to me like now he's thinking about living back here."

"What's wrong with that?"

"Well, for one thing, what's he going to do? He doesn't seem to have a job of any kind. And for another, that place up there is a mess. Why would anyone want to live in it?"

"Maybe we could help him."

"I really doubt that he'd appreciate any help we might be able to give him. You'd best just keep your distance, Katherine."

As usual, Katherine thought. Her mother would always try to avoid anything she thought might turn out to be unpleasant or hurtful. It was an attitude that was familiar and stifling, and it made Katherine feel short of breath.

"Well, Mother, I don't happen to agree, if you want to know the truth. I think it would be nice if we got to be friends. If we could somehow patch up all that ugly business of the past."

"Stick to your own business, dear," Libbie said. "That's my best advice."

Katherine smiled. "But wouldn't it be interesting, if the two of us, a Craig and a Von Vechten, turned out to be friends?"

"Your father wouldn't like it, Katherine."

"No," she replied, "I don't suppose he would."

*   *   *

Mudd was asleep, dreaming of herself and of her husband Roy. Outside her window were wild animals that had somehow been set free from their cages and allowed to prowl unrestrained through the rustling thick cornfields that surrounded the house on all sides like a rolling sea. The animals were crouched in the dirt under the front porch. Their shadows glided along the road and they walked, quickly, silently, on their heavy fleshy paws. They stopped at the creek to drink, slurping up the clear cold water with tongues as thick and pink as slabs of raw steak; they slept in the shadows under the bridge, their roars like a distant thunder rolling in the hills, and all the time Roy's hands were skimming Mudd's hips and grazing the down on her belly and rolling the hunch of her shoulders between his two thumbs, shaping them like soft clay.

There was the pure white mound of Roy's buttocks, the raised splatter of scars over his shoulders, the curly brown hair that was spread out across the swell of his stomach and the breadth of his chest. The shadowed outline of his legs, the hard knot of his ankle bones, the jut of his hips, his face moving above hers — straining, flushed, slick with sweat, stubbled with a day's growth of beard — his slackened jowl, and the hard weight of his belly sliding across the cushion of hers. His hands cupping her breasts and rolling over her nipples. His breathing, heavy and hoarse. The gentle waggle of his shoulders, the hard thrust of his hips.

Mudd's eyes snapped open. Her body had cooled, finally, and her skin was filmed over now with a sheen of sweat that seemed to cover her like the ice that coated each small twig end of the trees outside her window in the dead of winter-time.

* * *

"Don't slouch, Margaret. Lift up your shoulders, pick up your chin. Don't drag your feet. You walk like that, you look like a cow."

That was the sound of her sister's voice — Rayanne get-ting ready to go out on her date, Rayanne standing in her bare feet, Rayanne in her shiny white slip, pulling on a pair of cinnamon-colored stockings, sliding spiked pink plastic rollers along through the bouncy curls of her hair, while Mudd peered at the mirror, into her own gray eyes. The thin, downy lines of her eyebrows were so faint on her face that at a distance they were hardly visible.

"You ought to darken those," Rayanne said, handing her the eyebrow pencil. "Your face is just too plain." She reached out and brushed away the straggle of hair that had drifted over her brow. "Plain as rain."

Mudd's face was like a moon, or a plate, or a big, white flower, round and shiny, smooth and bland. She was big, too. She was hefty, and stupid-looking, she thought. Later, after Rayanne was gone out on her date, Mudd stood there in front of the mirror again, and she turned her body all around, twisting herself this way and that, studying her re-flection from all angles in the long, white-framed mirror that was nailed up onto the back of Rayanne's closet door, and what she saw were Mudd Butt Butler's puckered buttocks packed into a pair of white cotton underpants. And her plump breasts — "melons," she'd overheard the girls' whis-pers echo in the vault of the school gym — filling up the wide cups of her brassiere. The girls talked behind their hands, shaking their heads, disgusted by how big Mudd was already, saying she was fat, but that wasn't right. She wasn't fat; she was only large. She was well developed, the gym teacher had tried to explain to the girls. She was mature for her age, that was all.

She was only an exaggeration of what the other girls all knew they could expect themselves to one day become, and so, embarrassed and ashamed of their own fascination, they stole glances, took furtive glimpses of her, were irresistibly drawn to the sight of her bare flesh — of the dark smudge of hair in her armpits and on her ankles and between her legs, of her milky, blue-veined breasts floating, cloudlike, in the big cups of her thick-strapped rubber and wire and nylon bra, of the firm mound of her belly, her rounded shoulders, the damp doughy creases in her neck, her meaty arms, her bare skin, clear and creamy — as she changed back into her school clothes again at the end of the physical education class.

Some boys trapped her in the stairwell after lunch and, jeering, they gave her the nickname "Mudd Butt." They formed a circle around her, laughing. They poked their fingers at her "knockers," whistling "hooters," howling "jugs."

And she smelled, they said, and she agreed, wrinkling her nose. Her skin was always damp. Her hair was oily near her scalp and broken at the ends; it hung down onto her shoulders like a rag, drab and limp and dull. She sweated too much. She was too large. She was too hairy. She was too ugly. She was too dumb.

"You're a cow," she whispered to herself, frowning, shaking her head from side to side, pursing her lips. "Big stupid cow. Plain as rain."

Her legs were solid, and her ankles were stout, and her feet were blocklike, small and square, with rounded toes that looked like little bleached pebbles, shiny and white.

She walked home alone after school, with her books folded in her arms — pressed up against her chest to hide its wobble and breadth. She kept her chin tucked in and her head bowed down and her shoulders hunched forward, trying to

make herself seem just as uninteresting and commonplace as
a stone, wishing to be forgotten, hoping to be overlooked.
Her shadow stretched away from her on the grass, leaking
out of the ends of her feet, as if, she thought, that might be
her real self — a delicate smoky soul snagged on the heaving,
stinking, sweating, warm, moist flesh of a big, clumsy girl.

Sitting at her school desk, in the crushing stillness of the
classroom, a stupor overcame her. She stared at the dust
motes that swirled in a shaft of sunlight. An idiot, she was.
Lumbering. Slumberous. For all she knew, sometimes, the
world around her might just as well have been a part of the
long, slow tumble of a dream.

Margaret Mudd Butt Butler. She walked the school hall-
ways with her books clasped so tightly to her chest that her
fingertips turned white. She kept her head down and her eyes
on the floor, and, over and over, she had to remind herself,
"Keep walking, keep moving, don't stop. Don't look. Don't
talk." She didn't want to draw anyone's attention to herself.
She didn't want to make them turn their eyes her way. She'd
be sorry, she knew, if she did. She'd be sorry if they noticed
her, sorry if someone decided he wanted to talk to her. She
wouldn't know what he wanted from her. She wouldn't
want to hear whatever it was he thought he had to say.

Her legs were hidden under the folds of the long, pleated
skirts she wore. Her ankles were bound by the rolled-over
tops of her thick white socks, and her feet were tucked into a
pair of brown leather loafers. Just like all the other girls, only
bigger, that was all. She wore cabled wool sweaters and cotton blouses with rounded collars — but they always seemed
too thin and sheer, so if she took her sweater off anybody
could look right through and see the outline of her bra with
its thick rubbery back and wide straps. Damp yellow rings of
sweat flowered in her armpits, and she kept her sweater on
for as long as she could stand it, and that made her sleepy,
too, stupid and sleepy, nodding in the classroom, dozing off

sometimes, so that when the other kids looked at her, when the teacher called her name, when she was asked the simplest question, she would be struck dumb, and she'd stare, bewildered, shake her head, and murmur, "I don't know."

So who could blame her, then, if after a while she felt as if she hated everybody, not only herself, but all of them, every single one?

Margaret Mudd Butt Butler, standing on the steps during recess, looked down at the playground behind the school and watched the other children, and what she saw was the blur of their muscular legs, the sheen of the sweat on their clear faces, the pumping of their bare arms, the flip and flap of one boy's bright hair, the flutter of a girl's ribbony black braid. But what Mudd was imagining as she watched them was the deep, distant roar of an earthquake's hard and sudden surge. She thought up an unsettling shift of soil beneath her planted feet, allowed it a healthy gain in strength and force, let it hump and rise like the back of some huge hibernating beast that stretched its massive limbs and rolled over, restless in its sleep. As if she herself were the earth that they all stood and ran and walked and played on, shifting under their feet. She could hear the crackle and fall of plaster off the classroom walls in the building at her back. The moan of the wood straining in the ceilings and the floors. The bulge and the snap of the window glass.

She felt her heart struggle, pounding with the agitation of these images, and she thought that she could just about feel the devastation, it seemed so real to her, as if it were happening inside, within her own body, splintering the brittle sticks of her own bones, shredding her stringy muscles, wresting the rubbery ligaments of her legs, splitting her tendons and crushing her joints, like the savage twist and tear of green wood and flimsy bark in the saplings that had been planted along the sidewalk in front of the school, abruptly uprooted and torn free.

A flock of long-legged older boys in gym shorts and T-shirts was skittering back and forth between opposing basketball hoops. A piece of notebook paper had been blown up flat against the wire fence. And a dark pile of castoff coats and sweaters was wadded up in a mound that might have been a body hunched, sleeping, unconscious, dead, in an out-of-the-way corner of the court.

The recess bell was screaming. Mudd stood on the school steps and pressed herself back against the wall, watching the herd of her classmates come stampeding blindly toward her, afraid now that they might unthinkingly run her down and heedlessly crush her, trample her into the dirt.

They had all of them teased her, all these kids, at one time or another. They had all made fun of her. No one had any reason to talk to her otherwise, it seemed. Except for Roy Kimbel. He was the only one. Oh, he stood with the others sometimes, when they huddled around her, and in front of his friends, with everybody watching, he smiled and winked and snickered just about as much as the next one. And the truth was, she knew, that in a way he was ashamed of her. Or, at least, of himself and of how he felt about her, of how he liked her, in spite of what everybody else seemed to think. Beauty might just be in the eye of the beholder, he'd whispered, lying beside her in the dark, tracing his fingertip over the curve of her cheek. When he said that, she'd pictured a perfect, pure alabaster woman, armless and naked, with a gleam in her eye that would turn out to be the same perfect, pure alabaster woman, posed there inside her own eye.

Roy told Mudd that her bare skin was just about the softest surface he'd ever touched. He said he liked how she smelled, salty and milky and sour. And together the two of them had stuck to an agreement — he wasn't to ever call her Mudd, and she wouldn't expect him to stand up for her in public, against his friends. Because Roy Kimbel just about could not get enough of all that was Mudd. As much of her as there

was, it still seemed that he always could find a use for more.
He loved to look at her. He loved to touch her. He wallowed
in her, he floated in her arms, he rolled his body against her
flesh, and she knew she was the one thing in the world that
could make him happy, every time, she was the one warm
soft thing that would always be able to make him feel good.

*   *   *

Roy had lived alone with his father in Cedar Hill then, on the
west side of the river, next door to Rayanne Butler's boyfriend, Ridge Hamilton, in one of two houses that sat side by
side, perched up on top of a short swell of land above the
sidewalk, beyond a limestone retaining wall that was green
with moss, on a gentle mound of grassy yard. The houses
had been built at the same time by the same builder, and each
one was a mirror image of the other, different only because
Ridge, even though he was in a wheelchair, was able to keep
his place well tended and neat while Roy and his father —
who were both of them healthy and strong-armed and fit —
had anyway let theirs run down and then cluttered it up both
inside and out with all their collection of castoffs, what
looked to anybody else to be nothing but trash and garbage
and junk.

The houses were miniature mock Tudors, with thin slats
of wood bent across a heavy swirl of stucco that always re-
minded Mudd of rich white cream cheese frosting smeared
over the crumbly dark surface of a chocolate cake. Back then,
before she got to know Roy, she thought that her sister's
boyfriend — with his slicked-back black hair and his soft
brown eyes and his square, shadowy jaw — was just about
the handsomest-looking person she'd ever laid eyes on beyond the shimmering screen of a movie house, and that Rayanne was probably the luckiest girl in the world to be wearing
on a chain around her neck the red ruby stone of his high
school graduation ring. And besides that, his little house

looked to Mudd like it maybe couldn't even be real, but was just something that was pretend, a plaything that he'd borrowed from the pages of a picture book or taken from an illustration to a fairy tale, molded out of gingerbread or chocolate or sugared, jellied fruit. Just about too good to be true, she told her sister when she saw it for the first time, and Rayanne had looked at her and, proudly, grinned.

"Just wait'll you meet him," she said. "Just wait'll you see what he does."

Ridge was in his kitchen, sitting on the vinyl seat pad of his wheelchair with the soles of his black leather boots propped up on the footrests, caught there in the circle spotlight of a bright, unshaded overhead bulb. His red plaid flannel shirt was opened at the neck to reveal the tangle of dark hairs that swirled upward toward the smooth, hard curve of his throat, and his faded brown chinos, held up by a snaky-looking green belt, were worn so thin at the knees and along the tops of his thighs that the cloth was smooth and flimsy and gray. Ridge's head was bent over what at first Mudd thought looked like some serious and complicated work — in fact, she realized, it was the pieces of a plastic model airplane he was building, spread out over a sheet of newspapers on the surface of a wobbly-legged aluminum card table. She could see then that his house was filled with wooden and plastic planes — bombers and fighters and gliders and jets — all suspended from the ceiling by invisible strands of fishing line, all of them floating in midair, silently swinging and turning, slowly hitching on any occasional waft of breeze.

Ridge looked up and grinned at Mudd and Rayanne — his big Butler girls as he called them — reaching out to pinch Mudd on the leg. He'd been in a car wreck two summers before he got to know Rayanne, and he'd cracked his back and shattered one leg, broken it in so many places that by the time it was mended back together again it was changed — it came out of its cast an inch and a half shorter than it had been when it went in. He had no feeling in it anymore, and it wouldn't move. But if you didn't get stuck and dwell for too long on the looks of his bottom half, Mudd thought, Ridge was still an extraordinarily handsome man. His face was smooth and white and soft-looking, as if it had been carved out of soap. His arms and shoulders and back and chest rippled with the muscles that he'd built up to compensate for the uselessness of his legs. His injury had made it hard for him to get around, and impossible for him to work at a steady job, so he collected some kind of a compensation from the insurance and the government, too, because he was a vet, Rayanne said, and he stayed at home all day and rolled around his house and his yard and built his model airplanes, and Rayanne came by to visit with him whenever she had time.

"So, how's that Miss Margaret Butler, eh?" Ridge was smiling and squinting at Mudd.

He winked at her, and she blushed and murmured, "Hiya, Ridge."

She hardly dared to look back at him straight, he was so good-looking — right out of the movies, she thought — it was as if just the sight of him might be enough to cause some kind of a damage to her eyes. When Rayanne leaned over to kiss Ridge on the cheek, Mudd, embarrassed, turned her head away. Through the open window behind her she could hear a racket of competing noises — the rattle and scream of a washing machine's unbalanced spin in the house next door, somebody shouting, the rhythmic ringing bangs of a hammer, and the high, sharp whine of an electric saw. Ridge was saying to Rayanne that Frank Kimbel was out there slamming around in his work shed again, and that would be where all that noise was coming from now.

"He thinks he's an artist," said Ridge, looking at Mudd over the wings of the model bomber, sighting along the swell of its fuselage to the foreshortened cross of its tail. He shuddered when he laughed and jostled the little toy that he held

balanced on the flat fingertips of his hand, rattling its flimsy
wings and shaking its gluey joints, like the dark turbulence
within a cottony roil of clouds.

"How about you scoot on outside for a while and find
something for yourself to do now, Margaret, all right?" Rayanne had turned her sleepy eyes to Mudd and was flapping
her hand with its long, red-painted nails, shooing her sister
off, across the kitchen toward the back door. "Let me and
Ridge here have a little privacy? If you don't mind?" Again,
a wink from Ridge. And another warm, friendly smile. His
teeth gleaming bright white. Deep vertical creases cut in
around the corners of his mouth. Rayanne, with her hand on
her head, sliding down into his lap. Her voice turned husky.
"Give us some precious time to ourselves, okay?"

Mudd backed away, embarrassed, stopping in the doorway for just one moment to get another look at the pair of
them, Ridge and Rayanne, wondering as she always did, she
just couldn't help herself, what he must look like bare naked,
with that one bent leg of his twisted and warped as a gnarled
old tree branch, the other one skinny and wasted-looking and
scarred. He'd hooked his finger under Rayanne's chin and as
he pulled her face up closer toward his own, Mudd turned
and pushed away from them, out through the screen door
and down the slow slope of the wheelchair ramp to the
ground.

There was a wire fence that ran along a wavery line between Ridge Hamilton's yard and the land that belonged to
the house next door, and it separated one man's helter-skelter
from the other's well-tended flower gardens and close-cut
grass. But the disorder threatened to spill out over a sag in
the fence where it had been stepped on and brought down so
a girl with time on her hands and nothing to do and nowhere
else to go might wander off onto the property next door.
Wads of newspaper had blown up against the fence, and the
yard was cluttered with piles of old bottles and cans, heaps of

rusted metal, and an incinerator that was filled to overflowing with ashes and soggy newspapers and dried, dead leaves. Weeds grew in unrestrained disorder around a patch of wild-flowers, a clump of untrimmed bushes, and a twisted crabap-ple tree. The one splash of color was in the sprawl of wild roses that climbed along a short stretch of unpainted picket fencing on the farthest edge of the yard.

Drawn by the din of what Ridge had said was his neighbor Frank Kimbel's strange work, Mudd approached the wooden shed that stood over to one side of the gravel drive. She stopped just outside its open doorway, and, bending for-ward, she peeked around it to see, in the center of the circle of light that was cast by a bulb suspended from a long cord, a tall, thin man in a leather apron hammering away at the wide, flat flange of a metal contraption — a monstrosity that looked like it had been formed piecemeal from furnace and automobile parts, with appendages of circular ventilation shaft, a rusted-out washtub, the mechanical innards of some huge motor, spoked bicycle wheels, and a rubber fan belt and oily gears.

The man's face and hands were black with sweat and grease. Behind him was a long counter jumbled up with a huddle of small appliances, their cords dangling from their backsides like long, thin tails. An old car motor squatted on a folded towel, and there were empty gas cans stacked up in a pile on top of each other against a far wall. A washing ma-chine had been gutted, its innards spilled out onto the floor. A refrigerator stood in the corner with its door open, reveal-ing a smorgasbord of stove parts, pipes, ropes, wires, and cords.

"What you've got there, that's an artist at his work."

Mudd jumped back, as startled as if she'd been burned, and she whirled around to face a boy — Roy Kimbel, seventeen years old, and already about full grown. His body towered over hers, long and dense and hard. He had on gray sweat-

pants and black sneakers, and his sweatshirt, with the Cedar
Hill High School Track Team logo printed in a circle on the
front, was shadowy with sweat. He'd been running, and his
chest heaved as he gasped to catch his breath. His eyes were
so dark and dilated that they looked to Mudd to be without
any color at all, just shining a pure, deep, inky black.

"Aw, hey, I scared you now, didn't I?" he said, finally. He
raised his hands and held them out, palms up, to show her he
wasn't meaning her any harm. "Well, I'm not gonna hurt
you, if that's what you think," he said. He was surprised to
see how startled and scared of him she was. He kept his eyes
locked on hers, and his mouth twitched up into a slanted
smile. "I promise. I'm a nice guy, all right? I'm not like that,
see?" His face was so close to Mudd's then that she could feel
the whisper of his hot breath tossing in her hair. It smelled
like melted butter. And the solid clanging of the man's hammer was still ringing in her ears.

"Hey, but don't I know you anyway?" Roy was asking
her. "Aren't you that girl they all call Mudd?"

Well, that was the last thing she wanted to hear from anybody, especially not from this boy, outside Ridge Hamilton's
back yard, just then. She frowned at Roy, narrowing her eyes
and thinning her lips.

"Don't you call me by that name," she growled, clenching
her teeth to show him that she meant what she said. "My
name is Margaret. You call me Margaret." She smiled then,
having made herself clear, and bit her lip. She threw a quick
look over her shoulder toward Ridge's house, and added, just
the same way she'd heard Rayanne saying to herself in the
mirror sometimes, "Or you just don't bother to call me at
all."

Roy grinned. "Okay, Margaret. That's just fine, Margaret. I'll call you whatever you tell me I should. Margaret."
He shook his head, marveling to himself over what looked
like was nothing less than his own pure good luck. Because,

right there, he had Mudd Butt Butler herself. In the full flesh. Standing in his yard, before his very eyes, so close that he could smell her. Close enough to touch. He raised his eyebrows. He kept on smiling, trying to think of what he was going to do with her, what he ought to say next, and then he was squinting at her, with his arms folded over his chest and his elbows cupped in his palms.

"So," he said, "what is it that brings you this way, Margaret, out here into my messy old dump of a back yard?"

She took a look behind her again. "My sister —" she began.

The sudden hard burst of his laughter sounded like a cough.

"That's your sister?" he asked, incredulous. "That old gal who's in there sucking on Ridge Hamilton's wasted, shriveled-up dick?"

Mudd gasped, and Roy took one long step toward her, and then he was reaching out to her, and before she knew what he was doing, before she could pull away from him, he was squeezing her fingers, cupping her hand between both of his own, pressed up like a ball against his chest.

"Hey, hey, hey," he said, "I'm sorry, Margaret, don't back away from me, now wait."

He began to walk backward then himself, slowly pulling her along with him. He was wagging his head from side to side. "What's wrong with me? That was so rude. I can see why you might be mad. I shouldn't have said it, I know that. Hell, I shouldn't have even thought it, I guess. I'm sorry. Come on, over this way now. Don't be scared, okay? Shhh, where it's quiet, over here."

He was skillfully picking his way backward through the jumble of weeds and junk in the grass while he talked, and she was stumbling along with him, away from the shed and out of sight of Ridge Hamilton's back door, toward the bare bones of the picket fence and its snarl of climbing rose vines.

Roy was still smiling at Mudd, too, but, she thought, it wasn't like he was really mocking her or laughing at her anymore, it was more like he was just making some kind of small talk, only being friendly maybe, and normal, and nice. Roy stepped around a piece of twisted metal in the grass, and Mudd staggered along after him, until he stopped, and, still holding her hand, he brought his face up closer to her own again. "Can I tell you a little secret, Margaret?" he asked.

When she nodded, he smiled.

"I believe that any person could find some way to use everything there is on the earth if they just had enough time to look for how."

He let go of her hand and scratched his fingers through the sandy stubble of his hair. He cupped his hands under his arms.

"Well, I guess maybe that could be true," Mudd said.

She didn't know what to think, now. She wasn't sure what it was that Roy was trying to tell her. It didn't seem to her to be much of a secret that he'd decided to share with her, but she didn't want him to think that was because she was just too dumb to get the point of it, just too stupid to understand what he obviously believed was the seriousness and importance of his words. Her hand was warm and damp from how he'd held it. She squeezed it at her side and held her breath, feeling like she usually did when it came time in school for her to take a test, knowing that she'd know every answer perfectly well, right up to the moment when the questions actually got asked, and then they'd be flying right out of her head again, leaving her hollowed out, empty and blank.

"You know," Roy was going on, "I heard that Ridge over there talking one time, though, and you know what it was he said? He said he thinks my dad's a pig. And your sister? She agreed. They think that my dad and me, we live in our house just like a couple of pigs. But I want you to tell him for me, you tell him thank you, that must be a compliment, because I happen to know that in spite of what is popular opinion, pigs are the cleanest animals there are, see? And the smartest ones, too, by the way."

He stooped down and picked up a stick off the ground. He tapped its point against an overturned metal tub, and the sound of it rang out, drowned in the din that was still pouring out from inside the dilapidated wooden shed. "But that Ridge Hamilton, what does he know, huh, Margaret? He's nothing but a gimp anyway, isn't he? Don't you think? All cooped up inside his house all the time. Strapped in helpless to that chair. Making model airplanes. I'll just bet you that he doesn't know even one thing about pigs. What do you think, Margaret? Does he?"

"Well," Mudd said, looking around at all the piled-up junk and trash, "I guess this place is sort of a mess, all right."

"Sure it is. Sure. But that's only because it's my dad's work, see?"

She nodded. Because, well, the truth was, she did see. She did know what it was that he was talking to her about. She did, for once, understand. And just then, at that particular time in her life, Roy's notion of order, or disorder, seemed an important and serious one to Mudd — the idea that something that looked like just a big mess might after all be there for a reason, that it might have a function and a purpose, that it might be appreciated, then, just for what it was. Instead of always being despised for all of what it was not.

But Roy was moving again, and she sensed that she was going to need to keep her concentration in clear focus upon him. He'd stepped off to her side and was beginning to circle around behind her.

"So," he said, "now that we've got this little secret understanding of things between us, Margaret, you and me, well, that makes us pals, I'd say. And I got this kind of a game that I like to play. The thing of it is, though, you gotta have two people. Just can't be played by only one person all alone. So, when I find a pal, I ask them to play it with me. And since we're pals, well, now I'm asking you. Do you want to play it with me, Margaret? But you gotta be It first, though, see, on account of this is your first time, and you're the guest and that's the rule, okay?" She felt his fingertips on the back of her neck, skimming her skin. "Here, now, Margaret," he was saying, "I'm just gonna tie this thing over your eyes. That's all. Don't you get scared or nothing, though, okay? I promise you I'll be careful. Real gentle. See, I'm not gonna hurt you, didn't I say so already? Didn't you hear me swear it?" He brought his hands up over her head, and he pressed the soft folds of a gray rag against her face. It was damp with what must have been his sweat, and he was leaning so close to her then that she could smell him, too, dusty and sour, as he pulled the two ends of the rag tight and twisted them into a hard knot at the back of her head.

"Okay, Margaret, now you're It," he said. "And all you gotta do is touch me, see? It's simple. That's all."

Roy had clamped his hands down onto her shoulders, and he turned her around and around until she was dizzy and lost, and then when he let her go, she stumbled forward and fell onto her hands and knees in the grass.

All that Mudd could see was a haze of gray as the sunlight was filtered in to her through the folded-over rag — gray that seemed to be the very same flat color of her own eyes just about, as if in blindness her eyesight had been somehow turned back inward on her, reflective not of the outside world anymore, but now only of her own internal secret self. She brought her hand up to her face and heard him groan, "Aw, c'mon now, Margaret, don't you go and spoil this. Don't you cheat." She pressed her knuckles down into the grass and straightened her arms and pushed herself up to her feet. The racket from the work shed had stopped — it had dwindled suddenly, dimmed as if a cloud had passed over the sun and cast the world into its cold shadow for a while — and she supposed that Roy's father must have been taking a break, that he would have been standing back from his piece, with his face tilted upward, and his skin slickened with sweat, and his hands on his hips as he squinted a critical eye upon the progress of his work.

She opened her arms and combed the air around her with the fingers of her outspread hands. She craned her neck forward and poked out her chin. Sniffing, she thought that she could still smell Roy Kimbel — the dank, sour musk of his sweat and his skin and his hair — and she could hear him — the quick intake of his breath, the crunch of the grass under his feet, and the squeak of his shoes and the rustle of his clothing when he moved — and feel him — the heat that seemed to rankle off his body onto hers.

His voice, when he called to her, was a deep, low, distant sound. "This way, Margaret," he was saying. "I'm here, all right. Come on this way."

She heard a sniffle. Felt the slap of his bare hand against her leg. A car whooshed past on the road out in front of the house. A dog was barking. There was a distant sound of water running in a sink.

Mudd groped awkwardly through a grim, gray fog. First Roy's voice was in front of her, and then it was behind her. She twirled hard, lunging to touch him, and then lurched suddenly in the other direction, flailing toward the thin sound of his breath as it whistled through the spaces between his teeth. His foot kicked her, and she stumbled; his fingers snapped out and pinched her arm. She felt his hand flex around her breast, and then his breath was hot and dry against the back of her neck. His lips brushed her ear. When she tripped and fell against him, he caught her. She rolled her head on his shoulder and let the soft burden of her weight sag against the hard pillar of his body, while from behind he wrapped his arms around her and squeezed her so hard that she couldn't breathe.

She began to struggle then, squirming against his embrace until, finally, he opened his arms and let her drop away from him, forward into black empty space, and, crying out, she fell into the roses that grew up alongside the fence. Then it was the sharp thorns and hard branches that had hold of Mudd. They snagged in the thin fabric of her blouse and the heavier billow of her skirt. They wrestled with her, and dragged at her, pulling her downward toward the ground. It was as if they'd turned into the limbs of some living thing, an animal that snared its bony fingers in her hair and raked her face with its talons, yanked at her sleeves and pulled at her socks, wrapped its thorny arms around her in a sharp and stinging embrace. The strong, sweet perfume of the roses filled her head, and the petals brushed against her cheeks, soft as kisses, even as the thorns scratched at her hands and gashed her arms.

It wasn't until Mudd gave up and stopped struggling that the roses let her go. She rolled away and pulled the gray rag away from her face. She sat up, yanking at the hem of her skirt where it had flapped back and bared her white thighs all the way up to the leg holes of her underpants. Her shins and thighs and knees and bare forearms were traced with long, red, angry-looking lines that welled with beads of blood, as bright as the flowers themselves.

Roy was crouched down in the grass close to her, and his thick silhouette was outlined against an aureole of bright sunlight. He reached past her and picked up a handful of the rose petals off the ground. He crumpled them in his fist, into a ball that he ran over her skin, then, using it like a sponge to try to sop up her blood.

Mudd swiped at her face with the back of her hand. Roy took her by the elbow, and he helped her up onto her feet.

"I'm really sorry," he said. His voice seemed to have deepened, thickened, and slowed, while the muscles of his jaw worked, hard and round as rocks. "I never meant . . ."

She balled her hands into fists, and she squeezed her eyes shut and shook her head. The pricks and scratches smoldered on the surface of her skin.

"It's okay," she whispered. "It's just I'm clumsy, that's all. I'm a clumsy girl. Everybody knows it. Sometimes I'm stupid, too. Most times, I'm just a big, fat cow." Mudd opened her eyes and looked at him. What she didn't want now was to have him watching her so closely, the way he was. She only wanted him to let her go, now that he'd had his fun, to leave her by herself, alone. "That's what they call me Mudd Butt for. Just about serves me right, I guess. Just about fits the bill." She relaxed her hands and let them fall down to her sides. She turned away from Roy, moving slowly and deliberately, squeezing back tears, holding on to her breath as if it was something that she meant to keep.

Roy had come up behind her by then. He laid a hand on the spongy cushion of her shoulder, and, pulling, he turned her around to face him. He took her hand, and he brought it up to his mouth, and with the pink tip of his tongue, he licked away the blood that had dribbled down into the creases between her fingers. He cupped her face in his hand, and he leaned down over her, and he kissed her on the mouth.

And maybe later, that night, when she was in her own room, in the dark, maybe then she'd made the whole entire incident seem more important and more romantic than it really was, but even if she'd tried, she would not have been able to forget the stabbing pleasure that had come to her with that kiss. Or how soft and cool the rose petals had felt, too, when Roy crushed them in his fist and then rubbed them over the ravaged surface of her skin. Or the smell of him. Or his sound when she'd been blind. That night, in the dark in her bed in her room at home — with even the smallest scratch seeming to be screaming out for her attention, stinging and burning with so much wickedness that she could hardly keep herself still — Mudd had turned her mind to thinking about

Roy's father, that tall, thin, sweaty man in his ramshackle shed. How he went out and picked up other people's old, useless, worthless stuff. How he took it off their hands for them, and if he wasn't able to repair it and make it right, then he brought it out back behind his house and, with the most terrible racket anybody had ever heard, he made it all over again, he turned it into something else, something that it had never been before, something better than it was. He re-formed it, and he reshaped it. He hammered and he battered and he beat it, until he had transformed it into something that he could stand back and look at and declare to be art.

Over time, the importance of that idea had kept on nagging at Mudd. And holding hands along with it came the notion that what she had in her own self that was broken, maybe what that Mr. Kimbel did, how he worked and what he knew, maybe that was what would fix it. Maybe if she could only gather together the right bits and pieces of herself, if she could just figure out what it was that was wrong with her, then she would know what she needed to do to find the corrections that would make her right. And, at the very least, she might be able to turn herself into something that was useful. She could transform what she was into something else, something that was beautiful, something that was a pleasure to see.

So, whenever Rayanne said that she was going into Cedar Hill to see Ridge, then there was Mudd, standing outside by the car, begging for her sister to let her go along with her again, too. At first Rayanne guessed that it must have been Ridge himself that Mudd was drawn to, but when finally she began to understand that it was Roy, then Rayanne didn't have any objections anymore, and she let Mudd come with her if that was what she thought she had to do. Mudd would stop just long enough to say hiya to Ridge and let him pinch her leg, she'd make a big, appreciative fuss over whatever little plastic thing with wings he was building on at the time, and then she'd slip out the back screen door and disappear down the wheelchair ramp and over the bent fence and be gone to no one knew where for as long as she wanted to, until Rayanne stood out on the stoop and called to her that it was time for the two of them to get home.

Mudd was just a ninth grader, and Roy was already a senior in high school then. The Cedar Hill High School track team took the regional and then the state championship that spring, and Roy had been awarded a scholarship to Iowa State University in Ames in the fall. He was full of pride about it, and, even though somewhere in the back of her mind Mudd knew that his leaving Cedar Hill was going to mean that he'd have to also be abandoning her, still, she was proud of him for it, too.

But what happened instead was something else. Because in August Frank Kimbel got careless, and he let a spark from his blowtorch go flying off onto an old mattress that he'd left folded over in one corner of his shed. It smoldered there for hours, biding its time until the Butler girls had come and gone and everybody else was sound asleep before it burst into the greedy flames that licked up the dry wood walls of the shed and closed in on the pile of gas cans, to explode, finally, with force enough to shatter four windows at the front of a house across the street. The fire quickly jumped the fence into Ridge Hamilton's back yard, and it trapped him there inside his little house. It was all he could do to roll down off his bed onto the floor and drag his body into his bathroom, where he tried to escape the building heat by filling up the tub and pulling himself in. But the smoke got to Ridge before the fire did, and he passed out. He slipped down under the water, and he drowned. Both of those two cute little twin Tudor houses were destroyed, along with all of Ridge's model planes, and Mudd was forever afterward sorry about that part of it, too. But at least Roy got out in one whole piece, and that was all she had it in her heart to really care about by then.

When she went to see him at the hospital — carrying a bundle of flowers and a box of cookies that she'd baked and a whole big basket full of fruit — he still smelled like smoke to her; his face seemed smudged, he had some bad burns on his shoulders and his back, and the hairs on his knuckles and his hands and his wrists had been singed off. She closed the door of his room, and she climbed up onto his bed and wrapped herself around him like a blanket. She held him up so close against her, pressing his face into that big, soft pillow of her bosom, that she just about smothered him, while he moaned and wept, just like a little baby, in her arms.

The hair grew back on his hands. And the burns that were scattered over his shoulders healed over. But the smoke had stolen his wind. He lost the track scholarship because of it, and he enrolled in the community college out on the highway near the airport instead and took a job painting houses with a contracting company in Cedar Hill. He and Mudd were married three years later, after she'd graduated from high school herself, and they moved out into their house on Bell Road, and right after that Lee was born.

Mudd believed then that it was her son who was the proof if anybody'd ever needed it that what she'd done by joining her life up with Roy Kimbel's was good and right and meant to be. Sometimes things just work out for the best, she told Roy. Sometimes some things are just a part of an overall destiny. Because, Leland Kimbel — with his milky skin and his fine, fair hair, his deep gray eyes and the sweet pink bow of his mouth — Lee was just the most beautiful little baby that anybody had ever seen. Everyone said so, even Rayanne — anyone who saw him just had to ooh and aah and make a big fuss over Mudd's new baby, marveling about just how truly lovely a child he was to look at, and she was aware of it when they turned away from the sight of him to take another look at her, and she understood what it was that they were thinking, how they puzzled, how they wondered that this big, plain, clumsy woman could be the actual blood mother of such a perfect boy. But Mudd knew that Lee was hers. He was hers and Roy's, and they deserved to have him as their own. They'd earned him, she thought. And, she suspected, he was the one most beautiful thing that they would ever in their lifetime together do.

Mudd used to get up out of her bed and stand there in Lee's darkened room in the middle of the night, hidden in the shadows near his crib, and she'd watch him while he slept — hunched into a ball on his stomach with his knees tucked up under his tummy, his cheek on the sheets, his hand curled into a fist beside his face, his pinkish heels pressed against the diapered mound of his bottom, the perfect round pebbles of his toes. She'd chewed on the bottoms of Lee's bare feet. She'd nibbled at the ends of his fingers and kissed the soft folds of his ears. She'd nuzzled his hair, caressed the silky pale skin of his belly, and licked the creases in his wrists. Until Roy came in and told her to put the baby down, leave him alone, stop poking at him all the time, and let him sleep. But Lee was so pretty, it had just about hurt Mudd's eyes to have to look at him sometimes, it was hard for her to focus on him, so he seemed indistinct almost, enveloped in smoke, and smudged, his features blurred. Like maybe he wasn't really real. Like maybe he was only something in her own head, something she'd invented, someone she'd made up.

*   *   *

Mudd stood in the shadows of her room, and she watched out the window, studying the evening that had begun to hang like smoke across the fields and snag like black crepe in the branches of the trees.

Outside, Roy's truck had pulled up off the road and come to a stop at the side of the yard. She took her robe down off its hook on the back of the closet door and wrapped it around herself. Shivering, she pulled the belt and tied it tight.

She heard the scuffle and squeak of Roy's boots on the loose boards as he climbed the steps outside and crossed the front porch. The door creaked open, and Roy stumbled in. Moving forward, like a top once set into motion and then spinning dutifully away, he plodded through the hallway and into the cool shadows of the living room. He tottered, reeled, and fell on his back onto the couch. And then he was immediately snoring, profoundly asleep.

Mudd picked up a crocheted cotton blanket from the back of the chair and spread it out over Roy, covering him. She untied his shoes and pulled them off his feet. She put her hand on his forehead. Roy slept with his jaw hung and his mouth open — Mudd could hear his breath as it rasped in and out deep in the back of his throat. She let her hand slide down along one side of Roy's slack face, and then she held it for a moment over his opened lips, feeling the heat of his breath beating between her fingers like a softly gusting breeze.

She could forgive him just about anything, she thought, as long as he still loved her. That was all.

Headlights wheeled over the ceiling, and Mudd went to the window again and watched as Bader Von Vechten's black Mustang convertible pulled up to the gate that had been closed across the small road near the house. She saw him get out and wade through the pools of light from his headlights; he lifted the chain, unlocked it, and swung open the wide wire gate. He went back to his car again and let it roll through, shifting gears as he accelerated gently up the hill, his red taillights flickering like small cold fires in the trees.

*   *   *

Bader let himself into his cottage, and, skimming the floor and the walls with the cold white circle of light from his flashlight, he walked through the dark and empty rooms. What must it have been like here before, he wondered, first for Karl and Juniper, and then later for Wolfgang, hiding out, and then, finally, for Margot, aging and alone? Had she been haunted by the memory of her younger son? Bader could just about picture the figure of Wolfgang moving through this same space, watching at the windows, scared, wondering when they'd come to get him, how long it would take them to figure it out, what they'd do when they knew that Horace was dead, murdered, and by whom. His slim shadow slipping along after him. The bend of his long legs. The curl of his bony hands. The hard, shiny knobs of his knuckles. His flat, white feet slapping the hard polished boards of the cottage's bare wood floor.

Bader went outside to his car, and he pulled his rolled-up sleeping bag out of its trunk and the flask of scotch that he kept hidden at the back of the glove box, and the shotgun that Margot had told him was the one that Wolfgang had used to kill Horace Craig. When Bader turned and looked down through the trees, he could see that there were lights on in the white farmhouse there below him, at the bottom of the hill.

Another family, Bader thought, living a normal, peaceful, ordinary life. Bader wondered what it would be like to be a boy like Lee, what he might be doing just then — eating, bathing, sleeping, dreaming, talking to his mother, arguing with his sister, listening to his father, bent over a book, chewing on a fingernail, stopping, looking up, lost in thought?

*   *   *

Lee had locked himself in his room, off the back of the kitchen downstairs. He was standing in front of his mirror, naked, studying his own slim form, turning this way and that way to try and see himself from every angle — his flat feet, his long, thin legs, his narrow hips, rigid penis and puckered balls, smooth belly, flat chest, angled shoulders, long, graceful neck. He bent one leg and propped his foot against the opposite knee. He raised his hands up over his head, high, stretching, and tipped his chin, and let his eyes roll up, flutter shut. He could be a bird, he thought, poised for flight. He dropped his hands and let them hang, and he bent forward with them, curved over until his fingertips skimmed the floor, and he let his chin fall forward against his chest, and he bent one knee, then the other, feeling the tension in his legs quiver up through his buttocks into his back. He dropped, crouched on his haunches, bouncing gently, with his arms folded over his head. He was a rock, self-contained. He raised his head then, and he opened his eyes, and he allowed himself to be swallowed down into his own gray void, at rest in the gentle eye of his own storm.

He thought of Bader Von Vechten in his cottage up on the bluff. And he wondered, did he think of him?

*   *   *

Bader had propped the shotgun up in one corner of the cottage's main room, and he spread his sleeping bag out over the dusty hardwood floor. He sat down on it, with his back resting up against a wall, cradling the flask in his lap. Bader took a swallow of scotch, gasped, and leaned his head back.

The story of what had become of his family here was an argument that had underlined Bader's life. It rang in his ears, expressed in struggle, through the push and pull and the give and take of the masculine and feminine poles of his parents' opposing points of view. He didn't know whether what he remembered of it now had been a continuing discussion that was carried on between them over some long period of time, or whether it was only a conversation that had taken place on a single, particular evening — one night when Bader had, for once, been allowed to stay up for a while downstairs after dinner, listening to his parents' conversation before his mother remembered he was there and ordered him off out of her sight, sent him upstairs to his room to bed.

The way that Tom Von Vechten had seen it, when his newly widowed mother Margot married her deceased husband's single enemy, Horace Archibald Craig, she was doing the one thing that she could think of to set things right again, and that had been the one thing that was the most wise and the most shrewd and the most smart course of action she could think to take. What weapon did she have to fight the fact of her disenfranchisement at the time of her husband's death? Only her own self, that was all. And so, if she couldn't hope to win a business battle with Horace Craig, she'd do the next best thing. She'd marry him. How could Wolfgang have called her unfaithful to her first marriage, when Heinrich was, in fact, already dead? Margot, Tom explained, only used what she had in order to do what she could to try and save the Von Vechten name, for her children's sake and for the sake of their children after them. She was going to dredge it back up out of what was threatening to become the oblivion of their most recent history, and she must have believed that if she'd been given only half a chance she could have restored it to where it really belonged — on the factory and on the business and on the land.

But, Bader's mother had interrupted her husband, hadn't Margot forgotten to think about the boy? What about Wolfgang then, only just a child at the time, barely fourteen years old? How could a mother expect her young son to be able to find any kind of an innocence at all in a scheme like the one that Margot had contrived? How could he, she'd asked — putting her hand on Bader's head and ruffling her long, thin fingers through his hair, scratching at his scalp with the filed and polished tips of her smooth nails in the way that made him shiver with the comfort of it — how could he have understood that there could be such a thing as a marriage without any love? And even if she'd told him so, would he have been able even for a moment to believe that his mother's union with Horace Craig wasn't a romantic entanglement and it wasn't a holy sacrament, it wasn't bonded by affection or passion or, even, physical desire?

"But," Tom had answered, "I knew, didn't I? I understood. And I had no objections to what my mother was up to. No objections at all."

"You were older," was Eleanor's measured reply. "You were already gone out of the house by then. You were more mature."

Bader heard the gentle, silky rustle of his mother's stockings as she sat back in her chair and crossed her legs. "It was a business agreement, then?" she asked. "Something like," she paused, searching, "a merger?"

Tom, rattling the ice in his drink, had smiled. Exactly. His mother's marriage to Horace Craig had been nothing more and nothing less than a transaction, that was all. It was a contract, and through it she was hoping to be able to combine two separate interests under the sheltering umbrella of one single, unified, Anglo-Saxon name. Tom lit a cigarette then, and, when she put out her hand toward him, he gave it to his wife before he lit another one for himself. Whether or not, he went on, blowing smoke, she cared in any way at all for Horace, Margot Von Vechten had only been doing what she believed she had to do, and selflessly, too. She'd chosen to follow a course that was not what might have been most satisfying for her, but that she could see would be most useful to her family. She did what she thought was necessary, that was all. She did what she thought was smart. And whether or not even Horace Craig himself understood that fact, well, that would have to be beside the point, wouldn't it? Let him go ahead and think that Margot loved him, if that was what he wanted to believe. Coughing, Tom crushed his cigarette out in the crystal ashtray on the table. Eleanor leaned forward to tap hers against its rim. She picked up her drink and, cradling it, she sat back again, watching her husband's face. He looked away, studied his shoes for a moment, then stood and crossed the room to the bar in the corner to pour himself another drink. He paused there for a moment, weighing a handful of ice in the cup of his palm.

"You don't think she loved him, then?" Eleanor asked.

Tom laughed. "No," he said, dropping the cubes into his glass, then reaching out to pour the scotch. "Of course she didn't. How could she have?"

The widow Von Vechten had only wanted to marry Mr. Craig so that then the factory, the business, the invention, would be back in the family again, and half of it hers. And in exchange for that she would, well, do whatever it was that the situation called for. She'd make herself Mr. Craig's if that was what was required of her, to do with as he pleased. Tom sipped at his drink, smacked his lips, and leaned back, crossing one foot over the other.

"But," Eleanor asked, "what about you?"

Hadn't she forgotten her sons? Hadn't she neglected to take what must have been their strongest feelings into consideration, and hadn't she blinded herself to what was obviously their complete and dedicated devotion to her? And why wasn't that enough for her? Eleanor had sighed. A boy's love for his mother. You'd have thought it would have been more than enough. If all she'd wanted to do was to preserve her husband's name, why didn't passing it on to her sons do that? Let them turn it into whatever they could, whatever they wanted it to become.

Bader saw that there were pinkish kisses hovering on the rim of his mother's glass.

"Not sons," Thomas had corrected her, reddening. "Son. It wasn't me. I didn't care."

It was only Wolfgang. Tom's voice seemed to have deepened, it was louder, Bader thought, stronger, more solid and firm, as if now his words had fiber, muscle, sinew, and form. Because, that voice went on, Wolfgang had been a stupid, careless fool. No, he was worse than stupid, he was more

than careless. He was a coward. He'd turned himself into a
killer, for Christ's sake, a saboteur, a firebug, and, finally, a
murderer, too. For what? To defend his father's honor? He
wasn't a hero. He wasn't a soldier. He never did anything at
all in his life that could have been called noble or honest or
brave. He wasn't a man. He'd behaved the way a child
would, that was all, like a selfish and spoiled-rotten boy.

"I think maybe he just loved your mother more than you
do," Eleanor said, sighing. "That was all. He loved her too
much. And maybe she should never have asked for anything
more from her life than that." She closed her eyes and let her
head fall to the side, resting her cheek against the cushioned
wing of her chair.

He'd loved her so much, in fact, that he ended up just
about destroying her.

"Not to mention," said Tom, smirking now, throwing
back the rest of his drink, "Horace Craig."

* * *

Bader had two small photographs of his parents. Tom's was
of a dim figure, an older man dressed in somber gray flannel,
smoking the thin brown cigarette that he held between his
finger and thumb and whose ashes he flicked thoughtlessly
onto the creamy pile of the carpet at his feet. He was standing
with his back to the camera, his face in profile, as he gazed
out a tall, mullioned window at a vista of flooded grass, drab
sky, and dark rain. Eleanor's was only of her face, and it had
been touched up — all the small lines and wrinkles and freckles and shadows had been softened and blurred, so that her
skin looked silky and bland. A bit of sparkle had been added
to her eyes and an inviting wet gleam to her lips, and her
long, dark hair was brushed behind the intricate curl of her
ear, swooped back dramatically over her shoulder to settle in
a soft wave along the smooth curved line of her throat,
against the moonish sheen of a circle of tightly strung pearls.

There was a rosy blush of health and well-being in her cheeks, and a look of patience in her eyes, an understanding and a serenity in her expression that Bader was sure he had never seen at play upon her features when she was alive.

He recognized his father in his photograph, but when Bader looked at the one of Eleanor, it was always with a dizzy feeling of displacement, because that woman was a sudden stranger to him, not the one that he remembered was his mother — sharper-edged, more brittle, thin-fingered and pale-skinned, sleepy-looking, her thick, smoky lashes damp against the smudged pouches of fatigue under her eyes.

The rooms of his childhood, in the big Von Vechten house on Linden Lane in Cedar Hill, loomed huge and cold in Bader's memory, roaring with emptiness, crashing with silence, maddeningly undisturbed and intractably calm. Left mostly on his own there, he'd filled the vast, whooshing void of his loneliness with noises of his own making. He'd talked to himself, he'd sung songs, whistled tunes, recited limericks and doggerel, hummed the melodies that he heard on the radio or in his music classes at school. He rattled a stick along the stair rails and the balustrade from the first floor up to the second and then back down. He bounced a rubber ball in the passageway between the pantry and the kitchen, held steady by the comfort of its rhythm, thud against the linoleum and slap back into his palm, thud the question and slap its reliable reply. The hard soles of his shoes had clattered on the bare wood of the upstairs hall, his footsteps echoed and came ringing back toward him — to his ears they'd sounded busy, full of purpose, like the friendly rush and shuffle of a noisy, boisterous crowd. He took a run and then locked his knees, and he skidded on his heels, squeaking and screaming, black rubber on blond wood. He bumped down the carpeted back stairs on his bottom, step by step, groaning and gasping — "Oomph, unh, oomph, unh!" He slapped his hands against the plaster walls, and his fists joggled the edges of the paintings in their frames.

Until his mother's bedroom door creaked open, and then she was there, standing in the hallway with the fingers of one hand tangled in her hair, the others clenched into a fist against her throat, and she hushed him, spat his name, called out for the maid to come and take him away, now, outside into the yard or over to the park, someplace where he could run and yell and play and wear himself out and she would not have to be disturbed.

"For God's sake, the little animal, get him out of here, please, I have a headache, can't you see? I haven't slept all night. I don't feel well."

And the maid would take Bader's arm, and she'd yank him away, drag him off to the kitchen, sit him down on a stool at the counter, give him crayons and paper to play with, feed him cookies and Jell-O and apples and peanut butter and milk, while the radio on the counter by the sink played, clogging his brain with music and the jibber-jabber of the news, until he was full and drowsy, finally, and then he laid his head down on his arms and slept, and he didn't make any noise, and he wasn't a nuisance to the maid or to his father or to his mother, either, and he didn't bother anybody at all.

Bader's last memories of his mother came to him in a sequence of pictures as blurred and as vague as a strip of old black and white film — a woman in a powder blue wool suit, with a knee-length straight skirt and a brass-buttoned jacket, a shimmery white silk blouse, and a pillbox hat pinned into the coiled and braided mass of her waist-length hair. She had the plastic handle of a cosmetic case clenched in one fist. She was standing downstairs, in the entryway, and the front door was open behind her. The gardens and the trees outside were a riot of color, but against that background her skin was gray, as pliable-looking as old candle wax, and her body seemed sharp-edged and bony — her knees at the hem of her skirt were knobbed and her shins were long, flat, bruised-looking blades. He remembered the angled jut of her hipbones and the ashy dark circles under her eyes. She had set the suitcase down, or dropped it.

It was a square cosmetic case — Bader knew that it had a mirror inside its lid and trays that were filled with her bottles and jars and tubes of creams and pastes and makeup and perfume, because he'd seen it sitting open on her bed the night before. He'd stood in the closet, up to his shins in a tumbled pile of her shoes, sheltered by the curtain of her hanging clothes, and he'd watched his mother clearing her dressing table, emptying the contents of its drawers into the case.

"We're just going off for a little holiday, Bader," Tom had explained. "Your mother and I. We need a short vacation. That's all. And before you know it, we'll be back."

When Bader was summoned downstairs to say goodbye the next morning, Eleanor had dropped the cosmetic case on the floor and taken two or three unsteady steps toward her son. Her movements had been stiff and jerky and unsure, as if she were holding herself together, as if she thought she might fly to pieces at the least misstep — like a puppet, Bader had thought, a wooden marionette whose arms and legs and hands and feet were attached to its body by bits of string that had been pulled through tiny holes and knotted at the joints. Shuffling, she'd dragged her feet as if they were heavy, or, like the magnets in the set that Tom had given him for his birthday, under the force of some other hard, mysterious, invisible pull. She'd reached out toward Bader — her fingers were like twig ends, knobbed and thin, there was a large-stoned ring glinting on her finger and, when she turned her hands palm-side up, a snarl of scars entwined in the tender skin on the insides of her wrists.

Thomas had nudged Bader forward, and the boy had

stumbled obediently toward his mother, and he'd allowed her to grab hold of him, to draw him up against her, to fold herself over him, and her smell had been like the translucent petals — of gardenias and violets and roses — that he'd found pressed between the pages of a leather-bound Bible in the bottom of her bedside table drawer. He'd felt the cool, slick fabric of his mother's blouse and the soft folds of skin at her neck pressing against his cheek. Her lips had brushed his eyes, and the coarse wool of her suit had rubbed and burned his skin.

"Goodbye, Bader," she'd cooed to him. "Bye-bye."

*   *   *

Bader lay in the cottage in the dark, listening to the night noises of the woods all around him, closing in. And he began to feel a whole realm of possibilities, like small boxes nestled inside bigger boxes, beginning to open up and unfold themselves inside his mind. What he might do. And what he might become.

*   *   *

Mudd was still awake when Roy finally dragged himself off the couch and came upstairs to their bed in the middle of the night. She heard him using the bathroom, gulping down a handful of aspirin and a glass of tap water fizzy with antacid, before she felt him tumble down onto the mattress next to her. He kicked her once while he was at it, and scratched the back of her calf with the rough edge of a toenail, and she huddled away from him, scooched as far over toward the edge of the bed as she could get. She lay still and listened to his steady breathing and smelled the hot ferment of his breath, until gray light started to bleed up into the sky outside the window, and then she slipped out of the bed, put on a housedress, and came downstairs to work.

She was in the basement, sorting through the dirty laundry, emptying the pockets of Roy's pants when she found the list that Roy had written about her. She could just picture him, hunched over at the kitchen table, running the back-handed snarl of his writing over a piece of lined white paper. He'd ripped it out of Darcy's school notebook, and the three punched holes along the left margin were torn. Their spoiled, broken circles were as disturbing to Mudd as Roy's words.

Across the top, he'd scrawled her name — *Margaret Butler Kimbel* — and then below that, in block letters, all capitals — SHORTCOMINGS. The page was full, each paragraph lined up and numbered neatly along the margin, with a double space between, one to ten:

1. Lazy. Too bad she's not a princess or something, so she could lie around in the dark in her bed all day, eating candy and getting fat and sleeping and watching the TV and reading all those magazines and books.
2. Sloppy. This house is a mess ninety percent of the time.
3. Procrastinates. A person should never put off until to-morrow whatever it is that they're supposed to be getting done today. Everybody knows this.
4. Too many scruples.
5. No discipline. Also known as Lee-niency. Half the time she doesn't even know where the boy is. This is part of being lazy.
6. Forgetful. The beer in the freezer — exploded. The roast in the oven — what was left of it. The hose flooding the yard for six hours straight and then leaking down into the window wells so the basement had an inch of water in it and it cost me a hundred bucks to have Pete Hoddicker bring his equipment in to pump it out. Where she left her purse, where she put her glasses, where she set the keys to the truck down last, what she did with the mail.
7. Stupid. Not the same as forgetting things.

8. Fat.
9. Can't cook. If we have that macaroni and cheese with stewed tomatoes and green beans one more time this month, I'm going to have to give up eating at home.
10. Talks too much. If I wanted to hear what she thinks, I'd ask.

And then, on the back side of the paper, Roy had printed, in lowercase letters — *good points*. And another list, shorter:

1. Strong legs.
2. Good sense of direction.
3. Reads a lot.

The rest of the page was littered with his doodles, squares and cubes and circles, as if Roy had been trying hard to think of something more to say, but was at a loss for just exactly what.

Mudd folded the paper neatly in half and then in half again, and she tucked it into the pocket of her dress.

She swept the back steps. She watered the plants in the pots out on the front porch. She dusted the table and the breakfront in the dining room. She scrubbed the kitchen counters, scoured the sink, washed all the dishes from the weekend and dried each one and put them all away. She was wringing out her dirty rag mop into a bucket of soapy water on the floor when Roy came in. Flies buzzed at the back screen door, and a big black crow was making a racket up in the branches of the apple tree behind the house. Mudd poured Roy a cup of coffee and set it down on the table in front of him, trying to move slowly for him and walk softly because it was easy to tell just by looking at his face how bad he felt. His skin was ruddy and flushed, and she could see the glowy purplish spray of broken capillaries that were beginning to bloom alongside the shadowed edges of his nose. There was a gentle trembling in his hands, and a small fluff of shaving cream that he'd missed, caught in the curve of his ear.

She picked up her bucket and dumped the soapy gray water in the sink. With her back to him, she began to compose a list of her own, of all the things she didn't like about him, and she used its words like bricks, piling one complaint up on top of another, building them into a strong, hard wall around her.

At the base, then, a foundation in bold letters, all caps:

ROY GARY KIMBEL — HIS DEFICIENCIES. 1. Too selfish. 2. Doesn't listen. 3. Can't concentrate. 4. Too loud. 5. Drinks too much. 6. Gets mad too easy. 7. Big ugly feet. 8. Too hairy.

She might have gone on with it. She might have erected a whole, big solid fortress all the way around herself, on every side and even up over the top, but Roy had pushed away from the breakfast table and he came up beside her, reaching behind her to pour himself another cup of coffee. She stepped back and pressed herself against him. He set his cup down and put his arms around her body. He hugged her and rocked her, gently, swaying from side to side. She closed her eyes and listened to his breathing, feeling the steady comfort of its give-and-take moving in a rhythm against her back.

"So," she whispered, "you want to explain to me now about what you call my shortcomings, Roy?" She raised her hands up over her head and cupped them behind her, behind his neck, pulling his face down closer, next to hers. "You want to tell me about all that's wrong with what I am?" she asked. She arched her back and pressed her buttocks into him. The wall she'd only just begun to build was dissolving, falling, tumbling, crashing down. "What is it that's so awful about me now?" She began to sway. "Is it this, Roy?" she asked him. His hands slid up over her belly onto her breasts. "Or that?"

He moaned and buried his nose in the warm, damp hollows of her neck. He was clawing clumsily at her skirt, trying to lift it up; he was tugging at her blouse, tearing it, popping the small pearly buttons off so that they bounced and pinged against the snowy white porcelain of the scoured sink. He swiveled his hips and rubbed his body into hers. His heavy belt buckle poked at her; its hard, sharp corners bruised her back. And she began to feel then as if he might be going to rub her away. As if he could erase her, maybe. As if he could tumble her against him, like a pebble that was rolled over and over in the rushing waters of the creek, until it was clean and perfect, until it had been made small, and featureless, and smooth.

When he brought her around, face to face with him, she opened her eyes, and, looking past his shoulder, she saw Lee. He was standing there in the doorway, watching her, and when he saw that he'd been seen, he smiled and turned and slipped away so quickly, Mudd thought, it was as if he'd never even been.

*   *   *

Sunshine was streaming in through the open window at the front of the limestone cottage on the bluff, and it bathed Bader with its heat, scalding him where he lay inside his sleeping bag on the hard, warped, dusty planks of the wooden floor. He swatted at a buzzing fly and, groaning, rolled over onto his back. With his hands folded behind his head, he was looking out through the window at the treetops that were as far away and flat and still as paper cutouts against the solid blue of the sky. Already the day's heat had begun to build, its moisture thickening the air. The woods outside were noisy with an unfamiliar racket of squirrels and crickets

and singing birds. And Bader's mind was humming along
with the rise and fall of the cicadas' deep, steady whine.

"Here I am," he thought. "Here I am. Home. Home."

He sat up. First, he'd have to do some cleaning — scrub
the kitchen, replace the broken window glass, repair the
hinges on the front door, polish the wood floor, whitewash
the interior walls. He'd have to get the electricity turned on.
And the water. Install a telephone. He could buy some more
furniture maybe, secondhand. A chair, a sofa, a table, a desk.
A bed.

Anxious to get started, he disengaged himself from the
tangle of his sleeping bag and, shirtless, in his chinos still, he
went outside to the yard. He stood barefoot in the dust at the
bottom of the porch steps, beside the pump. He cranked it
and then cupped his hands under the spigot, splashing the icy
cold water onto his face and neck and chest. He stooped and
ducked his head under the spout and then stood up, gasping
and shaking the water from his hair as he turned. Behind
him, his black Mustang convertible shimmered in the bright
sunshine. Lee Kimbel was sitting in the front seat, with one
hand on the wheel, his elbow crooked in the open window,
and a look of pure pleasure open in his face.

When he saw Bader, he climbed out of the car carefully,
and pushed the door softly shut behind him with the outspread fingertips of both hands.

"I was just sitting in it, Mr. Von Vechten," he said.

His feet were bare in the dust. He was wearing cutoff blue
jeans; his shirt was unbuttoned and flapping open; he'd rolled
his sleeves up tight past his elbows. There was a pack of cigarettes tucked into the breast pocket of his shirt. And that
teasing slanted smile, tweaking at the dimple in Lee's cheek,
near the corner of his mouth.

"Nice car," he said, patting its back fender with the flat of
his hand. "Maybe you could let me drive it sometime?" He
leaned back against the car and crossed his feet one over the

other. He pulled the pack of cigarettes out of his pocket, lit one and handed it to Bader, then lit another for himself.

"Maybe sometime," Bader said.

"I guess Mr. Craig gave you the key to the road all right, then?" Lee asked.

Bader nodded. He sat down on the porch step and peered past Lee, into the dark overgrowth of the trees, where the ribbon of a narrow dirt path wound through it, headed, he guessed, toward the big white house that Lee had said was his at the bottom of the hill.

Lee, with his arms folded over his chest, and his hands cupping his elbows, followed Bader's look. "What do you think Mr. Craig wants with all this land anyway?" he asked. "He isn't farming any of it anymore. Not even keeping cows."

Bader looked at him. "Maybe he's using it to try and make a point," he said.

Lee considered this. He nodded. "Maybe," he said. "Or could be he has some other plans."

"What do you mean?"

Lee pushed off from the car and sat down on the step beside Bader. "Well," he said, "maybe Mr. Craig's thinking he'll use it, you know, develop it. Build a bunch of big houses out here, and then sell them off to all his rich friends in Cedar Hill."

Bader looked around at the woods and tried to picture it, a neighborhood here, a community of families in bright new houses with painted shutters and polished windows, broad driveways and clean sidewalks, lined up along a graceful curve of shaded white streets. Overlooking the wreck of Empire, beyond an entryway, where wrought iron letters mounted on a pillar spelled out the name — permanent now, enduring and indelible — VON VECHTEN ESTATES.

Lee's hair had fallen into his face, and when Bader reached out to touch it, to brush it away from his eyes, he felt the flutter of the boy's lashes against his palm, as soft and as frantic as the fragile dusted wings of a captured moth.

*   *   *

The Cedar Hill Country Club parking lot was glittery with the gleam of a hundred cars' bright paint, clear glass, and shiny chrome. In the swimming pool the water was clean and blue, flanked by high white lifeguard perches, broken by wooden buoys that bobbed on a twist of thick rope that had been strung from one side to the other between the deep end and the shallow waters where the babies and nonswimmers could safely splash. Older children played diving games and underwater tag, the girls squealing, the boys springing from the ends of the boards, throwing themselves into muscled back flips and front flips, high swan dives, slicing through the taut surface of the water with the knife blade of their folded hands.

On the grass around the pool, a mosaic of women's bodies languished in chairs and on bright towels, their leathery brown skin glistening with oil, tight elastic bathing suits hugging their thighs, their bare bellies soft and slack. And beyond the women were the men, their husbands and brothers and fathers and sons, moving over the clean green sweep of the golf course, some walking, carrying clubs, others bouncing along in the small white carts with their fringed canvas tops.

Bader stood by himself, off to the side, unnoticed and hidden in the spread shade of leafy branches. He could see Katherine Craig in the pool, taking dives from the high board, and he idly admired the beautiful slow arch of her body, snug in a bright, shimmery orange and yellow bathing suit, flying out like a tropical bird, outlined first against the dazzling blue dome of the sky and then the brilliant, black-lined turquoise bottom of the pool. She plunged in and burst up again, sput-

tering, and she swam with long, slow strokes over to the
ladder at the side.

He stepped out into the open, where his bright white shirt
reflected the afternoon sunlight like an overexposed photograph, or a space in a drawing, erased, left painfully unfinished, achingly blank, its tails hanging down over the flowered fabric of his shorts. Katherine, pulling herself up out of
the water, saw him and waved. He smiled, raised his hand,
waved back. He sat down on a cushioned wooden chaise, in
the shade, with a towel thrown over his long legs — pale as
lilies, Katherine said, smiling, touching his knee with her fingertip, tweaking the swirl of dark hairs on his ankle, laughing
at him, asking, Don't you ever get outside? With his eyes
hidden behind the dark, reflective lenses of his sunglasses, he
regarded her smooth skin — slick, wet, tanned — her slim
ankles, the sop of her hair on her back, her flat belly, her full
breasts, and her dainty feet. She sat down on the grass next
to him and leaned forward to towel-dry her hair. He watched
the muscles in her back move, and the sharp blades of grass
that pricked at the bare skin of her legs.

The day was a shimmer of silver sunlight and blue water,
clear, cold vodka and bubbly white tonic, green grass, green
limes. The bright bird colors of Katherine's swimsuit. The
red bicycle design on the back of a deck of playing cards.
Toasted bread, piled high with slices of yellow cheese and
pink ham, held together with fancy toothpicks — feathered,
orange and purple and green.

Late in the afternoon, Mrs. Craig came down to the pool
to tell Katherine that she and Mr. Craig would be staying for
cocktails and then dinner. He was still in the bar after having
been out on the golf course all afternoon, and she'd been in
the clubhouse playing cards. Her blond hair was gleaming,
shiny and sticky-looking as cotton candy, in the sun. She tottered on the grass in her pumps.

"Will you be able to get home, dear?" she asked.

Katherine looked at Bader, and he answered that, of course, he'd take her, he'd be glad to do it, it was on his way.

*   *   *

As they drove out to Edgewood Road in the open convertible, the sun was still pounding down on them, like a hot and hard punishment. Katherine threw her head back, exposing the long, graceful curve of her throat, letting her hair fly, drying in the wind, fluttering behind her like a trail of dim smoke.

Bader parked in the driveway and followed her through the cool, dark house. He sat down on the white wicker rocker out on the screened back porch. There was a badminton net strung up across the long lawn and the wire wickets of a croquet course laid out over the grass nearby. The house itself seemed filled up with a huge accumulation of personal things — family photos, glass ashtrays, china figurines, collected seashells, brass candlesticks — all of it put out on display to track the course of Katherine's family's life together, in such a way that brought to Bader a pang of envy and even anger, as if all of it were really not theirs, but only something that they'd come by after having stolen it away from him. They could walk through these rooms, he knew, and by way of the collection of these objects, trace over the outline of how they'd lived. This was a gift from Aunt Sadie. That came from the time they took that trip together to Sanibel over Easter break. Someone's mother picked this little clock up in Europe, isn't it exquisite? Bader sat in the white wicker chair, waiting for Katherine, and he absorbed all of it, he soaked it in, and he felt himself settling down into it, too, as if it might just as easily have belonged to him.

When Katherine came downstairs, she'd changed into a white summer dress with straps tied in small, tight bows that pressed against the nubs of her suntanned shoulders. Her hair was gathered at the back of her neck, held in place there by the loose knot of a sheer scarf. Bader still had on his white shirt and flowered shorts, and when Katherine looked at his flaming face, she took a small knife from the kitchen and cut an aloe leaf from a potted plant on the porch. She slit it lengthwise and peeled its two halves apart, exposing the moist slick flesh inside, and then she held it to his face, rubbing it over and over his cheeks and his chin and his nose while he sat still for her, with his eyes closed, feeling a cool, wet, soothing numbness creeping into his sunburned skin.

She poured white wine and lit the gas barbecue outside, and then she stood at the counter slicing ripe tomatoes and peeling cucumbers for a salad while he shucked the sweet corn at the sink. Fresh from the fields, she said. So sweet that you didn't even have to steam it, you could eat it just like that, cold and raw. The silk clung to his fingers; a fat green worm slipped out of the husks and crawled across the back of his hand.

*   *   *

Bader sat across from Katherine at one end of the table in the dining room, beside a long window that faced out toward the broad swath of the front yard. He rubbed the edge of a snowy white linen napkin between his finger and his thumb. He twirled the stem of a twinkling crystal goblet. He used a silver fork to pluck bits of meat and salad from the shimmer of a bone-colored, gold-rimmed plate.

Katherine sat back and looked at Bader — his dark hair, mussed, his blue eyes, sharp and clear, searching hers, the way he seemed to wince whenever his eyes met hers. Even though they'd only just met, she said, he seemed somehow familiar to her. His was a face and a presence that she remembered. She smiled. He might be someone that she'd always known, but had forgotten, someone who was so familiar to her that she'd taken him for granted. He might have been that

landmark oak tree whose ancient limbs were gnarled against
the sky down at the south end of Linden Lane; or the row of
battered mailboxes that bristled on the corner of the Old Post
highway and the county road; or the iron arch that straddled
the doors at the top of the courthouse steps. Bader Von
Vechten had always been here — but now it was as though
she'd been given a reason to look at him, to really see him,
maybe for the first time.

She was touched by the softness of his voice. She admired
the gentility of his hands. His awkwardness moved her — he
sat there so quietly, twirling the stem of his wineglass.

"Why do you think your father's been buying up all that
land out by Empire, Katherine?" Bader asked.

She looked at him, her green eyes bright, and she
shrugged. "He just likes to own things, I guess," she said.
"That's the way he is."

*　*　*

Outside, the sun had set, and the night was cool. Katherine
went upstairs to get a sweater, while Bader waited by his car,
leaning on the fender with his arms folded over his chest. He
watched her shadow moving in the window.

The sky was bright with the big, rising moon, and as the
Mustang skimmed along the paved black surface of the highway away from the colored lights of town, Katherine told
Bader where to stop and where to turn, onto a rolling stretch
of nameless gravel road, unlit and deserted. She reached
across his lap and switched off his headlights, and they
cruised over the roads that way — in his convertible, rolling
along back and forth, kicking up clouds of dust that would
settle behind them and dull the flat, broad leaves of the weeds
and the bushes and the trees in the ditches — weaving up one
road and down another, back and forth, like the shuttle in a
loom, between the planted fields. The landscape all around

them was gray and black and white, like an old photograph, flattened and colorless and dull. It was as if they were invisible, wasn't it? Katherine asked, turning her face up toward his. She snuggled up close to him, and he could smell her — the flowery fragrance of her perfume and the lemony scent of her hair. She curled her legs up under her, and sipped scotch from the flask that she'd found in his glove compartment. She leaned over close to him and held it to his lips, while the wind skimmed through her hair.

Finally, he stopped. He pulled over onto the soft shoulder of the road, and he took Katherine's hand and helped her out. They climbed a wire fence into an empty hay field. He put an arm around her, and she moved against him, and he began to dance with her, slowly, while she hummed, and he spun her and then threw her down, harder than he meant to, onto her back on the soft ground. At first he was afraid he'd knocked the wind out of her, but then she was pulling at him and dragging him down on top of her, and she wrenched at him with a force and a strength that shook him and scared him because her need for him seemed as if it might be even more desperate than his was for her. He rolled away from her, and they lay side by side on their backs in the grass. Her hand found him, she curled her fingers around his, and that was their only contact, just their two hands, touching, and he felt the grass against his back, tickling his neck, the wet stink of the soil seeping upward. When he turned to her and started to speak, she hushed him, and he could hear her breathing, and when he looked at her he could see her chest moving, and he could feel the thunder of his own heartbeat, slowing, and he could hear the racket of the country night — crickets droning in the grass and an owl calling out, the creech of the tree frogs and the flap of the bats.

Katherine whistled then, "Whoo-wheet, whoo-whoo-wheet," calling to the bobwhites, "whoo-wheet, whoo-

whoo-wheet," and she was answered back by the birds in the brush, responding to her just as Bader knew that he was, too.

*   *   *

Lee Kimbel had a way of appearing at the cottage without warning that summer. As if out of nowhere, at any odd hour, he'd show up. Bader would come outside to find the boy sitting on the porch, with his head back and his eyes closed, and his hands hanging between his knees. Or there'd be a knock at the door or a tapping at the window, and Bader would look up to find Lee there, his face pressed up to the glass or his shadow lurking beyond the screen. Bader could hear him walking around outside, his shoes rustling the grass, crackling through the leaves and sticks on the path, and he'd look out to see Lee standing in the shade of the trees, watching the cottage, studying it, with one hand brought up to his face to shade his eyes. Bader would go out onto the porch then, and he'd invite the boy to come in. He'd give him a cigarette. Lee would circle the room, touching things — admiring the fresh paint or the clean floor and examining Bader's possessions, as if he thought this was the way to get to know him better and understand what it was he did. He pecked at the keys of the typewriter that Bader had bought.

"What are you writing?" he asked.

"I thought I'd try to tell the story," Bader said. "Get it down on paper. What happened between Wolfgang and the Craigs."

"How can you write about something that didn't happen to you?" he asked.

"I don't know," Bader answered, shrugging. "I guess I'll have to make it up."

"Is that the gun?"

The old shotgun was standing up in the corner, behind the door.

"Yes, Lee," Bader said. "It is."

"You know how to use it?" Lee picked it up and broke it open, peered into the empty breech, then snapped it straight again and held it to his shoulder, sighting down the barrel, aiming it at a window, a lampshade, the door. "Pow! Pow! Pow!"

Bader told him no, he'd never shot it himself, and Lee asked him, How will you know how to write about how it felt to him then, and Bader admitted that he didn't know, he wouldn't.

And so the next time the boy came by to see him, it was with a pocket full of cartridges that he'd taken from his dad. Bader followed Lee down through the woods, along the dirt path to a clearing, and the boy showed him how to load the shotgun — break it, drop the cartridges in, snap it — and how to hold it, how to stand, how to aim and pull the trigger and shoot. *Boom!* Lee took it into his own hands, and he sighted down the barrel and when he shot, his body was rocked back, shaken by the force of the gun's hard kick.

The sound of it rang in Bader's ears, and he thought of Wolfgang Von Vechten, a boy like Lee, fifteen years old, moved to defend what he perceived to be his father's honor, pressing the cold muzzle of that same gun up against the back of Horace Craig's neck — folds of flesh, sweat trickling, ears burning, mouth moving, gasping, No! And then, *boom!*

"Of course," Lee said, squinting into the trees, "you still don't know what it's like to kill somebody, do you?" He brought the butt of the gun up to his shoulder again. And again, *boom!* The body of a brown squirrel came tumbling down through the branches, a dead weight that snapped the twigs, it plummeted, the plume of its tail flapping, and then landed with a soft thud and rolled against the grass.

Lee walked over to it, and Bader followed him. He prodded the bloody pulp of hair and flesh and bone with the toe of his shoe, and Lee stooped down, pulled out his pocket-knife, and cleanly cut the fuzzy tail off at its base.

"A trophy," he said, smiling, his eyes dark. He handed the shotgun back to Bader, and he put the knife away.

*   *   *

The walls of the ladies' room at the Cedar Hill Country Club were decorated with delicately tinted watercolors, representations of huge, single blossoms — irises and lilies, daffodils and hibiscus, camellias and pansies and crocuses and glads, that bobbed at the ends of their tender green stems — mounted and hung in heavy, carved antique gilt frames. The petals were soft-looking and fleshy, layered and folded back. The knobbed button of a stamen was dusted with pollen, and the colors of the petals bled into one another in great blotty-looking stains. Each blossom swirled inward, toward a murky core. Alternating with the paintings were tall mirrors that rose above shallow counters — glass-topped, dotted with bottles of perfume and jars of powder and tubes of lotion and cream, glass canisters stuffed with cotton balls, boxes of swabs and tissues and packages of scented damp wipes — and in those mirrors the women's carefully made-up faces looked like reflections or imitations or extensions of all the painted flowers in their heavy frames.

They perched their slim bodies — with ankles crossed and backs arched, long smooth necks stretching upward from bare shoulders, chins out and faces uplifted — on the edges of the round padded stools. They daubed lipstick, swiped on dark mascara, blended in dusty pink powder and creamy rose blush.

"Who's the young man I keep seeing with the Craigs?" one woman was asking, poking her fingertips in her hair.

"You don't know?" Eyes rolled.

"Where have you been?"

"That's the Von Vechten boy," another answered, tugging at the neckline of her dress to let it settle and drift against the slope of her breasts.

"Really?"

"Good-looking, isn't he?"

"Those eyes."

A cigarette was lit.

"Isn't he Tom Von Vechten's son?"

Lips kissing tissue.

"Well, of course he is."

"I think he's dating Katherine Craig."

"A Von Vechten? You don't find that odd?"

"What's he do?"

"Libbie says he's moved into Margot's old cottage. He's fixed it up, and he's living there. And he's writing a book, I heard."

"There must have been some money left, then, after all."

"Not very much, I'm sure."

And then the voices quickened and dropped to a whisper — a smooth, low, hissing murmur, like the rush of creek water over rocks.

"Well, of course I knew his mother. Who didn't?"

"She was something."

"Hard to forget."

"I remember the party here when poor Tom had to pick her up and carry her out to the car to get her to go home. He rolled her up under his arm like a rug, and he brought her all the way down the stairs to the driveway. She was squirming and wriggling and shouting the most terrible things — every bad word you could think of, and then some, she had quite a mouth — kicking her feet so she lost her shoes, and pounding him on the back with her fists."

"I heard she took off her dress in the pool."

"All the men went out onto the porch to watch her. They all of them just stood there."

"Well, she was quite beautiful, you know."

"Each one of those guys was shouldering somebody else aside, all of them hoping to get a better look at her, in the dark, with just that one little light that they used to turn on over the pool. And there was poor Tom, trying to salvage things."

"He did his best, I always thought."

"Standing out on the diving board all by himself, until finally the only thing he could do was to take off his jacket and his shoes and dive in himself to get her. They both nearly drowned. She fought him so hard, but he was stronger, and she was pretty drunk, probably, besides. He dragged her out, and he wrapped his jacket around to cover her up. We all went back inside then — it was so embarrassing, really, most of us could hardly bear to even look."

"I don't know whether she was trying to kill herself, or was she only having some fun?"

The shrug of bare shoulders. The sheen of tossed hair.

The pair of heavy doors, swinging outward from the powder room into the front entryway, revealed through the opening between them the women who had gathered inside. Some were standing, with their arms folded over their breasts and a hip swung out and one leg extended, a pointed toe. Some were sitting on the stools, gazing at their reflections in the mirrors, smoking cigarettes, tapping their ashes on the rims of the ashtrays on the tabletops, sipping white wine or rattling the ice cubes in their drinks. They examined their world, gossiping and laughing, gesturing with hands whose polished nails shone on their fingertips like gems. There was the glint of a diamond earring, the fire of a gold necklace, a silver bracelet, an emerald ring.

Out in the hallway, the men waited, their shoes shiny and thin-soled, slithery on the velvety low pile of the carpeted floor. And the women's high spiked heels left a million small pockmarks, like kisses in the rug as they climbed the stairs.

*   *   *

By the end of that August, a little more than six weeks after they'd met — not met, Katherine insisted, got reacquainted, maybe, because, she argued, we've always known each other, haven't we? — he asked her to marry him, and she said yes, but he couldn't help but wonder later whether it had been his idea after all, or was it only what she'd been planning on all along, even as early as he had, on that first evening when he'd come by to ask her father for the key?

When she called, he stood at the window in the cottage, looking out at the lush green overgrowth of the woods and listened to her voice on the phone, soft and low. She sounded out of breath, as if she'd been running or maybe had just got to the top of a steep flight of stairs.

"I had an idea, Bader," she said. "Are you up for it?"

"What?" he asked her. "Up for what?"

"Your house. Let's go see your house."

"My house. What house?" On the table near him, the pile of filled pages had begun to thicken and build. White papers, black ink. How Karl and Juniper Von Vechten came over together from Germany to Iowa, in 1850, when it was early springtime and the trees along the banks of the river had just that week begun to bud. How Herr Von Vechten hopped down off the train and stood on the platform with one big fist at his wife's elbow and the other wrapped firmly around the leather strap to the black steamer trunk that held all that they owned — a family Bible, some clothes and blankets and quilts, a pair of handmade lace curtains, a pewter pitcher and a silver tray, and the drawings for the ingenious cream can that would one day make them rich.

"The old house," Katherine said. "The one on Linden Lane."

"Doesn't somebody live there?"

"Just pick me up in half an hour, okay?"

*   *   *

The house that Heinrich Von Vechten had built sat at the top of a gentle sweep of hill that rose up between First Avenue and Linden Lane. Bader drove in, between the stone pillars and past the wrought iron fence, and the Mustang glided down the long driveway like a shadow. He pulled to a stop under the brickwork of the porte cochere. Standing at the bottom of the front steps, he felt a wave of memory move through him, and he saw his own child's hand placed there on that railing, his child's feet climbing those steps.

He remembered himself, how he'd been as a boy, in wool shorts and brown leather shoes, his thick dark hair wild with sleep. Some Sunday mornings he'd waked up to find his parents' friends sleeping on the sofas, in a chair, on the living room floor. He remembered a woman with pale white hair, sitting all alone in the kitchen, holding a vodka bottle in one hand, weeping into a bloodstained towel. There was a night when they'd all been drunk, all the grownups, shouting and singing around the piano, and his parents had been dancing together on the stairs, but his father lost his balance, and his mother fell and cracked her cheekbone against the banister rail. There was another time when his father jumped out of a second-floor window to the ground, explaining later that he hadn't been trying to kill himself at all, he only wanted to imitate how it must have felt to be a World War II airman parachuting down onto a field in France. He broke his ankle, and Eleanor scolded him for it, not because he'd made the jump, but because he'd been too stupid to consider that if he'd been a real paratrooper, he would have known enough to have worn boots.

Bader turned to look at Katherine, and he saw her smile, encouraging him to go on. She was wearing a black satin headband that pulled her hair away from her face so tightly that her eyebrows were arched up into a look of surprise and her eyes were big and bright. He took a step forward, reached out, and knocked on the door.

"Who lives here, Katherine?" he whispered, afraid of disturbing, who? The people whose house this was? The neighbors? The dead?

"The Magruders," she told him. "But they have a cabin on the river that they go to on the weekends, so they probably aren't even in town."

The house was silent, empty and still. Katherine skipped down the steps away from Bader, and he turned and followed her around to the side yard. Window wells had been cut into the ground around the stone foundation. Bader knew that if you dropped down into one of them and stood in the bed of dead leaves at the bottom, if you pressed your face against the glass, you'd be looking into the dark, dank shadows of the unfinished basement beneath the house. Katherine stood outside the dining room, next to the lilac bush, and she stretched herself up on tiptoe to peek in through the window with her hands cupped around her face. He imagined that what she saw was a square room with a long walnut table, eight cane-bottomed chairs, a marble-topped sideboard with pheasants carved into its doors.

He stood back and looked up at the outside of the house, remembering how huge it had seemed to him once. He followed Katherine as she rounded the corner to the back stoop, where she paused, looking around, listening. She put a finger to her lips, and he stopped, wondering, what? She bent her foot back and pulled off her shoe, then tapped its heel hard against a square of window in the top of the door. She hopped back out of the way, laughing, as the glass shattered, spilling into the house.

Bader's head was pounding; he felt dizzy and flushed.

"Katherine," he said, "you can't . . ."

But, she already had. She was reaching in and flipping the locks, and the door swung inward, opened. She turned to him and grinned, her shoe still dangling from one hand.

"Can't what?" she asked, rolling her eyes at him.

They were standing in the empty kitchen. The house seemed to Bader like a huge, gaping, hollow shell. The hum of the refrigerator roared in his ears. There was the counter where he'd been made to sit. The radio had been in that corner there. That cupboard was where the glasses were kept. His mother had hidden boxes of chocolates and bottles of gin way up there.

Katherine led the way, and Bader followed after her, touring the big house as if he were a stranger in it, relieved to find that much had been changed — this wasn't his furniture here, he'd never seen that sofa, this table, that chair, the rooms didn't smell the same, the sounds didn't resound, he wouldn't go upstairs and see his mother sitting at the dressing table in her slip or his father behind her, at the mirror, fiddling with his tie.

Katherine found a bottle of champagne in a bar refrigerator in the study, and she opened it, squealing and jumping back as the cork popped and the wine foamed over. She brought out glasses, and she poured, and they made a toast. She said, her eyes serious now, "To the Von Vechtens." And he said, smiling, "To the Craigs."

Her shoes clattered against the hardwood floor; she made so much noise it scared him, so finally she slipped them off and then she wandered barefoot from room to room, snooping in closets and opening drawers. She found a stack of leather-bound magazines full of pictures of naked women and a bottle of Jack Daniel's hidden behind it, at the back of a bottom desk drawer. They went upstairs, she leading, he following, and she pulled out a huge rubber corset from a dresser in one of the big bedrooms, and she waved a pair of bright pink silk boxer shorts over her head like a flag, laughing.

The wallpaper had all been changed. The paint was different. The carpet was the wrong color. And although the general layout of the rooms was just the same, still nothing was as it had been and that was, to him, a huge relief. Here was the place in the hallway where he had hidden, listening to them talk. That had been his bedroom there.

She slipped away from him when he wasn't looking, and she disappeared down a hallway, hiding while he tried to find her, whispering her name. She held her breath behind a bedroom door, and when he came in she jumped out at him and grabbed him, she pulled him down on top of her on the peach-colored satin spread on the mattress of an old oak bed. And he was so overwhelmed, so moved by the whole experience, by the terrible sense of violation that he felt, by the danger and the dreadful risk that they were taking — what if someone came in? what if they were caught? — that he told her right then, he said it out loud, he loved her.

And he felt himself come apart, splitting off, sitting in that bedroom looking at the rubber corset on the floor at his feet, with its wires and laces and bent metal hooks. It was stretched and misshapen and yellowed with washing and wear, and Bader could just about picture a large woman stepping into it, squeezing her flesh down into its hard firm form.

He asked Katherine to marry him.

And she said of course she would.

*　*　*

When Katherine came home that night, she found her mother in the darkened living room. Her father, she knew, was upstairs, asleep in bed.

"He had a little bit too much to drink, maybe," Mrs. Craig said to her daughter, sighing. And she herself couldn't sleep. "I shouldn't have had that coffee after dinner, I suppose."

Katherine's eyes shone.

Libbie sipped at her glass of sherry and felt its sugary warmth move through her, throbbing in her throat, leaving an ache behind in her teeth.

"Bader asked me to marry him," Katherine was saying. "And I said yes."

Libbie's heart was pounding. She looked over at her daughter and wondered, a little girl? But then, she thought, how old was I when Archie proposed to me? Younger even than this. Why not? she asked herself. Why not?

"But you hardly know him," she said.

Katherine frowned. She pulled the band from her head and her hair spilled over into her face. "You know that's not true," she said, tossing her head to throw it back. "I've always known him, Mother. Just like you and Daddy. I remember him from way back, when I was just a little kid."

Mrs. Craig put her glass down on the table.

"I want us to have a big, formal wedding," Katherine said. "In the church downtown, and we'll invite everyone we know."

"And a reception at the country club?" Libbie asked.

Katherine nodded, smiling. "And a dress with pearls sewn in around the neck and cuffs."

She went upstairs to bed. She stood in front of her mirror and studied her own face. Mrs. Bader Von Vechten, she thought, and she wrapped her arms around and hugged herself. She loved him. She looked forward to when they'd be together again with a need that frightened her. She longed for the sight of his face, his dark hair, mussed, his blue eyes, sharp and clear, searching hers.

Katherine believed that something serious and important was happening to her; for the first time in her life she felt that what she was about to do was truly dangerous. Nothing else that she had ever done seemed of any consequence to her now. She'd only been floating along through her life, it seemed, happy and careless, never looking or asking for much more than what she already had.

Her mother, who had once been as young and beautiful as Katherine was now, had aged. She seemed withered, battered by decades of neglect and abuse — too many cigarettes, too many drinks, too little ambition, no direction, no meaning, no plan. Libbie's had been a wasted life, Katherine thought, taken up by a string of trivialities — bridge games and cocktail parties, evening dresses and place settings, mornings spent arranging flowers at the Garden Club, luncheons at the country club, afternoons dribbled away with shopping trips and committee meetings. Winters in a beach house in Florida. Summers in a cabin on a lake in Minnesota. Trips abroad with her husband, five- and ten-day whirlwind tours. All of it to no purpose, because nothing stayed and nothing stuck.

And Archie, like a big wind, blustering in and out of rooms, knocking into things and people, too, as if the world were slightly too small for him. He had spent his whole life making deals, doing business, negotiating purchases and sales, buying up farmland, selling off livestock, squabbling over deeds to property that had been in the family now for years and years.

Mrs. Craig sat alone in the dark downstairs, with her eyes wide open, hard awake. Her sheer nightgown was a bright blooming spot in the darkened room. And on his back in his bed, Mr. Craig, sleeping his drunk into a hangover, snored.

*   *   *

There were parties, then. Everybody wanted to meet Bader Von Vechten, Tom and Eleanor's only son. Katherine introduced him. She brought him along with her, to the dances and the parties, the movies and the concerts and the picnics in the grass. They made a handsome pair, everybody agreed, Bader Von Vechten and Katherine Craig, pulling up to the clubhouse in his black convertible — she was so pretty and warm and cheerful in the cool shadow of his more sober diffidence and shy reserve. They looked good together, everybody said. A perfect match.

And Bader was happy. He enjoyed the noise and the commotion of so much company. The loud laughter. The firm handshakes and hearty slaps on the back. Of course, he'd have to join the country club now, wouldn't he? Did he play golf? Tennis? Cards? The winks of understanding, and the jokes that were shared with him. The drunken confessions and the secrets that were whispered in his ear, with the expectation that because he was a writer — wasn't he writing it all down, putting it into a book, about the families, about Cedar Hill, what a wonderful idea, what a challenge for a young man, what a marvelous enterprise for him to have undertaken, and now he was going to marry Katherine Craig besides, it was all too perfect, wasn't it? — they expected him to understand them and have insights into who they were and what they did that only an outsider like himself might see. Maybe he could use some of what they told him, too, maybe it would help.

"Here's a story for you, Bader," they said to him. "Listen to this."

All the dancing and the drinking and the eating. He and Katherine went to dinner parties on the weekends. Sometimes, there were two or three in one single night, and they'd leave one place and move on to another. He took her home to the house on Edgewood Road, and then he drove back out to Empire alone, up to his cottage in the woods, where he collapsed in his bed.

They followed along in a caravan of cars into the country, brought picnic baskets and bottles of beer and champagne, and they spread their grandmothers' worn quilts and crocheted blankets out over the grass. He and Katherine rode her father's horses along the paths in Old Indian Woods on a Sunday afternoon. She found an arrowhead and a bit of rock that looked like it might have been a shard from a piece of pottery. Or a splinter of bone. There were football games on Saturdays, where they sat together in a group in the cold sunshine, cheering loudly, sipping bourbon from the flat silver flask that Katherine kept hidden inside her sweater, warmed by the flush of her bare skin.

Just so, Katherine began to draw Bader out of his world, lonely, and into her own, crowded full of friends. There seemed to be so many of them, in fact, that he had trouble, sometimes, telling them apart. They looked so much alike — clean-cut young men with scrubbed faces and glistening hair, their eyes friendly and their smiles quick, and women with styled hair and diamond earrings, pearl necklaces, lipstick that matched the colors of their sweaters, ribbons that matched their dresses, purses that matched their shoes — and he couldn't keep track of who was married to whom, or which one was which; each of them seemed to be an only slightly altered version of another, with just the least variation in their height or their hair color or the way that they dressed. It bewildered him, sometimes, to look at them, and he became confused, searching for a connection. They only thought that he was absent-minded, and they forgave him for it. He was a writer, after all. With bigger things in mind.

Because, of course, everybody understood who Bader Von Vechten was. They knew all about him, they thought. They'd heard the stories about the Von Vechtens and the Craigs and the cream cans and the flu and the war. And if they hadn't heard, Katherine told them. That Bader's uncle had murdered Katherine's great-grandfather. That Wolfgang had hanged himself afterward, in despair. That the factory had been burned down. And that now Bader was living in the old cottage in the woods above Empire, and now he was going to write an important book about it all. And they'd all of them be famous someday. And they'd all of them be rich.

How could Archie Craig possibly disapprove?

Because, wasn't it just lucky that Bader and Katherine had

met? And wasn't it just fitting that he'd asked her to marry
him? And wasn't it just the most perfect thing anybody could
imagine that she'd told him that she would?

*   *   *

Bader, working, heard a noise outside his window. Lee was
there, standing in the dirt, tossing his pocketknife at the
ground. Bader took a bottle of beer from the refrigerator and
went out onto the porch. Lee looked up at him and squinted.

"I heard you're getting married," he said.

Bader nodded.

"It said in the paper you're marrying Katherine Craig."

"Yes," Bader said.

Lee flung the knife at the ground. It stuck in the dirt. He
stepped toward it, picked it up, and wiped the blade clean on
his pant leg. "Why?" he asked.

Bader put his hand in his pocket and leaned against the
porch post. He took a swallow of beer, shrugged. "I love her,
I guess," he said.

"You guess?" Lee asked. He flung the knife at the ground
again.

"No," Bader said, shaking his head. "I do."

Lee retrieved his knife. He fingered the gash in the dirt that
it had left.

"Or is it something else?"

"Like what?" Bader asked.

Lee shrugged. "I don't know," he said. "Revenge?"

Bader laughed, and Lee brought the knife back behind his
head and hurled it at Bader. Bader watched the blade flash
and spin toward him, and he flinched to dodge its bite. He
ducked his head to the side and brought his shoulder up, too
high, so the blade struck him before it hit the wooden post
and clattered off. Bader's hand opened, and the bottle of beer
fell, turning, and spilled and shattered on the stones of the
porch.

Blood seeped into the fabric of his shirt. Lee, his face white, came toward Bader with his hands outstretched.

"I didn't mean to hit you," he said. "You should have stayed where you were. You shouldn't have moved."

Bader's fingertips were dappled with blood. He staggered backward, away from Lee, his boots crunching over the bits of broken glass.

* * *

Roy and Darcy and Lee had been up and out of the house since daybreak, working their way alongside the creek, clearing the broken limbs and the fallen trees — some blown over by the wind, some old and rotten, some lightning-struck — out in the woods behind their house. The sky was a crisp, distant blue, thin as glass, and even though the sun was high, it was winter, and the air was still cold enough to burn their breath and turn it to smoke.

Roy had a cigarette clamped between his teeth. Darcy picked up a twig and brought it to her lips. She sucked on it and exhaled an extravagant stream of vapor, like smoke.

"Oh rally, Daddy dahling," she said, holding the twig in her fingers, pretending that it was a long, gold and black fancy cigarette holder and that she was all dressed up, not in her bulky blue jeans and heavy parka, but in a tight-fitting sheer silk dress that slid against her skin and followed the rolling movement of her hips, with impossibly high-heeled shoes on her feet and a snow white feather boa wrapped around her neck. She might be on her way to the country club with Lee's friend, Mr. Von Vechten.

"I must say, you do look stunning, rally, absolutely, uh, delectable in that charming chapeau. Where in the world did you buy it, dahling, rally, Daddy, did you say?" She flicked make-believe ashes and pursed her lips and batted her eyelids while Roy and Lee both stood with their hands hanging at their sides and stared.

Roy — in his oil-stained black and blue checked wool shirt, the pair of plastic goggles that protected his eyes from flying wood chips, a leather, fur-lined hat with the flaps pulled down over his ears — smiled, finally. His heavy suede gloves made his hands look big and clumsy as a bear's paws. It was Darcy's silly vamp that made him smile, she knew, not because he could understand what she was saying to him about his hat, which he happened to like, but because the truth was that Darcy herself was so far from being the woman she was trying to portray that it was a joke in itself. Darcy was still just a skinny little knock-kneed kid, thirteen years old, with chapped lips and a freckled nose, straight hair tied up in a ponytail, torn and faded dungarees with plaid flannel lining, bunched at the waist and rolled up at the cuffs, a quilted green parka zipped up to her chin over layers of a sweater and a flannel shirt, a turtleneck and an undershirt. Her fingernails were chewed down to the nub, and there were bruises on her forearms, and there was dirt smudged on her forehead and on one cheek. The farthest cry from Bader Von Vechten and his fiancée, Katherine Craig.

The edges of the creek had already begun to film over with its first thin icy crust. Roy turned back to his work, and the chain saw screamed in his hands.

He had Lee doing the hauling for him. The boy picked up a log and swung it onto his shoulder, heaving it into the bed of the truck. Darcy had a hatchet, and she was chopping up some of the smaller twigs and branches. When she'd gathered enough for a good-sized bundle, she tied the kindling together with hairy twine that burned her fingers when she pulled it tight.

There was the whack of Darcy's hatchet. The scream of Roy's saw. The grunt and heave of Lee's lifting and tossing. As she worked, Darcy was hot inside the layers of her warm clothes.

"Bundle up, Darcy," Mudd had told her. "It's cold out there. It's going to snow. I can smell it."

But Darcy was suffocating. She was burning up. First, she took off her parka. Then her sweater. Then the shirt and finally the turtleneck, until she was down to only her thin cotton undershirt. She lifted her hatchet up high and cracked it down hard on the twigs again. Like breaking an old man's fingers, she thought. The muscles in her arms and her back ached, but it was a pleasurable, warm pain. Her skin was rosy and damp and flushed a healthy pink.

She climbed up onto the bumper of the truck and pulled herself over the edge of its bed, into the back with the logs. She yanked off her gloves and slapped them together, listening to the sound, like applause, echoing off through the trees. When the wind sucked in through the gully, it snatched her breath away, strangling her. She scrambled to the top of the pile, where she sat and watched while her brother and her father continued their hard work. Bare-armed, Darcy steamed in the wintry cold, until Mudd came out of the trees with a thermos of hot cocoa and three mugs and saw her sitting there half-naked on top of the heap of logs, and then she yelled at her to put her clothes back on.

"You'll catch your death, Darcy!"

She slammed the metal thermos and the cups down on the hood of the truck. When Roy came up behind her and put his arms over her shoulders to hug her, she rolled away from the weight of his embrace, turned, adjusted the scarf on her head, and pulled the folds of her coat in tight around the barrel of her body. She craned past Roy to look up at Darcy again, squinting in the white sunshine, her mouth cruel-looking, her lips firm and tight with anger.

"Darcy," she chided, hissing her daughter's name with a sound that was sudden and hard, "you heard me. You get yourself dressed. Right this minute. Roy, you see to it she does." She turned her face toward the sky again. "It's going to snow," she said. "I can feel it coming. There'll be snow."

* * *

"Who is she, Daddy?" Darcy had asked her father, point-blank, on a morning when he drove her in to school instead of making her take the bus. She was sitting right there next to him in the cab of the truck, with her hands curled over her books and her hair fallen forward to hide her face, looking at her chewed nails, the chipped polish, the cracked leather of her shoes. She'd tied a red plaid ribbon in her hair. After he dropped her off, she would hurry in to the girls' bathroom and put on the lipstick that Mudd would never let her wear.

"Who?" he'd asked. She knew he was going to try and deny it. He was pretending that he didn't know what she meant.

But she'd turned to face him then, her eyes level and knowing and holding his, until he'd had to look away to watch the road. She saw the blush of shame and embarrassment that came creeping up like a fire from his chest to his neck and onto his face, flaming in his ears, buzzing in his head. With one hand on the wheel, he'd pulled his wallet out of his pocket. And, fingers groping, clumsy and thick, he'd told her, "Here, Darcy, steer this for a second." She'd reached out and curled her own small hand over the wheel, squeezing so tight her fingertips turned red, then white, while she steered the truck for him, with her heart pounding, as they climbed the long hill of the parkway away from Empire and toward Cedar Hill. Finally he had hold of it again, strong and sure; he accelerated and the truck bounded over the crest. And the small, square photograph that Darcy held in her hand was of a woman's face. She had freckles, and a halo of bright red hair.

"Naomi," Roy said, his voice rough with all the vowels. "Her name's Naomi."

Darcy cleared her throat. "That's pretty, I think," she said. She looked up at her father, then down at the photo again. "Prettier anyway than Mudd."

She leaned over and took his wallet from him, and she tucked the photo back inside.

"Well, do you love her?" Darcy asked. She held the wallet in both her hands and gazed out the side window at the passing land — houses, barns, silos, fields, as they approached the outskirts of Cedar Hill — waiting to hear his answer.

"I don't know, Darcy," he said, finally. "I might. But I just don't know."

Then Darcy had been silent, clutching her father's wallet in her lap, all the rest of the drive to the school. She hadn't said a word, until he pulled up to the curb alongside the playground, and then she'd handed his wallet back, and when he took it, she leaned over closer, and she wrapped her long thin arms around his neck, and she brushed his rough cheek with her cold lips.

"Well," she sighed, "I know I love you, Daddy." And she pulled her face away to look at him again. "No matter what."

Her eyes had been bright then, shining with the secret that she and her father shared. She'd turned and climbed down out of the truck, and she'd pushed the door shut behind her with one hard thrust of her flat hip.

* * *

The chain saw rumbled, hanging from Roy's fist. Lee handed Darcy up her shirt, and she climbed down from the rolling logs. She looked at her mother's face, round and flat and frowning at her, blaming her, it seemed, as if Roy's infidelity were somehow her fault, just because she was young, and he loved her, and she didn't take after Mudd. She knew that her mother was thinking that Darcy had betrayed her somehow, and maybe, Darcy thought, she had. By taking his side. By understanding him as she did. By loving him back, no matter what, not because he was perfect, but because he was her dad. She pulled her turtleneck over her head, slipped her arms back into her shirt and buttoned it up, yanked on her sweater and zipped her parka up under her chin, bringing the hood up over her head to hide her face. Holding her hatchet, she turned away, toward the trees, squinting upward at the snake of white smoke that coiled from the chimney of the cottage that was poised there in the clearing on the bluff. She forgave her father his faults, she thought. But she couldn't forgive her mother hers.

*　　*　　*

From where he was standing, leaning with one foot up on the bottom rail and his elbows planted on the top of the fence that encircled his cottage and enclosed his back yard, Bader could look down the hill, through the gray shadows of the barren trees, and into the gully, all the way to the edge of the creek — a curling silver thread — where Roy and Darcy and Lee, diminished and toylike, worked. Their voices came to him in shreds and spurts, carried on the wind in ragged bits and pieces, drowned out now and then by the chain saw's raw shriek.

The air was wintry and crisp, full of the smell of wood smoke and pine sap. The ground had begun to harden and freeze; the grass at his feet was crunchy with the frost.

Bader shivered. He blew on his hands as he turned and headed back toward the cottage. Smoke was billowing up from its chimney in a way that seemed to Bader to be comforting and ordinary and warm. He crossed the yard and climbed up onto the porch, and he went inside to try to bring some order to the disarray of all the Christmas decorations that he'd bought. They cluttered the living room, along with the shopping bags that held his unwrapped presents — a fisherman's sweater for Katherine and a long knit scarf, a pair of cashmere gloves for her mother, a crystal decanter for Mr. Craig — and rolls of shiny paper and strands of ribbons, bows and cards and scissors and tape. The noble fir on its stand in the corner had been strung with lights and popcorn, but it was still only partly decorated, and the box of ornaments that Bader had bought was on the floor nearby, opened and overturned, its contents — glass balls and brass snowflakes, wooden figures, china candy canes, silver icicles and paper stars — all spilled out in a jumble on the braided rug. A painted plaster crèche sat on the kitchen table, each of its pieces still wrapped in tissue.

Bader turned on the radio beside his typewriter, and it filled the cottage with soft music, the familiar strains of the Christmas carols that he'd listened to, alone, all his life. Never before had this holiday held so much meaning for Bader. Never before, he thought, had he felt the strength of its spirit move him more. Because he had a family now. Because there were people to whom, finally, he belonged.

He slipped out of his black wool overcoat and hung it up on the iron hook behind the door. He sat on the sofa and unwrapped each small plaster figure — angels and sheep, shepherds and Wise Men, Mary, Joseph, and the baby Jesus himself. When he was finished, he would shower and shave, dress and drive into Cedar Hill to pick up Katherine and take her to the annual Christmas party out at the club.

*　*　*

Later, everyone would say that it was the worst blizzard to hit the area in more than fifty years. Twenty-seven inches of snow in less than twelve hours. Bone-chilling arctic winds tearing through the trees at fifty miles an hour. A night when the world around Cedar Hill and Empire turned killing cold and blinding, deathly white.

*　*　*

Tangled in her bedsheets, her nightgown twisted and pulled up above her waist, her big white breasts shiny with sweat, Mudd Kimbel was dreaming of her husband Roy. She could feel his shadow cast over her, like a cloud, long and cool, roiling and dark. She could feel the glide of his palms over her hips. His breath, the soft hot breeze of his sigh, in her eyes. His mouth moving against hers, strangling her. The long, hard muscles of his thighs, his square knees, the flat blades of his shins. His furry belly and broad scarred shoulders and the wide, moving mound of his chest. His heart thudding. The hard swallow of his throat; the steady pounding pressure of his pulse. The veins on the backs of his hands; the knobs of his wrists; the bones and muscles turning in his arms. Smooth, bluish skin on the tops of his bare feet. The roaring song of his whisper in her ear. The dark bristle of his hair against his temple. Three deep, parallel lines carved into his brow. The spread of his nose, the splinters of his beard, the flutter of his lashes, the deep, black hollows of his eyes.

And her own limbs, twined around Roy's body like flower stems. And her hands moving over him. And his thumbs pushing, pressing into her belly, the spread of his fingertips squeezed against her spine. How delicate her feet. How pliable her flesh, how breakable her bones.

*　　*　　*

White twinkle lights had been strung up around the windows and along the eaves of the brick front of the country club, and a stream of cars glided in between the stone pillars, coursing up the long drive to stop at the top, outside the door, and unload their cargo — children, mothers, grandparents — before the dads coasted back down to the lot at the bottom of the hill to park. There was a treacherous sheen of ice on the steps, sprinkled with sand and white salt.

Inside the clubhouse, the cloakroom was filled with hanging coats, and the ladies' room was busy, the doors opening and closing, the chatter inside as noisy as it was out. On the table next to a love seat by the window was a tray of cookies and a bowl of ribbon candy. A coffeepot was brewing. Green garlands draped the mirrors and the picture frames, too.

Little boys in velvet trousers and red bow ties and older youths in gray flannel pants and navy blue blazers with brass buttons slid their slick-soled loafers over the carpeting at the top of the stairs. They grabbed food, jostled each other, splattered cups of punch. The girls wore green and red plaid Christmas jumpers, white blouses with lace collars, white tights and round-toed patent leather shoes, and their hair was curled and tied or braided or drawn up into pigtails or twisted into buns. Their fathers stood together in their dark suits, snow white shirts, and red and green striped ties. The mothers wore creamy wool dresses, shiny stockings, black leather pumps. A quartet of singers in Dickensian dress harmonized carols outside the ballroom door. And in a minute, Santa Claus would appear, he'd come ho-ho-hoing up the stairs, with his bag of presents thrown over one shoulder, and in it was something for everybody, a present for all the boys and girls, both the bad ones and the good.

When Santa Claus finally emerged from the smoke of the card room in the Men's Grill, his beard was crooked. Mrs. Craig stood on tiptoe to straighten it, and he put his hand on her back and pulled her toward him and kissed her on the mouth. His bright green eyes were twinkling. His nose was shining, red. He was holding a glass of bourbon and ice in the heavy curl of his fist. Katherine Craig brought him a cup of coffee to drink, but he was clumsy, and he spilled it on himself, staining the white fur trim of his suit, scalding the back of his hand. He cursed her for that. When Bader Von Vechten came up and put a hand on his arm to restrain him, St. Nick grabbed him by the front of his shirt and pushed him away so hard that he stumbled back and banged his

shoulder against the wall. Santa turned away and trudged up
the carpeted stairs in his heavy black boots, his voice reverberating, "Ho-ho-ho!" He took a cup of spiked eggnog from
a table near the entryway, slugged it down, refilled it, and
drank again. Beads of the sticky yellow cream caught in his
mustache and clung to his beard. A cluster of small children
surrounded him, clamoring. The pillow under his jacket had
begun to slip, so he stopped, reeling, and straightened it,
hoisting it back up into place over his belly with both his
hands. He was handed a bag of toys, and he slung it over his
shoulder and pushed his way onward through the crowd.

A chair had been set up in the ballroom for him, on a raised
platform, under the darkened skylights, like a throne. Teen-
age girls were dressed up in red velvet skirts and green tights
to act as elves to help him serve the younger kids, but when
he came in they knew that something was wrong with him,
and they just stood there and stared at him while he staggered
up to his chair, sat down in it heavily, closed his eyes, and
sighed.

Parents were standing back and staring, too. Nobody
knew what to do. It was too embarrassing, really, wasn't it?
Their hushed whispers hissed in his ears. What's wrong with
him? Is he ill? He's drunk. But the little ones weren't afraid.
This was Santa Claus, after all. They clambered up onto the
platform and crowded around him, pulling on his jacket and
his sleeves, touching his hands, reaching for his beard, grabbing at the black bag that they knew was filled up with toys.

And Archie Craig grinned and howled, "Ho! Ho! Ho!"

While Mrs. Craig stood against the wall watching him,
with one arm wrapped around herself and her other hand at
her face and her finger curled over her lip.

*   *   *

Mudd, bleary-eyed, nose stuffed, throat red and raw, plodded barefoot down the hall to Darcy's room. Darcy was sit-

ting on her bed, leafing through a teen magazine that Lee had swiped for her from the drugstore in town.

"Where did he go tonight, Darcy?" she asked, standing in the doorway, in her nightgown, her hair damp with sweat. "I know that you know. And I don't want you to lie to me."

"I don't know anything."

"He's still seeing her, isn't he?"

Darcy bit her tongue and shook her head, turning pages.

Mudd stepped into the room and crossed over to the bed. She took Darcy's shoulder and shook it. "Who is she?"

"She isn't anybody." She shrugged her mother's hand away.

"Have you met her, Darcy? Have you talked to her?"

"No."

"Then there is someone? You admit it?"

Darcy turned and looked at her mother. "Well, she has red hair," she said.

"He told you that?"

"I saw a picture."

Mudd stepped back. "Is she pretty, Darcy?" she asked, begging. "Is she?"

Darcy cocked her head and chewed on her lips, considering. "Well," she said, finally, "I guess she's prettier than you."

And Mudd saw in Darcy then, in her own daughter, in that face — the way she was holding herself, the way she was looking at her, that critical squint — she saw there all those other girls, and they were whispering, "Mudd Butt, plain as rain, big fat stupid ugly cow," giggling, poking, prodding, and tormenting her. Before she knew what she was doing, Mudd's hand came out, like a big bird, and it swooped toward Darcy and smacked her, heavy, stinging, hard. And in the pocket of her robe, creased and crumpled, folded and unfolded so many times that it had become as soft as tissue paper, its ink rubbed and smeared, erased and hardly legible,

was Roy's note about her, Roy's assessment of her, Roy's list
— SHORTCOMINGS.

*   *   *

It had begun to snow, softly and lightly, dusting the ground
like powdered sugar sprinkled over gingerbread. Lee, outside in the yard, tipped back his head, and he let the snowflakes fall on his face, in his hair, in his mouth, and in his eyes.

*   *   *

Santa had pulled one little boy up onto his lap. His face was
round and clear, as perfect as a doll's, with shining skin and
glassy eyes. "And what do you want for Christmas, son?"
The words caught on Santa's tongue, slurring them. "What's
your name?"

"Jack Hamer," the boy said.

Santa put a hand in his beard and rubbed it thoughtfully
with his gloved fingers. "Hamer," he murmured, puzzling
over the name. "Hamer. Hamer. Would that be David
Hamer, son? Is that your daddy's name? David?"

The little boy nodded, eyes wide, full of wonder that this
man would know his father's name.

"Your grandma Edna still sick, Jackie-boy?" Santa asked
him. And when the child nodded, he went on, "She still shitting in her bed, son?"

Jack Hamer stared at Santa Claus for a moment before he
began to struggle and pull away. He scrambled down from
Santa's lap and fell back off the platform onto the floor,
bumping his head. His father, David Hamer, was pushing
through the crowd of children, and Archie stood up on his
chair, opened up his bag, and lobbed the wrapped toys out at
the children.

Bader was the first to get to him. He took hold of Mr.
Craig's arm, firmly, and dragged him down.

"Aw, it was only a joke," Archie protested, struggling weakly against Bader's grip, shaking his head. "Come on, jeez, I was only kidding. Christ!"

Some of the children had already gone back to their tables, and were opening up the gifts that they'd gathered off the floor. Libbie and Katherine each took one of Archie's arms, and they helped him down the carpeted stairs, glistening with chips of shattered ribbon candy, through the doors, to Bader's car that had been brought up to the top of the drive. Halfway down the hill, Archie pulled off his beard and tossed it out the open window. He unbuttoned the front of the Santa suit and pulled out the pillow and threw it out, too, and it landed on the road behind them, bounced and broke, and feathers flew, like snow.

*   *   *

The Mustang pulled up into the Craigs' driveway and stopped. The house was dark, the lights on the tree in the window turned off. Bader knew that there were piles of presents accumulating under it already and that there were three stockings hanging by the fireplace and that Mrs. Craig was working on a fourth, for him.

Mrs. Craig unlocked the front door, and let Mr. Craig stagger off on his own inside. She stopped and turned to Katherine.

"I think it's best if we just call this a night now, don't you?" she asked, and then she followed her husband in. Bader heard him calling out, "Hey, dammit, I was only kidding. Hell. Come on, what's the big deal?" And then Mrs. Craig shut the door behind her, slamming it hard.

Katherine looked at Bader. "I'm sorry," she said. He smiled and brushed her hair from her face. "He can be pretty awful sometimes."

"It's all right, Katherine," he said. "I've seen worse, remember? Way worse."

She leaned against him, grateful for his understanding. "He's not a bad man, you know."

Bader shook his head. "No," he said, "he's not."

"He's my father. And I can't help it, Bader, I love him."

She was bundled up in a long, dark fur coat and matching muff and hat, and he pulled her aside, out of the way, into the shadows, and it was so cold, and snow had begun to fall and stick, and her breath was hot in his face when he kissed her. He pulled off his glove and slid his hand in under the plush fur of her coat — she was wearing only the thinnest little crepe blouse — and ran his fingers over her bare skin, damp and silky and warm.

*   *   *

Darcy had thrown a blanket over her shoulders, and now she grasped its corners in her fists and pulled it around her, tight. One hand drifted up to her face. She pressed her cheek lightly with her fingertips, bewildered by the tenderness that she felt there. From her mother's slap. From her mother's hand, swinging, flapping, clapping her anger onto Darcy's face. Mudd was upstairs now, shut away in her bedroom, and the house was quiet, dignified-seeming, cold and empty-feeling and dark.

The snowfall whispered outside. Still holding her blanket against her chest, Darcy bent over and plugged in the Christmas tree lights, and they blinked on and off in a pattern — red and yellow and green and blue — bathing her, flickering over her, caressing her with a blend of color, like a bruise. Outside the windows whose corners Lee had frosted with a spray can of white rime, the sky was aglow with snow.

So maybe it would be a white Christmas this year after all. There were some packages piled up already under the tree. Darcy loved this holiday; she reveled in the sparkle of excitement and secrecy and anticipation that brought it on. Mudd hid wrapped presents out of sight under her bed, and Darcy would sneak in, late in the afternoon, as the house darkened, and she'd lie on her side on the rug and stare at the magic-seeming shapes there in the shadows, among the dust mice on the floor, longing for Christmas to hurry up and get here soon. Not that there was all that much of anything special in the boxes. Handmade things, mostly, that smelled like Mudd, a sachet of sour vinegar and rosewater perfume. Knit scarves, and slippers, useful things like underwear and socks. A new winter coat, maybe. A pair of warm gloves. Fur-lined boots. But whatever it was, no matter how practical, still it came to her wrapped in the dazzle of gold and silver paper, bright with colored ribbons and huge fancy bows.

Right now, thinking about all the Christmas holidays that she could remember, when she was little and didn't know anything and didn't understand what anybody was up to outside of her own self, Darcy was beginning to feel like she'd been caught in a vise, held here between her childish wishes and a stronger, stranger longing to be grown up, as if she were being squeezed between them, so tight that she could hardly breathe.

She looked around the living room and saw the spatter of homely ornaments that decorated the tree — icicles and candy canes, sequined balls, cutout angels and paper stars — that she and Lee had made in their Sunday school classes over the years. Mudd had tacked up the cards that came in the mail — from family and friends, in town and out and at the church — all around the frame of the doorway that led to the hall. There would be the lighting of the Advent candles at Peace Christian on Sunday mornings now, where a family would walk down to the front of the church, and the father would read from the Bible, and the mother would light a long stick and touch it to the candles to rekindle the flames. Of love. Of hope. Of joy.

Except that her father was in love with somebody else right now. Except that maybe he was going to leave them to go and be with her. Except that maybe nobody here was good enough for him anymore. Except that he wasn't here now, and her mother was mad, and Darcy couldn't blame her, and everything was all messed up.

"Lee?" she called. It would be all right if she could see him, talk to him, feel his calm gaze and watch his dimpled smile and hear his gentle voice.

She felt her way along the darkened hallway, past the kitchen to his bedroom at the back of the house. She tapped with her knuckles, turned the knob, swung the door open wide, and gasped against the sudden stinging cold. Lee's window gaped, the curtains flapped and blew, snow flew in and drifted like talc on the windowsill and the floor and across the quilt that covered the bed.

Because Lee was gone.

*   *   *

The ghost of Wolfgang Von Vechten was known to haunt these woods. He was a shadow in the trees. He was a scream on the hillside. He was a howl that echoed through the caverns of the limestone caves. Lee, trying to picture Wolfgang, thought of Bader Von Vechten instead — younger, with pale skin and black hair and blue eyes, full of passion and murder, killing Horace Craig, ambushing him, shooting him in the head. And Horace Craig a big old fat satisfied man, with wormy-looking lips and freckles and hair that looked like the bristle on the backside of a pig.

The world seemed secretive and silent, muffled by the falling snow, and the air felt heavy and thick, like a pressure, building, as Lee tromped through the woods alongside the creek, following a looping path that led him up the hill and then south again, in a wide circle around the Von Vechten parcel at the top of the bluff. He was drawn toward the old cottage with an attraction that stiffened his movements and made him feel jagged and tense, like a bundle of iron slivers brought up to a quivering point in response to a magnet's hard, smooth pull. He spiraled inward, like a whirlpool or a cyclone that was all chaos and churning on its outer edges, but at the core remained untouched and untroubled and unspeakably calm.

Lee was thinking he might freeze to death here, in the blizzard that they said was on its way. Maybe he could lie down, curl up, go to sleep. Like a bear. He'd be a snow-covered mound. A blanketed bundle. He would be mistaken for a large rock, maybe. A small hill. At least until spring, until the snow melted and was washed away.

He picked up a stick and stooped over to prod its tip into the rocks and chalky blocks of limestone on the ground. The leaves and grass were frosty underfoot, and the snow was still falling and blowing, coming down faster and harder now, thick enough, he thought, he hoped, to stick. When Lee turned to look behind him for a moment, he could see the dark slate roof of his house rising up through the trees. The lights from its windows spilled out into the night, and from where he stood, it looked safe and warm, snug even. Lee could believe, looking at it, that it sheltered a happy family, that it enclosed normal, simple people who all got along, who understood each other and who loved themselves and one another and who lived in an ordinary world, leading ordinary, unspectacular lives.

*   *   *

There was snow, the sky was white with it, it was coming down steadily, in thick fat flakes that blanketed the fields and made the world around him look changed and unreal as Bader, in the Mustang, sailed down the empty parkway toward Empire, out of Cedar Hill. The fields were breathtakingly beautiful. Tomorrow, when the storm was over, the snow-laden trees would sparkle in the bright sunshine. But now it was nighttime, now it was dark, now the sky was filled with a dangerous swirl of falling, blowing snow.

*   *   *

First, Lee saw the pair of headlights that came swooping over the crest of the hill and barreling down its incline toward him. Then he heard the groan of the trailer truck that was lumbering up at his back. He was buffeted by the semi's blowing backdraft as it roared past — gears grinding, huge tires plowing, heavy treads throwing back big chunks of hard-packed snow. And then, in one slow, fluid motion, the truck was taking the long curve of the parkway wide, and the black Mustang was veering off into a graceful, looping, sweeping skid — horn blaring, headlights losing the road, skimming the trees — and thumping down off the roadbed, over the shoulder, into the ditch.

The truck rumbled onward, up the hill — without stopping, without slowing, maintaining its momentum, its traction, its heaving, struggling speed — until it had mounted the crest, humped over it, dipped downward again, and disappeared.

The trees stirred, their branches waved and swayed, like dancers, in the snow.

*   *   *

Lee was in the front seat of the Mustang, at the wheel, and Bader was behind it, pushing. "Give it some gas!" he hollered, and the tires spun, spewing snow, then leaves and grass and finally great globs of black mud. The air was filled with the acrid smell of burnt rubber. The snow was falling hard and fast. The woods were dark, and the trees seemed to be crowding nearer, looming, leering, closing in. The wind gusted and howled, battering the Mustang and strangling Lee.

Bader slammed his fist on the back fender of the car. "Fuck!"

He tromped in an angry little circle. Lee got out and stood, was buffeted off balance, his sneakers skidding, filled with snow. His socks were wet; his toes were numb. His hair was whipped around his face, stinging his eyes, blinding him. Bader caught him and led him back into the refuge of the car.

* * *

There was a wool blanket in the trunk. And a flask of scotch in the glove box.

The wind was screaming through the trees.

The headlights were reflected back against a smooth white wall of falling snow. Lee shivered. Under his parka, he only had on a thin T-shirt and jeans with holes ripped out of the knees. And on his feet, his canvas tennis shoes, red wool socks, soaked through. He pulled off his sopping socks and rubbed his bare feet, groaning as the feeling came aching back into them again. Tears shone in his eyes.

So, finally, Bader reached for him. He hugged his arms around him. He pulled his body close to his own, to warm him. To warm himself.

* * *

Darcy and Mudd kept a watch at all the windows, moving from one room to another, peering out, circling inside the house, through the living room, the dining room, the kitchen, Lee's bedroom, and back, listening, wondering, did they hear his cries out there in the howl of the wind? They talked about going to look for him — Mudd went so far as to pull on her coat and her gloves and her hat, and she stood outside on the porch with the snow swirling all around her, so thick and blinding that she couldn't see anything much past the railing. She was afraid, and she would forever afterward be ashamed of that fear. She went back inside, shouldered the door shut against the wind and blowing snow. Darcy made tea, and the two of them sat together at the kitchen table sipping it, praying — "Please God, please God" — until finally Darcy put her head in her arms and fell asleep. And then Darcy dreamed that it was she and not Lee at all, out there in the woods, in the storm, cold and lost. She imagined her own body falling, freezing, buried in a drift of deep, deep snow. First you're drowsy, she'd been told. Then you fall asleep, you sink down into yourself, away from the cold, away from the snow, away from the ache and the pain, until the least last little bit of heat inside you has flickered out, and then you're dead. You freeze over, like a pond, from the outside in, until the merest glimmering of your consciousness has been blacked out, solid and unforgiving and hard.

*   *   *

The snow swirled around the Mustang, trapping Lee and Bader inside, as if in the make-believe hollow of a glass globe. They dozed — there was a smell of whiskey on Lee's breath, his head rested against Bader's shoulder, his body was nestled in his arms — and when Bader came awake again, his hands were inside Lee's coat, his fingers were against the boy's skin, on his belly and his back.

Bader held Lee. He rubbed his cold hands between his own, he massaged his icy feet.

"Will we die?" Lee asked, his face long, solemn, a cold, stark white.

Bader shook his head. No. They would not die.

He touched Lee's hair, brushed it away from his face.

"I'm cold," Lee said.

He shivered and clamped his teeth shut to still them. He brought his hands up and wrapped his arms around Bader. Bader smelled his hair. He turned Lee and pressed his body up even closer, curling his back, fitting it like a socket into the curve of Bader's belly and chest and drawn-up knees.

Bader wrapped his overcoat around the ball that their bodies formed. He drew the blanket up over them. Lee rolled under him. Bader nuzzled the soft skin at the back of his neck. On the undersides of his arms. The veins and slender tendons in his wrists. His knuckles. And, moaning then, Lee was moving, gasping, arching, and grasping at Bader, surprisingly supple and strong. His eyes were closed, his head thrown back, his nostrils flared. His chest heaved. The flex of his feet. The suck and flutter of his belly. He raised his arms and stretched them out, he straightened them behind his head with his elbows locked, and he strained and pressed his palms flat against the window, fingers spread. Bader breathed in the smell of him and the taste of him, salty and sweaty and sour. When Lee took his hands away from the glass there were two fog-edged palm prints there, and they faded slowly; they diminished and disappeared as Lee's breathing slowed.

Bader was on his knees. His face was slack, his eyes wide, startled, shocked. Lee rose to his elbows — his parka fell open; his shirt was unbuttoned and folded back, exposing his bare belly and its soft straight brownish hairs, the angles of his hipbones, his penis, glistening, the tender pinkish tissue-paper crumple of his balls — he sat up and looked at Bader, studied him, with his head tipped to one side and his hair fallen into his eyes. Blinking, he regarded him — there was moisture on his eyelashes and his mouth looked swollen, his face was rosy now, cheeks reddened and flushed. And then Bader was reaching for Lee again. He pulled the boy toward him. He held his head against his chest. Lee heard the hammer of Bader's heart as he hugged him, held him, rocked him. He licked the salty tears from his cheeks. He kissed the ribbon of his mouth. He groaned and strained against him, until his own slow moans and the sough of the wind in the branches of the trees had become a chorus to the tender melody of the boy's soft, gasping cries.

And outside, beyond the confines of the car, the wind

blew, and in the fields and in the ditches, in the trees and in the bushes, on the houses and on the roads, the walkways and the driveways, the mailboxes and the fences, in the ravines and in the gullies, in Empire and in Cedar Hill, it continued to snow and snow and snow.

*　　*　　*

There was a pale light — the same drab blue-gray hue of Lee Kimbel's eyes — filtering through the gauzy snow that was piled up on the windows and the windshield of the Mustang — black as a beetle, mired in frozen mud, buried in new snow. The wind had stopped blowing, and the snow had stopped falling; the sky was a low, white scowl, and the world outside the car seemed muffled, muted, silent and deathly still. Lee was curled up, asleep, against the curve of Bader's body. The black wool overcoat was wrapped around the boy, and the blanket covered them both. Bader felt the soft rise and fall of Lee's chest moving against him as he breathed. His nose was a button, red with the cold. His face looked smooth and childish, his skin clear, flushed, cheeks rosy, lips dry, white, chapped. His hand was flat against his cheek, its fingernails ragged and gnawed. A faint white vapor was curling around his nose as he breathed, like smoke.

And with the rocking motion of his breathing and the warmth of the boy's body mingling with his own, Bader felt himself begin, again, to stir. He reached behind him and pulled down hard on the door handle, struggling with it, desperately — it had frozen; it was stuck; it crackled with ice and cold. When he drew himself back and slammed against it with his shoulder, groaning, the movement awakened Lee.

Blinking, confused, the boy drew back and pulled away to look at Bader with drowsy eyes. He shivered, yawned. Closed his eyes again and smiled. And then the door was swinging open, and Bader was tumbling out backward into the bitter cold of a deep soft cushion of snow.

A windblown drift had buried the Mustang's nose. When Bader stood, he was up to his hips in the white powder. It filled his shoes and burned the bare skin of his ankles above his socks.

The cold was sharp, and he gasped against it, strangled, his breath gone. He opened and closed his mouth like a landed fish. The trunks of the trees in the woods all around him were white with the blown snow that clung to them like a heavy, sticky gauze. Their limbs were burdened by its soggy weight, strained, bending down, as if bowing, like old women hunched around the curves of their crooked spines. A branch cracked, and the sound of it echoed like a gunshot through the frozen woods.

Lee had climbed out of the car and was standing in the snow now, too, his face a gray blur inside his parka hood. He struggled toward Bader, stumbling, and then fell against him with a moan. Bader put an arm around the boy's waist and held him upright; Lee teetered and went limp against him. His knees buckled and his head rolled back, throwing off the parka hood, exposing the sinew of his bared throat. Lee's hands were open, white, fingers stiff with cold.

Bader bent and, groaning, he scooped the boy up into his arms. And he thought, then, I could kill him, drop him, let him fall into the snow, roll him over and press his face down, smother him with the cold of it and then leave him here to freeze over, buried until the snow has all melted away and someone finds what's left of him in the spring. He shuddered, shifted Lee's body in his arms, brought him up closer, tighter against his chest. Lee's head lolled against Bader's shoulder. His lashes fluttered, his slack arm swung.

The reproachful stillness of the woods closed in. And Bader, with Lee in his arms, began to walk, pushing himself

forward through the deep snow, bearing the soft resilience of
the boy's body, trembling, shivering, shuddering, against his
own.

*   *   *

There was a breaking up, a coming apart, a slow and steady
hard crumbling, as if something in Bader had begun to crack
off and pull away. As if some part of him had separated itself
and was sliding out of his grasp, beyond recovery, floating
wayward and drifting off. He felt it in his body — a painful,
wrenching knot, like a fist flexing in his gut. And he heard it,
too — a tearing sound inside his head, a crackling in his ears,
a loud, sudden, thunderous boom that knocked him awake
in the middle of the night and withheld from him the forgetful luxury of sleep.

Alone in the cottage, Bader sat at his desk, punching at the
typewriter keys, watching the pile of his manuscript pages
grow, the hard blocks of its paragraphs ornamented with corrections from his colored pens. How Heinrich had married
Margot. How Margot had had two sons. The cottage drew
itself in around him, and it huddled over him. As if it would
protect him, he thought. Or suffocate him. As if it might
swallow him. His loneliness welled up, drowning him, and
his longing began again its gentle, aching tug and pull.

"What is it that you want, Eleanor?" Those had been his
father's words, the refrain that Tom Von Vechten had sung,
the sentence that he always came back to, the question that
he asked his wife, over and over again. Every night, it
seemed, but it couldn't have been every night, could it? It
must have only been a few times, once or twice maybe, when
things started going from bad to worse, near the end. But it
was that phrase, that combination of words, that Bader could
best recall. And it was the question that, crouched in the
shadows of the staircase, he had overheard.

"What do you want?"

She'd put Bader to bed too early, and he wasn't tired, and he waited, and then he crept out of his room again, and he padded barefoot down the hall, curious, wondering what they did, the two of them, when there was no one around to watch them. When he was asleep, and no company came, and they were all alone. He listened for the sound of his mother at the piano, music that came wafting up to him the way it did sometimes, as comforting to him, as soothing and as gentle as her touch. He peeked down through the slats of the railing that encircled the stairs, past the open entryway, toward the living room where he'd expected them to be. But that room was empty and dark, and what he saw instead was the movement in a room across the hall, in his father's study, where his mother glided past the doorway, and her shadow trailed along on the carpet, rippling out after her as if she were wading through water, splashing in a creek. She was pacing the room, and arguing — "But it wasn't an argument, Bader," his father had corrected him at breakfast the next morning, "what you heard was only a discussion, a conversation, not a fight. Your mother and I don't fight. We talk." But while they talked, she moved, she was circling him, she came close and then she turned away again, as if she were following some intricate choreography, a complicated sort of a dance. The flames in the fireplace had thrown a chiaroscuro of light and shade out through the open doorway and onto the ceiling of the hall. And Bader could just about feel the fire's heat, burning in his face. He closed his eyes and listened to the murmured sound of his parents' voices, the gentle rising and falling of their mingled words.

His father, it seemed, was posing the same question, over and over again to her. But, it was true, he didn't shout. He never raised his voice at all. He only asked her, insisting, pressing for her answer, quietly, calmly, repeating the words, his voice sinking sometimes to a hoarse whisper, strained and tight, "What is it, Eleanor, that you want?"

"I don't know." Finally, those were the only words she could find to answer him with, and she did it with a scream. She took off her shoe and threw it at him. She sobbed and whined and growled, "I don't know."

But why didn't she? Why didn't Eleanor know? And if she didn't know, then who did? Bader believed that if she'd only been able to tell her husband what it was she wanted, he would have found a way to give it to her. He would have done anything for her. Whatever it was, he would have seen to it that it was hers.

"What do you want, Eleanor?" he asked her, over and over again. But she never had an answer. If she knew, she never said.

So, Bader thought, maybe that was what was wrong with him now, too. Maybe he'd been afflicted with that same vague, nameless longing, that same strained yearning that had been hers.

There it was, echoing in Bader's mind, his father's question. What do you want? Katherine? But, when he closed his eyes, what Bader saw, what came rising up before him, uninvited, moonlike, full and bright, was the picture of Leland Kimbel's gray-eyed face — and it was painfully undeveloped, achingly unfinished, and dazzlingly young.

It had been an aberration, Bader thought. With the storm and the cold, what they'd done. It had only had something to do with dying. With survival. With the most elemental feelings and needs of a human being. That was all. It wouldn't have happened any other way. And it couldn't ever happen again.

But when he drove the retrieved Mustang down the hill from the cottage to Bell Road, passing through the open gateway, he slowed, craned, tried, hoped, longed to get a glimpse of Lee. Maybe he'd be outside, shoveling snow. Maybe if he timed himself exactly right, he'd pass the boy at the spot in the road where he knew Lee stood on some mornings to wait for the bus that would carry him to school in Cedar Hill. Maybe one time it would be all right, and he could stop, he'd have a reason, he'd offer him a ride. Maybe Lee wouldn't be afraid of Bader. Maybe he'd say sure. And smile. And toss his hair. Maybe he'd climb into the Mustang again and maybe the two of them could ride together, side by side, for a few miles, and Bader would be able to feel Lee's warmth then, and he'd see the small, nervous movements of his hands, he'd hear his voice, the hard hollow cough of his laugh, and he'd feel nothing more than what was proper, a fatherly sort of fondness for him; he'd drop him off outside the school, where Lee would turn away, like any other boy, murmuring thanks, goodbye, he'd wave — and nothing else would happen, and nothing else would be said, and then they could forget about that night, as if nothing else had ever passed between them at all, everything was normal, as it should be, unremarkable, unsullied, and unchanged.

But when Lee did happen to be there, if Bader did happen to see him, to catch sight of his face, his form, his shape, his shadow stretched out, long and thin, against the snow, then his heart lurched in his chest, and his stomach clenched, and he could feel his pulse drumming in his throat, so hard and fast that it dizzied him, and he gripped the steering wheel, he squeezed it tightly with both his hands, and he didn't have the courage even to turn his head, he couldn't look over at the boy or wave at him, much less stop for him and open the door and beckon him in. Instead, he fiddled with the radio or adjusted the rearview mirror, he pulled the visor down, pretended to be preoccupied, acted as if he hadn't even noticed that the boy was there.

And at night, when he came home again after stopping in at the club for a drink at the bar, if it was already dark outside and the windows of the Kimbel house were all lit up, he peered at it as he cruised past, slowing, his brake lights brightening, and he studied the movement of the shadows

that he thought he'd glimpsed inside, and although he wondered, Was that the boy? Or that?, he never saw him clearly,
and he never could be completely, absolutely sure.

Roy had come up to the cottage to talk to him. Bader had
found him standing outside on the porch, with his fur-lined
leather hat in his bare hands, his fingers bluish-looking. Big
boots, paint-splattered, steel-toed. Oil-stained blue and black
checked wool shirt. Bader, in his underwear, with a bathrobe
pulled around him, had stood in his doorway, protecting it,
unwilling to let Roy come in. The cold air had shocked him,
and Roy had looked at Bader with tears in his eyes. Or was
it only the wind and the cold, reddening his nose?

He had a debt to Bader, he said. He owed him. And
wanted to thank him. Because if it hadn't been for him, hell,
his son might be dead.

"It was nothing," Bader said, shaking the man's hand.
"Forget it, Roy. All right? Never mind."

Because Bader's shame had begun, then, to grow within
him, like a flowing dark stain, like a cataract that would
cloud his sight, slowly dim his vision, and finally leave him
blind.

He was having trouble working. It was hard to concentrate. To remember what he'd written. To recall to what part
of the story he'd come. He studied his own words — about
cream cans and dairy cows, Germans and Englishmen, a war
in Europe, an influenza epidemic that spilled over from England into New England before it began to spread out west-
ward toward Iowa — and none of it made any sense to him
anymore. A factory in a warehouse? A bargain sealed with a
handshake? A war? The flu?

It made him impatient with himself, and with Katherine,
too, for no reason that he could find an explanation for, only
that he was bothered by a nagging, insistent tweak of dissat-
isfaction, with his work, with her, with himself. There was
much about Katherine that irked him, and yet he was unset-

tled less by her than he was by the painful twinges of his own discontent.

He almost confessed everything to her one night. They'd been sitting in the dark in the cottage, drinking red wine. She'd lit a candle, and it threw shadows around the room like moths.

"That night," he'd begun, "in the snow."

She'd leaned forward close to him, and tangled her fingers in his hair.

"What?" she'd asked. "That night?"

He could see her eyes, sparkling. "It was cold," he said. And then he didn't have the words to tell her any more than that — how could he describe it to her, what had happened to him, how Lee had looked, how he'd smelled, how he'd felt? He knew what she was thinking, that it was just that he'd been afraid, that he'd thought he was going to die, to freeze to death out there.

"It must have been terrible," she said. But she didn't know. How could she? She didn't understand.

That when he closed his eyes, when he was making love to her, when he ran his hand over her hip or cupped her shoulder or pressed his cheek against her breast, what he was seeing was another face, what he was remembering was another body. Someone else. A boy.

* * *

That spring, Bader Von Vechten and Katherine Craig were married in the sanctuary of the Cedar Hill Presbyterian Church, at six-thirty in the evening, on the upswing of the hour, for luck, according to Mrs. Craig. Every pew was full, and traffic became so snarled afterward, with everybody leaving at the same time, all of them pouring out through the church doors in one big crush, that Third Street had to be closed off completely, and a policeman was dispatched to direct the traffic over to Second until the line of limousines and private cars had crept off onto First Avenue on their way up to the Cedar Hill Country Club where the reception was held.

When clouds began to gather and spit rain, Libbie Craig said it only meant that good fortune would pour down upon the years of her daughter's married life.

Bader rode in the limousine next to Katherine, and he held her hand sandwiched between his own. He touched her fingertips to his lips and eyed the diamond and emerald ring that Mrs. Craig had given him to give to her. He had the marriage certificate there in his pocket — signed and folded and sealed — and he had a gold band on his own hand — with his initials and her initials and the date engraved on its inside curve — and the minister had said it — everybody had heard it, he'd called it out to them, he'd pronounced it loud and clear: Bader Von Vechten and Katherine Craig were husband and wife.

"I, and everything I am, and everything I will ever be, belong to you," Katherine had vowed. He'd taken her into his arms. He'd lifted the mist of her veil, and he'd kissed her. Katherine Craig — and, incidentally, everything she had, including access to the eighty acres of Von Vechten land on the bluff overlooking Empire — was, finally, for better or worse, his.

*　*　*

From where Lee Kimbel stood, outside the clubhouse, beyond the tall French doors and windows off the ballroom, the Craig–Von Vechten wedding reception looked like some kind of a dream world, a whirl of light and movement and color and warmth — the men in their sober dark suits and the women in their glorious dresses, all dancing and laughing and talking, touching each other, holding hands, raising glasses, circling the room, swarming the food tables and the bar.

The bride was followed wherever she went by a flock of her admirers, ladies of all ages in pastel chiffon dresses, who took her hands in their own and pulled her toward them, leaned in to brush her cheeks with their lips, men who tipped her chin with a finger and kissed her on the mouth. They slapped Bader on the back, and winked at him, and remarked, out of the sides of their mouths, on what a lucky devil he was.

And in the crush Katherine's train, a long spill of beaded satin, was stepped on and trampled, and she was snagged for a moment in the crowd, ensnared by it so that she couldn't pull away, and she was unable to move. She cried out for her husband then. She found his face — the pale plane of his brow, his shadowed jaw, the deep blue gleam of his eyes — floating in a sea of faces. For a moment it bobbed before her, and then it was gone, as if caught in the swell and the trough of a surging wave.

Mr. Craig's voice was booming. And Mrs. Craig's laughter chimed. And then the music started up again, and everyone was dancing, and the room was spinning, and Katherine thought that she might drown.

Bader, craning to find her, caught the look of panic that was like a yellow flame beginning to blaze up into her eyes, and he pushed his way toward her, parting a path through the crowd, shouldering people roughly aside, until he found a place beside his wife. She fell against him, her body yielding and limp, and he cupped her elbow in his hand, he wrapped an arm around her waist, he yanked on her train, releasing it and gathering it up against her, and he steered her away. He guided her through the throng and out of danger, up onto the dais where the bridal table had been set.

Lee pressed his cheek to the window glass, and he closed his eyes, and he let the muffled roar of the party — the clatter of the silverware and the china, the chink of the crystal glasses, the swish of satin and silk, the shuffle and tap of the

dancers' shoes, the surge of voices and laughter and music —
flow around him, swamp him, engulf him, and, finally, close
over him, like a warm and rolling sea.

*   *   *

Bader stood outside the clubhouse in the drizzle, lighting a
cigarette, cupping his hand around the flutter of the match's
flame. He squinted through the smoke at a sky that was roiling with dark clouds. The rain had thinned, but overhead the
branches of the trees were being tossed in a building wind.
He looked first at his watch, and then over his shoulder
toward the sober facade of the clubhouse, through whose
heavy door, in a moment, Katherine Von Vechten, his bride,
his wife, would walk. To be helped into his car, to be driven
away with him, to be taken home. The Mustang was parked
in the middle of the driveway, waiting — adorned with a
soggy drape of crepe streamers and paper flowers, a squirrel's
tail swinging from the antenna, a string of tin cans tied onto
its back bumper, "Just Married" scrawled across its sides
with soap.

There was a furtive rustling in the bushes behind him, and
Lee's form separated itself from the shadows of a juniper
bush. He stepped out into the open onto the grass. He rubbed
his hand over his face, reddening, and he flashed his crooked
smile at Bader.

"Oh, hi," he murmured, as if Bader were the last person
in the world that he'd expected to find there, outside the club,
waiting for his new wife, in the rain, on his wedding night.

Lee's face was wet; his hair was soaked and slicked back
from his high, white forehead. He had on Roy's putty-
colored raincoat, and it was much too big for him, the sleeves
so long that their cuffs fell past the curl of his hands, and his
shoes were all wet and slimy with mud.

He'd been wandering around outside all night in the rain,
it seemed, peeking in the windows, standing on his tiptoes,

with his fingers pressed against a window ledge, his nose pushed up to the glass, straining for a glimpse of the women in the powder room, of their silken stockings and their lacy underwear and their clear, white skin.

"Nice wedding," Lee said, spreading his arms. The over-size coat diminished him. It made him look younger, child-like and frail.

"How did you get here, Lee?" Bader asked. "You're wet. You must be cold."

Lee shrugged again. "I'm okay," he said. "I was just having a look, that's all."

Bader blew smoke.

"I put that tail on your car there," Lee went on, smiling. "It's sort of like a gift, I guess."

Bader turned and saw the squirrel's tail, hanging like a brown rag from the antenna of his car.

Lee stuffed his hands down into his pockets. He shook his head, looked down at his feet, laughed. Then he turned to Bader and held his gaze.

Bader flicked his cigarette onto the asphalt, and it skittered, sparking.

The darkened clouds seemed to be snagged in the swaying branches of the trees behind Lee, and his face was bobbing and floating among them, like a moon — his skin was so white, luminous, slick with rain.

"Anyway," he said, finally, "I guess, congratulations."

"Well, Lee, thanks," Bader answered, nodding and smiling. "Thanks a lot."

"Lousy night," Lee said.

"Hey, you know, now it's not so bad." Bader stepped toward him. He could see that Lee was shivering. Bader reached over, and he clasped his arm around the boy's shoulders, hugging him up close to him hard, crushing his body up against him, and squeezing his breath away. He turned his head and pressed his lips against Lee's warm temple, feeling the pulse that was pounding there, and inhaling the soapy smell of his damp hair.

There was a stirring behind them, as Katherine appeared on the steps, changed out of the snowy flow of her bridal gown into a more practical skirt and blouse and sweater and coat. Bader took his arm away from Lee, and he moved toward his wife. As the crowd of guests boiled out of the clubhouse, Lee slipped in through the open double doors. With his chin tucked down and his hands in his pockets, he left a trail of wet footprints on the carpeting as he took the long stairs up, two at a time.

Outside, Bader waited in the middle of the driveway, beside his car, with his hands in his pockets. His heart was scudding in his chest; his breath was short. Katherine stood on the steps and tossed her bouquet back over her shoulder toward a scrambling gaggle of young women and girls.

Lee had stopped at the top of the stairs, breathless, gaping at the rich furnishings — the heavy tables and bright brass lamps, the plush upholstery and the heavenly twinkle of the huge chandelier — the whole soft, silent expanse of the clubhouse's empty main room.

The wedding cake, by then a tumbled ruin, had been served from a small, square table set up near the wall on the far side of the room. Lee approached it and stood in front of it. He reached out, pulled back the sleeve of his coat with one hand, and slipped the fingers of his other into the glop of frosting and crumbs. He moved his tongue over his fingertips, lapping at the sticky mess. It was so heavily sweet that it made his mouth ache.

A silver cake knife had been wrapped in a napkin and set aside. The gleam of its handle caught Lee's eye, and with one quick, fluid movement, he snatched it up and tucked it away, out of sight, under the folds of his rubber coat.

Outside, in the driveway, Bader Von Vechten opened the car door for Katherine, and he helped her climb inside.

Lee sucked the rest of the frosting off his fingertips, and then he turned slowly, and, with his silver treasure tucked under his arm and held there, snug against his body, he walked away, across the room toward the stairs and down, past the straggle of returning guests.

And the Mustang sailed down the driveway, with the streamers flying and the squirrel's tail waving and the paper flowers waffling and the tin cans rattling against the asphalt road.

* * *

It was raining, in hard thrusts and timid splatters, pouring down with a fierce violence one moment, sprinkling with a soft, fine diffidence the next. Dim flashes of far-off lightning were followed several seconds later by the sullen murmur of a distant thunder, like an old man, clearing his throat. To Lee Kimbel, the sky looked like wet cardboard. It was low, with a scowl of hanging gray clouds.

Lee slopped through the muck of weeds that pressed against the base of the Von Vechten cottage, until he had rounded the corner to the back side, where a high casement window faced out toward the presumed privacy of the leafless trees. He planted his feet flat in the mud under the window, took hold of the sill with both hands, and stretched himself up to chin height, just enough to allow a clear peek through the open chintz curtains into the Von Vechtens' living room beyond.

Looking past that frilled and ruffled edging was like peering through a peephole of swirled icing, from one world — dull and drab, cold and wet and gray — into another sort of place altogether — a springtime diorama hidden within the hollow center of a candy Easter egg, a perfect country setting with robin's-egg blue skies and emerald green grass, and crayon-colored rainbows and a majestic white billow of clouds. Inside, beyond the window glass and the curtains, Bader's charming little cottage seemed to Lee to be welcoming and warm, comfortable and cozy and dry. Home sweet home, Lee thought. A love nest. A honeymoon suite.

He could feel the press of Bader's lips, still soft against his temple. He could smell the smoke in his mouth. He could feel his arm, hard and solid on his shoulders; his hand, his fingers, pressed, warm, against his throat.

In the buttery spill of light from the chimney of an antique brass lamp, Lee could see a tangle of trampled bedclothes, peach-colored satin sheets, and a lumpy, soft comforter, a pile of pillows. On the floor, an empty champagne bottle lay dead on its side. Lee thought of the games of spin-the-bottle that he'd played with other children, on the cool square of concrete underneath the rise of metal steps behind the elementary school. He'd had to kiss a girl with crooked front teeth, and he'd held his breath and closed his eyes, and he could feel the nubs of her teeth behind her lips, like pebbles under a blanket of snow, or seashells half buried in the sand, twisted and lumpy and sharp. The bottle's glass was a deep, dark, inky green, and beside it lay two long, thin champagne glasses, their stems twisted like twirled licorice, one of them upturned. A beribboned gift basket on the table was overflowing with nuts and fruit and cellophane-wrapped crackers and softened wedges of cheese. Boxes wrapped in white and silver wedding paper were strewn around the room, some of them stacked up in a tidy pyramid against a bare wall. There was Bader's desk. His typewriter. The stacked pages of his manuscript.

A pile of logs lay on the hearth, and kindling blazed in the fireplace. There was a round braided rug and shelves of books and a console television set with a record player built into the top, Wolfgang's shotgun standing up in the corner, an overstuffed chair and ottoman, and an oak rocker with wide arms and a padded seat.

To Lee Kimbel this place was like some kind of a dream

world that Bader had, in the past year, invented for himself, created out of nothing, just about before his very eyes, like magic, a dove conjured from a magician's closed fist. He'd taken the empty cottage, cleaned and scrubbed and white-washed its walls, and then, as if it were a blank page, or a bare canvas, he'd filled it up with his things, bit by bit, piece by piece, like a puzzle — furniture, rugs, lamps, a bed, a chair, a wife — making a whole, complete picture in it, fi-nally, of domestic harmony and matrimonial bliss. It was a fantasy, Lee thought, that was all. It was a figment that was just too homey, too comfy, too pretty, and too snug to be anything that was in any way real.

He moved around the side of the cottage, slopping through the wet grass toward another window closer to the front. Rainwater streamed down Lee's face, in rivulets that traced his cheeks. It soaked through his hair, onto the ledge of his brow. It poured off the tip of his nose, it dribbled from his chin, down his neck, inside his collar, and it oozed against his skin. Its icy chill seemed to be trickling in his veins and then seeping down further still, into the deepest dark marrow of his bones.

Now he was able to make out what was the outline of Katherine Von Vechten herself, standing with her back to the window, unaware of Lee's face pressed against the glass. She'd wrapped her body in a patterned Indian blanket, and she was turned toward the bright hot burning glow of the fire. The coarse wool fibers rubbed up against the surface of her bare skin, scratching it, Lee thought, like diamonds on glass.

When Bader came up behind her and touched his hands to her shoulders, the blanket slipped away, and it puddled at her feet. His hands were turning her, until she'd come full around to face him. Lee caught the wobble of Katherine's heavy breasts, the shadowy smudged triangle of her hair, and the sheen of her long, thin thighs as she knelt on the floor in front of her husband. Her hands held his waist, her fingertips probed the line of his spine. The flesh of his buttocks quivered. He wove his fingers into her hair, and, finally, he pulled her back up to her feet again before him. She bent one knee and lifted it, squeezing the firm, flat surface of Bader's bare hip. She raised her foot and wrapped her leg around him, and she allowed him to ease her down gently, sideways, onto her back on the bunchy drift of the blanket on the floor.

Lee, watching, felt as if his own body had been turned to stone, frozen solid, rock hard, even as at the same time his flesh seemed to be melting, liquefied, molten and inflamed. His heart scudded and his pulse was pounding, a loud, hard throbbing in his ears, and his blood seemed to be surging wildly, foaming, smoking though his veins like dry ice, so cold that it seethed and scorched and steamed, thudding in his temples, racking him with an impossible blend of hot pleasure and freezing shame. His hair was plastered to his skull. The rain had begun to come down hard, pouring on his head and his back and his shoulders and his face, and he was struck by the sudden memory — as bright and as vibrant in his mind as a color photograph — of his mother, of Mudd, giving him a bath. Filling up the huge, clawfoot cast-iron tub in her bathroom, bending over to add powdered soap and then to test the temperature of the water. He'd been sitting on the floor, pulling off his socks, and when he looked up, he'd seen the insides of her legs, where they rubbed against each other up under the tentlike folds of her skirt, the turned-over tops of her stockings, and the lumps of flesh that had spilled over them like risen dough. Her soap-sheened breasts. Her strong hands cupped under his armpits as she held him, squealing and squirming, in the air above the tub. She'd dipped him in and lifted him out again. She'd pressed his steamy body up close against her own. She'd nuzzled her nose into the nest of his damp hair and she'd breathed in his ears. She'd tickled him and then propped him up against the pillow of her chest, and she'd let him slide down the long, mountainous slopes of her body, swoop over the curve of her bosom, hang in midair for one breathless instant before he splashed into the water and, breathless, sank. The slither of his slick flesh against hers and the deep chuckle of her laughter, his own high excited squeals of both terror and delight, the splatter and splash of soap and water on the walls and the ceiling and the floor. Mudd's bare skin glistening and sleek, veined, bruised, downy with hair, puckered and rippled with folds of muscle and fat. The feel of her leathery nipples against the soles of his feet, and the great soft cloud of her bosom against the hard bare bones of his butt.

Afterward, she'd wrapped him in a towel and brought him with her into her bed, and he'd snuggled up close to her while through the slits of his half-closed eyes he studied the mounds of her doughy flesh and swam in the warmth that radiated from her body and rolled with the sway of her movements, content to drown in sleep upon the waves of her mess of blankets and sheets.

Bader had pulled himself away from Katherine. He rose, first to his hands and knees, and then to his feet, staggering, lumbering, awkward as a bear. His shadow was cast across Katherine's body — she lay on her back on the rug, her arms flung out from her sides, her face turned toward the fire, mottled by the flames, her knees brought together, bent, and angled away. Her skin was orange in the firelight, glowing, rosy and silky with sweat.

Bader turned toward the window and stopped. He was naked, his penis still stiffened; it poked out, glistening and slick, and it bobbed with his movements, between his slim hips, long legs and bony feet, beneath his furry belly, his heavy shoulders, his broad chest. When he lifted his head, he was looking directly at the window, past the curtains, through the glass, right into Lee Kimbel's widened eyes. Lee's heart lurched hard, jolting him with a sudden stab of fear and embarrassment and shame. He gasped, as if he'd been punched, dropped to his knees in the mud, and scrambled through the high weeds, away.

Water sloshed over the rims of gutters that were clogged with leaves. Lightning flashed, closer and brighter. The thunder was terrible and loud, rolling so near now that it chased Lee, followed on his heels, and drove him forward, to the edge of the bluff and over the fence rail and down the hill, like some huge boulder tumbling and rolling wild and heavy and fast along the path behind him. Lee slopped through the puddles, and the mud snickered. He gasped for breath, he sputtered and flailed, as if he thought he could be swimming for his life, as if he thought it just might be possible for a boy like him to drown in a sky full of falling rain.

*   *   *

By morning, when Katherine woke up, the storm had passed, and overhead the sky was clear and blue. She looked at her husband, sprawled beside her, asleep. Outside, the trees dripped. Their trunks and branches were blackened and wet. Battered leaves and twigs and sticks littered the yard. Sunlight was pouring in through the window in the front room, spilling out over the pile of presents, waiting to be opened. In a small white satin-covered book there was the list of the thank-you notes that she would need to write. She pushed through the screen door and went outside. The woods were hushed in the aftermath of the storm. The grass was wet and cool under her bare feet as she walked across the yard toward the trees. A baby bird lay dead, washed from its nest, drowned in mud. Katherine scooped it up and cradled its small gray body in her palm. She poked at the wet feathers with her fingertip, and then she stood up and flung it off, into the trees. When she turned to walk back to the cabin, there was Lee, standing behind her in the grass. She jumped back, startled by the sudden sight of him. His hair was wet, slicked back from his face, and his shoes were caked with mud.

He was smiling at her. "I didn't mean to scare you," he said. "I'm sorry if I did."

"I didn't expect to see anyone out here, I guess."

Katherine was aware of the fact that all she had on was Bader's shirt — its long tails hung down over her thighs and stopped just above her knees.

Lee had taken a step toward her. "Lee Kimbel," he said. "I live down there." He pointed through the trees toward the gray slate roof of his house.

"Katherine Craig," she said. She paused, smiling. "Von Vechten."

Lee reached out and took her hand in his. He turned it over, and studied the ring that gleamed on her finger in the sunlight. He looked into her eyes and smiled.

"Congratulations," he said.

His eyes held hers for a moment, then slid past her face, and she turned to see that Bader had come outside and was standing on the porch.

"Lee," he said, "this is my wife, Katherine."

She smiled. "We've already met," she said. Lee let go of her hand and she wiped it on her shirt.

Bader had stepped down onto the grass. He bent over Katherine and kissed her. "Good morning," he said. He had a blanket folded over his arm, and he shook it out and draped it over her shoulders. "You must be cold," he said.

She wrapped the blanket around her, grateful for the cover, and then turned to Lee. "Would you like to come inside?" she asked. "Have something to eat?"

Lee smiled at her and looked at Bader.

"I'm sure he's got other things to do this morning," he said. "Don't you, Lee?"

He shrugged. "Sure," he answered, nodding, squinting up

into the bright sky. "Sure I do." He turned away. "Well, bye," he said, waving his hand over his shoulder. He stopped and looked back at them again. "Nice to meet you, Mrs. Von Vechten," he said. He hurdled the fence and disappeared into the trees.

"That was rude, Bader," she said.

He put his hand on her shoulder and turned her around to face him. "You shouldn't have asked him in," he said. His face had reddened; bright pink circles flushed his cheeks.

"Why not?" she asked.

Bader smiled. He rubbed his hand over his face and shook his head. "Because it embarrassed him, Katherine," he said. He could feel a knot of annoyance begin to tighten in his chest.

"I don't think he looked embarrassed," she replied. "I think he looked wet."

He sighed. "I don't want to argue with you," he said.

"Then don't." Her eyes were bright and defiant, glittery and green.

Bader thought he could hear Lee crashing through the woods behind him, charging down the hill toward his house, as Katherine turned and crossed the yard, walking back to the cottage, dragging the blanket behind her, trailing it over the thick, wet grass.

"Hey," he called after her. He hurried to catch up to her. "I'm sorry," he said.

She stopped and turned, her face softened, and she was smiling at him again. She let the blanket fall away from her. She stood up on tiptoe and wrapped her arms around his neck. "All right," she said, nuzzling him, brushing her lips against his skin, feeling the hard pulse that throbbed in his throat, "it's all right."

*　*　*

When Mrs. Craig came by to visit the newlyweds, she brought a bouquet of fresh flowers and a chicken and mushroom casserole that she'd made. She stood in the cottage with her arms outspread.

"But you need more room," she exclaimed. "This place is so small. How will you ever be able to do any entertaining here?"

And Mrs. Craig was right, the cottage was small. Lying in bed, Bader could hear Katherine's movements in the kitchen — the splash of dishwater in the sink, the hum of the refrigerator, the grind of the garbage disposal, a cupboard door snapped open, thumped shut. The chime of glass, the clatter of pots and pans. The squeak of a stove knob turned, the whoosh of gas, the pop of a flame.

If he listened, he could know from the evidence of all these small noises where Katherine was and what she was doing. He could turn in the embrace of the cottage's snugness, but he was grateful, too, when she went out and left him there alone.

They'd been invited to have dinner at the club with a group of Katherine's friends, but Bader didn't want to go. He had work to do, he said. He couldn't sit through an evening of their conversation, listening to their stories, laughing at their jokes. "Please," he begged her, "don't make me go."

So instead, she went by herself. She took his car and left him alone with his work. When she came home later, he could see that she was drunk.

"We had caramelized duck," she told him. "And boiled shrimp. And escargots."

On the desk beside his typewriter was a plate with a crust of bread, a bottle of scotch, and a glass. She took off her clothes and left them in a pile on the floor. Bader was hunched over the typewriter in his undershorts and bare chest

— working on slaughtered cows, fires, and tainted milk. Katherine came up behind him and put her hands on his shoulders; she skimmed her lips over the back of his neck.

He shrugged her off. "Please, Katherine," he said, "not now."

She poured scotch over ice and stood in the doorway, looking out at the night sky that rose up beyond the huddle of the dark woods.

"It's almost summer again, Bader," she said.

The air felt warm with it. Soon they'd open the pool and she could go out there in the mornings to swim.

She sat cross-legged on the bed, in a sheer, flowered nightie, and the way the light shone from behind her, he could see the shadowy outline of her body, her hips, her belly, her hanging breasts. She had her hands up behind her head, trying to braid her hair in a fancy way that she'd seen, but she couldn't get it right, her fingers were clumsy, and the braid kept bunching up too much on one side, so she yanked it out, combed her fingers through it, and started over again. Her glass of scotch and ice was on the table.

"I saw a man standing by a fence tonight," she said. He had his pants undone, and his hand was moving, and he was looking right at her. He saw that she was watching him, and she sat there, in the car, frozen, staring at him, unable to turn away.

Katherine's cheeks were flushed, pink. She smiled. Her laugh was a high, tight squeak. "His face was so white," she said. It was like a blur, his features dark smudges, as if he weren't real. He was wearing a dark wool coat, even though it was so warm, and his hand just kept moving and moving, his mouth opening and closing, his eyes locked on hers.

"I never used to be afraid of anything before," Katherine said. Bader turned and looked at her.

"What do you have to be afraid of now?" he asked.

She shrugged and took a swallow of her drink. "I don't know," she said. "You. Me. Us."

He frowned at her. "That's crazy," he said.

She smiled. "I know."

Katherine turned on the television, with the sound down low so she wouldn't disturb him, and she lay back against the pillows, cradling her drink against her chest. It was an old movie, a love story, in black and white. When Bader came into the bedroom later, he found Katherine weeping.

"It was a sad story," she told him.

He gave her a tissue, and she blew her nose, coughing. He took the glass of scotch from her hands and pulled the covers up over her. He bent and kissed her temple, and she turned and curled her body away from his.

She looked like she might be a child, Bader thought. In her little nightgown, Katherine Craig Von Vechten looked less like a grown woman sometimes than she did a young girl. He studied her perfect profile, high aristocratic bones, and he wondered why he didn't love her as much as she wished he did. He wondered what deficiency it was in him that kept him from needing her.

Because there was still that boy, Lee Kimbel, and there was still Bader's searing memory of him. Like a small flame flickering in snow. How many times did Bader stop what he was doing — look up from his typewriter or his book or his newspaper — and freeze, with his heart skittering, his glass raised halfway to his mouth. And how often did he listen, closing his eyes, holding his breath, thinking, had he seen a movement at the window, were eyes watching him, was there a face — pale, gray-eyed, young — pressed up against the glass? Wondering, was there someone prowling in the bushes or standing, watching, waiting in the shadows of the trees? Hoping, had he heard footsteps, the slog of a boy's shoes in the grass, from a distance a shrill whistle, or, closer, a playing child's spirited whoop and wild cry?

Sometimes the body of a dog that's been struck and killed
by a speeding car on a black back road on a snowy night in
the dead of winter gets shoveled up by the plow during the
earliest dark morning hours when it makes its first round; it's
pushed aside and buried under the drift that's built up in the
ditch. Maybe it's missed by the boy who owns it, maybe its
loss is mourned all through the cold, hard winter months. He
posts signs up around the neighborhood, and he places an ad
in the local paper. He checks in with the animal shelter every
week, with faith, never giving up hope. But then, when
spring comes, when the snow has melted, when the water's
run off and the ground is thawed, he'll be walking along the
side of that same road, and he'll stumble upon all that's left
of his dog, and it won't be the beautiful animal that he lost
anymore, it won't be the warm, furry, friendly pet that he
loved. It's a carcass, stinking, dead, it's a pile of gleaming
bones, a clump of soggy fur and decayed flesh.

Just so, Bader could feel that his affection for Katherine
had begun to fade away from him. Under the heat of his
obsession with Lee, it melted from his body like snow and
left exposed the bare bones, the rotted remains of what he
had begun to believe must be his own unloved and unloving
self.

*　　*　　*

And so, that was when it was, summertime again — the
heavy swelter of the warmest evening of the hottest summer,
in the middle of July. On a Saturday night. At a semiformal
dinner dance, at the country club. Katherine would wear a
dark blue dress. A diamond-studded barrette. An opal on a
platinum chain. She came out of the shower with her hair
wet, and she stood in the bedroom doorway, looking like a
child again, or some wax figure, a doll, melted, shrunken,
diminished inside her robe, its sleeves too long and dangling
past her hanging hands.

Bader was riffling through the closet, and he couldn't find one white shirt that was clean and pressed. Katherine was sorry. She'd forgotten. She'd iron one for him right now. But he was impatient. He was angry. He yelled at her. "What kind of a wife are you?"

She balled her hands into fists, and her face was red with rage. She came out with it then, what she'd been thinking all along, what it was that had been playing in her mind. Her suspicion. Her fear. She thought that he had a lover.

He laughed. Stepped toward her and laughed, and scotch sloshed out of his glass and splattered on the floor. Moaning, she put her hand out, gripped the crystal ashtray — a wedding gift — brought it back behind her head, and with a small, helpless squeak, she heaved it at him. He watched it sail, turning over and over, tumbling toward him, until he ducked aside and it flew past him, at the window behind him with an explosion of shattered glass.

She could have killed him with that.

Tears glistened in her eyes. Her hand was pressed against her mouth. She whimpered, "Oh God, Bader, no, I'm sorry. I didn't mean it." And then she stopped, looked at him, her face crumpling with confusion and despair. "What's happening to me?"

While his guilt continued to bloom, taking on its dark, heavy, spreading shape inside his mind.

She got out the ironing board and stood in the bathroom and ironed his white shirt until it was perfectly crisp and smooth.

After he was dressed, he found her in the kitchen. Her dress was midnight blue. Her earrings sparkled. He came up behind her and pulled her away from the sink. Her hands came out of the dishwater, soapy and steaming and wet. The diamond of her wedding ring sparkled like a chip of ice.

"Hey, leave that," he whispered, turning her, nuzzling

her, pulling her up close to him. "Don't worry about it now, Katherine. Come on."

And she laughed and rubbed her nose with the back of her wrist, and he took her by the elbow, pressed his fingers against her skin, brought her up close to him and kissed her.

"Let's go," he said. "We'll be late."

He guided the Mustang down the long winding roadway, through the gate and past the darkened Kimbel house, wondering, in spite of himself, was the boy there, had he gone to bed, was he out somewhere, was he sleeping, was he thinking about him?

*   *   *

Mudd was circling Lee's room. She moved around and around, and Lee was lying on his back in his bed, smoking a cigarette, exhaling extravagant, long, wafting streams of smoke while, in the heat, he thought about snow, and Mudd kept moving, around and around, past the window, past the door, past the lamp, a shadow, circling and circling, around and around. Sweat glimmered on Lee's temples, and it shimmered in his hair. He was wearing a pair of blue jeans, torn, and no shirt. And she kept asking him, over and over again, "What?" She wanted to know, she wanted him to tell her. "Where?" While her big body moved, like a planet, a wheel, a top, revolving, it went around and around, circling and circling. And there was a fan in the window, and its blades were turning, too.

Mudd had a photograph in her hand — she held it out, to show him, gripped between her finger and her thumb, and it fluttered with the fan's whiff, a small square colored picture of a young woman, with pale skin and a halo of red hair. Who? Mudd asked.

She'd found it in Roy's wallet. He'd left his wallet on the bathroom counter, and she was looking through it — she

needed some money, change for the market — and this was
what she'd found, this picture, this person, this woman, instead. And now she wanted Lee to tell her, Who was it? What
was her name? Where was she? Had he met her? Did he know
her? Where did she live?

Lee's gray eyes followed his mother as she circled him,
turning, spinning, moving, around and around his room. He
blew a stream of smoke out of his mouth and then sucked it
back in again through his nose. He sat up, propped on one
elbow, and leaned forward to flick his ashes into the mouth
of a beer bottle on the floor.

"Naomi LeSage," he said, finally, without looking up at
her, without raising his eyes, "her name is Naomi LeSage."

*   *   *

Roy and Darcy were down the hall, at the front of the house,
together in the den, watching a comedy show on the TV.
Roy was sitting on the couch; he had a beer, he was smiling,
and Darcy was in the chair, smiling, too, holding a bottle of
soda pop, her legs curled under her, her feet tucked away.
They neither of them even noticed that Mudd was there.

She crossed the hall into the kitchen, and she found the
Cedar Hill telephone book in a drawer. Landers, Larson,
Lehman, Lerner, LeSage. Naomi LeSage, 424 Memorial
Drive, Sky View Trailer Courts, Cedar Hill. She picked up
the phone, dialed the number, and, holding her breath, she
listened to the voice — soft, high, girlish — on the other
end, the TV playing in the background, the same stupid
jokes, the same canned laughter, and that voice — small,
childlike, faint — said, "Hello? Hello?" And then, "Roy?"
Mudd hung up, quietly, quickly, as if she'd been burned. She
picked up the keys to the truck off the counter and slipped,
like a shadow, out the back door, down the back steps, across
the back yard, to Roy's truck. She started it up, wincing at

the sound, hoping he wouldn't hear, or if he did, he wouldn't think, or if he did, it would be too late, she'd already be gone, and she rolled slowly around to the front of the house, with the headlights turned off, tires crunching over the gravel and the grass, and she backed down the driveway onto Bell Road. She pulled away, drove off, turned, and headed up the parkway toward Cedar Hill.

*   *   *

Bader and Katherine had sat down to dinner. There was too much to drink. They always drank too much when they went to the club, they expected it, anticipated the hangover that they knew would be waiting to punish them for it the next day. There was white wine and red wine, chilled champagne and warmed brandy. And then they were dancing, and it was too hot, and she couldn't stand it, she said so, and he was wondering, what, she can't stand what? The heat? Him? The swelter and the noise and the constant, hard jostle of the crowd? He bought her a drink, vodka and ice. She drew him up close to her; she pressed her shoulder against his arm; she threw her head back, collapsed in helpless laughter at something funny someone said. Her dress shimmered, midnight blue. She'd brought her hair up into a loose bundle, held with a diamond-studded clasp. Her necklace was an opal on a platinum chain, nestled in the hollow of her throat. He enfolded her hand in his. She smiled, laughed, leaned against him. He kissed her. She sat on his lap.

And then they were leaving the ballroom, and she was leading him into the front room, where it was cooler, and quiet, and then he was following her, up a staircase, where it was private and dark. And then she was pulling him toward her, and he was kissing her again, and then she'd tripped away from him, she was at the end of the hall, a door, a crystal knob, she was turning it, she was opening the door, and she was moving off, stepping out, dancing away from him, into that room.

* * *

Mudd pulled up to the last aluminum trailer far at the back of the courts, at the end of the road that was marked with a sign: MEMORIAL DRIVE. The numbers hanging next to the door shone in the truck's headlights: 424. A dim light leaked out through a crack in the pulled curtains. There was a car, a little red Volkswagen, parked on the berm to one side.

Mudd left the truck running and climbed down. Her shoes slipped over the gravel as she crossed to the trailer's door. She knocked and waited and then knocked again, but no one came. She called out "Hey!" but no one answered. The closest neighbor was farther up the road, several yards behind her — they were having a party there, she'd seen a group of people gathered around a barbecue when she drove by.

Mudd crossed back to the truck, and she was about to open the door and climb back up into it and drive back home again — as if nothing had happened, as if she didn't know any more than she ever had, about what her husband wanted, about what her husband dreamed of, about what her husband did — but she stopped first, she turned, and she took one last look over at the trailer again. This was where Roy went, then, she thought. This was where he was, when he wasn't at home with her. She could hear faint strains of music playing now, coming from that other trailer, up the way. People laughing. And then a woman's shout. And then silence again. Moths hovered around the bulb of the lamp that hung over the door. The license plate on the Volkswagen read YLDTHNG.

Mudd studied it, sounding it out, letter by letter, as she squinted at the glare that was thrown back by her headlights on the car's chrome and silver and glass. YLDTHNG. She stepped around behind the truck and she looked into its bed. There were paint cans. A ladder. Dropcloths. Brushes. And a short wooden closet pole, painted white, which Mudd reached in and fished out. She locked her knees and planted her feet flat, and she swung the pole around her head a few times, testing its weight in her hands, loosening up, limbering the joints of her shoulders and the muscles in her arms, warming the power in her wrists — and then she pivoted suddenly, she raised the pole up high over her head and she brought it down with a stunning force against the hood of the little car. She battered it, and she beat it. The windshield shattered; the side mirror snapped off. Dimples gleamed in the fenders and the bumper, the white and silver headlights were blinded, knocked cockeyed, the yellow turn signals were smashed. The front license plate swung: YLDTHNG. One hubcap popped off — it wobbled drunkenly and careened away.

Squinting through the crazed surface of the windshield, Mudd could see that there was a faceted glass ball hanging from a thread of fishing line that was wrapped around the stem of the rearview mirror, and it was glinting and winking in a crazy way, refracting hard shards of the truck's headlights as it jumped and jerked in response to each reckless blow of her pole. And Mudd imagined that she could just about make out the hunched shoulders and reddish head of that woman, Naomi LeSage, inside her red car; she had the fantastic impression that Naomi was actually in there, cowering behind the wheel, scrunched down into her seat, with both arms wrapped around her head. Mudd watched with increasing pleasure the flinch and the shift, as the chassis was rocked and her shoulders shook and her head wagged and Mudd's own heart was swelling and pounding with the relief of it, finally — *thunk! thunk! thunk!* — each time that the pole made contact with the car.

When she was done — she was gasping, panting, her face

red and painfully flushed, her body swimming in sweat —
Mudd threw the pole back into the truck bed, went around,
climbed up into the cab, and drove away. And if she'd looked
behind her, if she'd turned to see, she might have noticed, at
the window of the trailer, the flames of a woman's hair and
the stark white smear of her frightened face.

*   *   *

In Cedar Hill, on the dance floor at the country club, there
were bodies moving, dancing, men turning, women twirling, a voice singing, music playing, laughter ringing, heat
rising. And a presence overhead, a shadow, huddled, an
eclipse, a cloud bank rolling, a bird flapping, an angel with
outspread wings. Some few looked up, wondering, and they
saw it, that shape that hovered over the frosted glass of the
skylight, and there seemed to be a pause in the music then,
and a murmur ran through the crowd, and the chitter of the
glass, the ping of her shoes as they tapped against it, and then
the dark shape spread, spraying glass, shimmering, like ice,
like rain, like snow. The flight, the fall, the thunk as Katherine landed on a table and then bounced and then rolled, the
sounds reverberating away, like an echo, a peal of thunder, a
gasping wave of panic and horror and surprise that surged off
through the crowd and broke against the shoal of Bader Von
Vechten's soul.

*   *   *

All Saints Hospital was only a few miles from the club —
straight up Cedar Drive, then west along First Avenue
toward downtown, north on Tenth Street to A Avenue, then
half a block west again to the emergency entrance — but that
night, twenty-five years ago, in the summer, when it was so
hot, the trip there seemed to Bader as if it would never end,
and even when he craned his neck for a look outside to get
his bearings, all he could see was the stricken white mask of

his own face reflected right back at him in the darkened window glass. He was humped up in the back of the ambulance, crunched down next to Katherine as close as he could get, his legs too long, his back painfully curved, his knees stiff, and his ankles sore — he was awash in the red and blue and white sweep of the lights and swamped by the drowning sound of the siren's wail as he bounced and jounced with every bump and turn, afraid he'd lurch and fall on top of her, cause her more damage, injure her further, harm her somehow, with all his clumsiness and reckless weight.

He'd turned away from the open doorway of that closet at the end of the hall upstairs at the club — the yawning ragged-edged hole in its floor, with the image of her broken form below him, so far away and small, the converging shapes of the dancers in the ballroom, some with their faces upturned toward his, others huddled and bent over Katherine, their cries of shock and surprise echoing and bouncing up toward him, a roar of accusation that kept ringing in his ears — and he ran, fled, flew the length of that long corridor, with its bank of ivy-covered windows, and he tumbled down the narrow back stairway, past the row of botanical prints — the pomegranate fallen, its glass shattered and its paper torn. And when he burst into the swarming dining room, it felt to him just like he was being split into two, like he was coming apart from himself at the seams, and there was one part of his mind that was still holding back, separate from his body, as if he couldn't have been that raving stumbling, horrified man at all, but was another person instead, an observer who could be wholly objective and totally detached, mildly curious maybe, but mostly unsympathetic and untouched. Like one of the older fellows who was looking at him, maybe, that man in the dove gray jacket who stood with his back against the far wall, who cradled a drink in his hand and leaned in closer toward a thin woman in a long gold dress. The one who had stopped speaking and was looking up now, startled by the sight of Bader Von Vechten scuttling down the narrow stairs and bounding over the last grouping of steps, landing on both feet, regaining his balance and bursting into the crowd. A murmur of surprise had begun, and it moved from one end of the room to the other, surging away from him as Bader pushed through the crowd that was pouring out of the ballroom now.

As if some one of those people, gaping stupidly — that man there in the gray jacket, or this woman here in the gold dress, the girl with the bobbed blond hair or the youth with the peeling forehead and sunburned cheeks — as if maybe they were suspecting some criminal intent, thinking that for some reason what had happened had been planned, that Bader meant for the night to end this way, that he'd known all along it would, he'd been expecting it, he'd led Katherine away from the dance floor with a knowledge of exactly what was in store for her up those stairs, down that hallway, through that door, and maybe the two of them, maybe they hadn't been kissing at all, maybe they weren't making love, maybe they were arguing, and he was angry with her, because she'd accused him of something unspeakable, and so he'd pushed her away from him, to protect himself, or he'd put his foot out and tripped her or he'd picked her up and thrown her through the glass, and even though he knew that this was not how it had happened and that none of it was true, still he wanted to defend himself, to cry out to all of them, over and over again, "It was an accident!"

He wanted to take that boy there by the shoulders, to slam him against the wall and shake him. Slap him. Make him believe, force him to understand. "Oh, Christ! It was a mistake!" Because at that moment he had begun to think that the mob of party-goers was going to turn him on, that they would want to blame him for what had happened to his

wife, and that they would grab him and trip him and knock
him to the ground, hold him there, trample him, kick and
pound him until he blacked out, or was dead.

But it hadn't even been his idea, had it? And wasn't it just
the kind of thing that Katherine could have been expected to
do, to leave the ballroom and sneak off upstairs to the attic,
to take him away to make love to him in a part of the clubhouse where he'd never been before, in a hallway that he
hadn't imagined was there, that he'd never even known ex-
isted until that evening, a place that he himself wouldn't have
dreamed of going to, if it hadn't been for her? Katherine, it
seemed, had explored the clubhouse from top to bottom, and
she'd laughed at his surprise when she told him so. Of course
she had, she and her friends, since the time when they were
little children here, left to amuse themselves while their parents ate dinner in the dining room or drank cocktails at the
bar. Everybody did it, didn't they? Katherine and the rest of
them had run loose, scampering around the building like
mice, creeping into the bar to steal a paper umbrella or a slice
of lemon or orange or a red maraschino cherry, peeking into
the ladies' room downstairs, crawling into the cloakroom to
hide among the furs. And sneaking up the back stairs, too,
up into the extra rooms there, into the attic, into rooms that
were, for some reason, off-limits on the third floor.

She'd touched her finger to his cheek and asked him, Had
he never done anything like that before? And Bader had been
ashamed to say that he hadn't, knowing how cautious he
could seem to her, how guarded and reserved, dispassionate
even, distant and cold. She'd squinted her eyes at him and
tilted her head to the side, amused, and it was clear that some
of what she loved him for was just that, what must have
seemed to her to be his virtue and his inexperience. He was
always such a good boy, wasn't he? Because the truth was
that as a child Bader had come out here with his parents only
a few times, for dinner, on special occasions, a birthday,

Thanksgiving, and they had sat together, at a table for three, and he had eaten in silence and waited patiently, a well-mannered young gentleman, disturbing no one and biding his time, until the dessert had been served, and coffee, and his father had signed the check, and then he could go home.

If anyone was to blame for what had happened, it was the person who had left the lock turned on that door. If it was anybody's fault, it was theirs, not his, the men who had made the decision to remodel the clubhouse, the men who had told the builders to closet in the skylights instead of spending the money to have them removed. And among those men, Bader knew, was none other than Archie Craig himself.

If he could have, Bader would have run away right then. If he could have, he would have stumbled farther, down the second flight of stairs — brightly lit and framed by the curved sweep of two brass banisters that were bent outward like a graceful welcome of open arms — through the heavy double doors, into the merciful blacking over of the night. He would have escaped to the safety of his car; he would have left the whole of it, his life, behind him. If only he could have, if only he'd known how. The country club and Cedar Hill, the cottage, the land, his life here, his book, even Lee Kimbel, every bit of it — he would have abandoned all his plans and all his obligations, deserted Katherine and her family and her friends, he would have hit the road and high-tailed it away, and he would have just kept on driving on and on forever and ever across the far, flat fields, until he'd lost himself in the distance, until he'd become a stranger, a refugee, an outsider who'd been gone away for too long to ever have a hope of remembering how to find the right way back again.

She'd lost her shoes. He saw one, with the heel broken, kicked off to the side, on the floor under a table, amid a scattering of shattered glass. He noticed, too, that her stockings were torn, that her underwear was black, and that she'd painted her toenails pink. Her dress, that scant shimmer of

midnight blue, was in shreds. He could see that there was
a network of cuts and gashes, blood-smeared, like brush
strokes, marking her arms and her legs, the spread of her
chest, her shoulders and her throat and her bare back. And
on the floor around her head, that thick, red-black blossom
of blood.

"It was an accident," he kept saying over and over again.
"I didn't mean it. It's not my fault." Because there was a part
of him that would always understand it, that in a fundamental
way, of course, it really was.

When he took hold of Katherine's hand, he was surprised
and repelled by how heavy and warm it was. He fiddled with
her ring — that crisp, bright diamond chip embedded in a
platinum band and encircled by the green sparks of tiny emeralds — and he mumbled, repeating over and over again as
he rolled her fingers between his own, in a rhythm that
seemed to correspond to the eerie sink and swell of the siren's
wail, "Oh, don't die, Katherine, don't die, please, Katherine,
don't die."

He had a feeling that if he really tried, if he truly concen-
trated, he could will her to survive; his own strength and
health might seep into her body and bring about its mending
through the simple connection of touch, from his hand into
hers. And that it was somehow his responsibility to do that,
to maintain that healing contact with her. If he let his own
doubts take hold of him, he thought, then he would lose her.
If he allowed his concentration to be broken, then she would
die.

Her face, which had always seemed to him to be so pretty
and childlike in its expressions — her easy smile and the look
of surprise or curiosity that appeared so often in her eyes —
was solemn now, and drained and pale. And he was able to
see every detail of it clearly, and separately — as if it might
have caused him an excruciating blinding pain to take in the

sight of her face as a whole, he only picked up bits and pieces of it, her eyelashes, long and dark and feathery against her cheeks, the shallow fine pores of her skin, the delicate hairs of her eyebrows arching upward, the fragile folds of her ears. Her nose, her lips, her chin, the soft pulse that fluttered in her throat.

The ambulance careened around the last sharp corner and bounced up into the hospital driveway, and it threw Bader off balance, away from Katherine, as it jerked to a stop. With his fists squeezed up to his chest and his body pressed against the back side of the driver's seat, he looked like he was doubled over on himself, curled in pain maybe, while the ambulance attendants were roused into action, yanking open the doors, sliding the stretcher out, flipping down its wheeled legs and rolling off, bearing her away from him, through a pair of doors that glided open, silently, and then whispered shut.

Bader hopped down to the pavement and waded through the swirling pool of red and yellow ambulance lights. He could still see Katherine through the window glass — the mound of her body was receding from him, down along the length of a narrowing corridor until the gurney rounded a corner, and then she was gone, absorbed into the labyrinth that was the hospital, where Katherine would become indistinguishable from all the others who were there, clothed in the same faded flowered gown, wearing the same unhealthy hollows in her face. Passing the open doors, peeking in, all a visitor could see was the skin and bones of the patients' bent knees and wasted bodies tenting thin gray bedsheets.

The emergency room doors opened for him as Bader approached them, and when he stepped inside, it was suddenly cool, and the air seemed to hum, as if the hospital were some kind of a living, breathing thing. He was met by a nun with black hair and blue eyes and blotty skin and a pair of thick-lensed glasses that hung from a silver chain that she'd looped over her head. She'd placed herself in front of Bader and put her small hands up to his chest to hold him back.

"Stop here," she was saying. Her fingers were like a bird's sharp feet, white and bony, gnarled beyond the heavy soft black cuffs of her habit's sleeves.

"I can't," he protested weakly, as he craned to see around her, when the truth was that he was grateful to her in a way, to find himself so restrained, because he might not have been able to control himself otherwise. She kept him from cracking, from shattering, from exploding into a million small, sharp glittery pieces.

"That woman they just brought in?" he asked, through clenched teeth, as if it were a question, he wasn't sure, he didn't know. "She's my wife?"

The nun's hand floated up to his shoulder, and she was squeezing him, digging her fingers into him with a strength that took him by surprise as she peered up into his face.

"Maybe you need to sit down," she said.

And so he allowed her to take his elbow then, and he leaned on her, this small woman, surprised by how effortlessly she seemed to be able to move his body and bear the burden of its weight as she brought him over to a metal chair beside a cluttered desk. The soles of her square-toed black shoes squeaked against the glossy speckled surface of the waxed linoleum floor.

"Now then," she went on, putting on her glasses, rolling a clean sheet of paper into her typewriter. "We'll have to fill out some forms. Just a few small questions, if you don't mind? Not too much trouble, I don't think."

Her voice was businesslike and flat, raised not quite to a shout, but with a clear and crisp and slow enunciation of every word, as if she were thinking that Bader might be hard of hearing, so stunned by what had happened to him that his shock had left him slightly deaf.

"First, tell me what happened." The nun's hands were poised over the keys of her typewriter, waiting for his answer.

"It was an accident." Bader's hands were trembling. He squeezed them into fists to steady them and rolled his knuckles up and down along the tops of his legs. "We were dancing." He shrugged, as if that was all, as if it were just as simple and as uncomplicated as that. "She fell."

He saw a man across the room look up from the magazine he was reading and eye Bader over the half lenses of his glasses. Was that a squint of accusation in his eyes? he wondered. Was his lip curled with contempt at what he saw? You don't deserve her, the man's look seemed to be telling him, and Bader, cringing, agreed.

"I have to call her parents," Bader said. "They should be here."

But someone at the club must already have telephoned Mr. Craig, because there he was, storming into the emergency room. He was pushing people aside and bellowing, "Where is she?"

When he spotted Bader, he barreled over to him and grabbed him by the lapels and picked him up out of the chair.

"What the hell did you do to her, Von Vechten?" he growled.

Bader raised his hands and shook his head, letting himself go limp in the older man's grip, half fearing and at the same time half hoping that Mr. Craig might just go ahead now and pop him one, hit him hard enough to knock him out. To slip into unconsciousness just then would have been a relief.

But Mrs. Craig's quiet voice intervened. "Archie, please," she said, so softly that the other people in the room, who were staring at Mr. Craig and Bader, turned instead to look at her, and they craned to hear what it was that she would say. She took her hand away from her mouth to reveal her ruined smile.

And at that moment the whole room seemed to have stopped moving. Everybody was locked into position, as if they were all of them frozen there in their places, and the sudden silence roared like rushing water in Bader's ears. Mr. Craig's breath was thick with the smell of bourbon, and his face loomed so large and close that it filled up Bader's whole field of vision. It was only after he'd opened his fist again and let go that the normal sounds of the hospital resumed — a baby crying, an old man moaning, a woman coughing.

Mr. Craig allowed his wife to pull him off Bader. He turned away then, rubbing his hands on his jacket, and went striding off to find his daughter, directing the brute force of his wrath and fear, like a big wind that bends the trees, toward anyone and everyone who was brave or stupid enough to stand in his way.

Mrs. Craig collapsed in a chair, looking just as lost as if she were an abandoned child. Ashen-faced, dull-eyed, stunned and exhausted, she looked like one of Katherine's old dolls, its body worn, soiled, ragged and frayed, but lovingly costumed in an expensive outfit of brand-new dress-up clothes.

Because, there in the emergency waiting room at All Saints Hospital, after midnight, on the night of Katherine's stunning fall, Libbie Craig was dressed in a neatly pressed navy blue linen suit, with covered buttons and a round white collar, a straight and seamless skirt with a kick pleat at the back that showed off the snowy lace hem of her slip, and blue and white spectator pumps. She would have been in bed already, Bader thought, sound asleep, with her husband snoring, flat on his back beside her, when the phone call from the club came and jangled her awake. And she'd listened to that thin, distant voice on the other end telling her that there had been a terrible accident, that her daughter was involved and had been quite badly hurt, head injury, broken leg, a fall of some kind, that Katherine was unconscious, that she'd been

taken to the hospital in an ambulance, and Mrs. Craig's second thought, after that first choke and groan of sharp fear,
had been, "Oh my God, but I'm a mess." Because all that
she'd had on then was some little mint- or salmon-colored
nylon nightie and cream on her face and plastic curlers in her
hair.

Hanging up the phone, she would have wondered, what
would she wear? How was a lady like herself supposed to
dress for an emergency like this? What could she put on that
would be right for a trip to the hospital in the middle of the
night? And the first thing that Mrs. Craig had come to was
this suit, which she'd taken out of her closet last night and
laid out to wear in the morning when she went to church.
She'd washed her face and brushed out her hair and pinned it
up, and she'd slipped into those dressy clothes, with the end
result that now she looked strangely formal and out of place
there among all those other ordinary victims and common
family members in their bare feet and their slippers and their
sneakers and bathrobes and unbuttoned shirts.

"Mrs. Craig?" Bader croaked.

She stood up and looked at him, bewildered, with her head
cocked and her eyes sparkling. Then she leaned toward him
and took his face in her hands, and she kissed him.

"Katherine loves you, Bader," she said.

He felt her breath brush against his cheek, rustling in his
hair, warm, moist, and foul, like browned lettuce or gray
meat or wet bread, and he had to rear away.

*   *   *

At the cottage, standing in the kitchen, in the blackest hour
of early morning, Bader blinked back the painful glare of the
unshaded overhead light, thinking that maybe he could draw
out some kind of a comfort for himself from the abiding
sheen of the waxed floor, the warm, yellowy wood of the
pine cabinets, the scrubbed surface of the tiled countertops,

and the bright, enduring glint of the chrome on the refrigerator and the dishwasher and the stove.

When he looked down at his hands he saw that some of
Katherine's blood was caked in the creases of one of his
knuckles, ground in around the edges of a fingernail, as black
and thick and crumbly as dirt. He could just about imagine
Wolfgang Von Vechten standing here, just this way, in this
cottage, at this sink, with Horace Craig's body laid out on
the floor behind him, its head torn apart by a blast from the
barrel of the boy's shotgun. Wolfgang washing his hands,
and then turning to roll the body up in a blanket, drag it out
onto the porch, bump it down the steps to the yard, come
back in to sop up the blood, the gore — a fluff of gray clinging to the rug like lint, white bone glinting, black blood
gleaming, sticky and wet — scrub the floor, find a rope,
climb up onto the table, and jump.

Bader shuddered, and he struggled out of his coat. He un-
knotted his tie, and when he went to roll up his shirtsleeves,
he saw that their crisp white cuffs were stained, too, spattered
with a delicate fine spray of Katherine's blood. He turned on
the water in the sink, and he let it run hard and hot while he
soaped up to his elbows, lathering his hands and scrubbing
his nails and the backs of his wrists and his arms. Then he
peeled off his shirt — it stuck to his skin, damp with his
sweat and the summer's humid heat — and he lathered his
belly and his shoulders and his chest. He unbuttoned his
pants, he stepped out of his shoes, he yanked off his socks,
and he was standing there naked, sponge-bathing his body,
sudsing up and then splashing himself clean. A puddle of
soapy water spread out on the floor at his feet; bubbles slid in
sheets down his legs; steam billowed up from out of the sink.
The water was so hot that his skin was flushed and reddened
as he washed himself, determined to get rid of every speck of
Katherine's blood as well as all of his own sweat and grime
from his hair and his creases and his dimples and his pores.

And still his mind was screaming, crying out, "It was not my fault!"

Outside the windows, the sky had begun to brighten with the sunrise, to become again its unrelenting cloudless summer blue. Naked — his skin so pale that he might have been transparent, as shapeless as a mist, unreal and insubstantial — he crossed from one side of the cottage to the other. His bare feet slapped the floor and left behind him a track of wet prints. He stood in the frame of his front door and looked out through the screen at the turmoil of the summer woods and the glowing eastern sky beyond. He studied the gentle filigree of ironwork flowers and vines that decorated the porch railing, and he knew how sturdy and solid and enduring those blossoms were — how delicate they looked, how intricate and complicated and fine, but they were not soft and they were not frail. And he sent out a wordless prayer for Katherine, wishing that she would be strong, hoping for her health, and that she would recover, longing for her eyes to open, for her to awaken and, unaltered and unblemished and unbruised, come to.

*   *   *

The window in the living room was broken; the crystal ashtray lay on the floor amid a bright sprinkle of broken glass. Without Katherine in it anymore, the cottage seemed to Bader to be unbearably empty and, at the same time, impossibly small. Alone, he tripped over chairs and knocked into walls. He reeled in the doorways, staggered from one room to another, hunching, stooped, feeling clumsy and awkward and slow.

Washing dishes, he knocked a bowl against the hard edge of the sink, and it shattered in his hands. He dropped a heavy china platter on the floor. He had no strength. His legs wobbled. His hands felt weakened and feeble; everything seemed to be slipping from between his fingers, sliding out of his grip and out of his control, but then when he turned the handle on the faucet in the bathroom, he pulled it around too far, and it came off in his palm.

He started in the kitchen, and he moved through the empty cottage, methodically, from one room to the other, straightening, tidying, opening up all the windows to the night. He unhooked the chain and threw the bolt on the back door. He opened the curtains and turned off all the lights, except for the lamp over his desk, and when he sat down at his typewriter, the racket of the nighttime wood sounds came to him in full force. The rasp and scrape and squeak of crickets and tree frogs and toads, the hum of the cicadas, the low soft call of an owl far up in the highest branches of a tall tree.

And there was Wolfgang again, skulking in the woods, holding a box of matches, a can of kerosene. He set fire to one of Horace Craig's houses. Smoke rose. Flames crackled. Children screamed. The blaze was visible to the farmers who stood out in their yards to see it, from miles away.

And dreaming this, recreating it in black words on white paper, Bader didn't hear the scuffle of Lee's feet on the porch outside, and he didn't know that the boy was there with him, watching, until his slim shadow fell across the page, and then, when he looked up, there was Lee, at the door, a silhouette outlined, his shoulders and neck, his hair, his lank, slim body.

Bader had been working barefoot and shirtless. The night was warm and muggy, and even with all the windows open, the cottage was hot.

There was a bottle of scotch on the table. And a glass, with ice, melted.

Lee had come inside. The hinges on the screen door creaked. He'd fingered the pile of manuscript pages, leaving a smudge in one corner of the title sheet. He'd touched the lip of the bottle of scotch. He'd picked up the glass, run his

finger over its rim, made it sing. He'd taken the pack of cigarettes, shaken one free, lit it, exhaled smoke, and smiled.

Was that how it began, then? With just that simple thing?
Had the boy put his hand out, handed the cigarette to Bader?
Had he come up behind him to read what he'd written? Fire,
smoke, wind, flame. Had he touched his shoulder? Had he
leaned closer to see, in the lamplight, his own shadow as it
played across the page?

Bader was standing. He'd turned. He had hold of Lee, and
he was lifting, hefting him up, with a groan, into his arms.
Carrying him, he felt the bones of the boy's back against the
inside of his wrist. Lee's long arm was thrown around Bader's neck, his hand clasping, holding on. Lee's cheek was
pressed against Bader's chest.

He was standing at the window, in the bedroom, a pale
silhouette in the darkness. And Bader was a darker shadow,
looming, looking out.

Lee's belly was flat, trembling, quivering. There were
long, straight hairs growing in the hollow of his chest. His
ribs were sharp.

Lee's hand was on Bader's knee. His fingers roved. Lee's
hair fell forward into his face. His eyebrows seemed to glim-
mer.

While Katherine was enclosed, kept like a rare butterfly in
the gauzy safe cocoon of the darkened room on the third floor
of All Saints Hospital. Bader sat in a chair beside her bed. He
held her hand, and he traced the features of her face, over and
over, with his eyes.

While Lee stood with his back to Bader, studying his own
reflection in the long mirror on the back of the closet door.
He wrapped one arm around his chest, crossed his feet,
clasped his own shoulder with his hand, raised his eyes to see
that Bader was watching him, smiled.

While a wall of Venetian blinds, half closed, laid down a

delicate pattern of black and white lines across the hills and the valleys of Katherine's inert limbs.

While Bader's hands moved over the mound of Lee's hip, pressing the delicate soft skin, kneading the harder muscle underneath.

Katherine, lost in a pitch-black blindness all her own.

Lee, his head thrown back, his throat sinewy, thick, exposed. His hair curled against his neck. His eyes closed, his lips parted, his throat gurgled, his lashes like feathers, stirred.

And Mr. Craig was in the corridor outside Katherine's room; he was shouting, angry with the nurse who was asking him to leave. Because he was drunk. Because he wasn't making things any easier for anybody. Because he was in the way.

Lee's clothes were in a heap; they might have been a body, huddled on the kitchen floor. Bader's big shoes, polished leather loafers, sat next to Lee's torn canvas sneakers, laces hanging, tongues lolling.

Lee, shuddering into the press of Bader's hand.

And the doctors huddled in the hallway, talking in hushed voices, discussing in whispers. Their eyeglasses flashed in the light. Their lips moved, forming words, like bubbles, that floated off — subdural hematoma, edema, intracerebral hemorrhage, lesions, seizures, coma. Death.

Lee sat at Bader's desk, in the straight-backed chair, and Bader stood behind him, and the small silver scissors snickered in his hands. Blond hairs fell, like rain, like snow, they stuck like slivers on Lee's bare shoulders, they caught in the creases behind his ears, they clung to Bader's fingertips. Bader leaned forward, whispering, blew them, dusted them away.

Katherine's head was cradled on a pillow, shaved smooth, cracked like an egg under a turban of wrapped bandages.

Bader awoke in darkness to find Lee's gray eyes, close up, watching him, a vast, bottomless void into which he himself might fall, lost, and disappear.

He came home from the hospital and heard the shower running. He looked into the steamy bathroom to see the boy's shadow moving, like a moth trapped in a lampshade, against the white shower curtain.

Red blood blooming on white gauze.

Lee wearing one of Bader's suits, standing in the doorway, with his shirttails hanging, suspenders dangling, barefoot, smiling.

Clear, cold, sugary liquid dribbled into Katherine's veins, from glass bottles, through plastic tubes.

Lee's sounds, cries and whimpers, mewling, mingling with the crickets' creeching and the squeaking of the bats.

Lee standing in the doorway, wearing a pair of Bader's trousers; they hung on his hips, below his bare belly. One hand, in his pocket, jingled change.

The gleam in Lee's eye. His crooked smile. The dimple in his cheek.

And Bader sat in the hospital room, holding Katherine's hand, listening to her breathing, the brush of a nurse's shoes as she passed by in the hall, the dimming of the light under the door, flickering, the neon floating in through the window, and Katherine's face white, shining, cold, as still as a moonlit drift of frozen snow.

* * *

Inside the clubhouse, in the Men's Grill, in a leather chair under a lamp by the window in the corner, sat Archibald Craig. His face was a huge, round, livid moon, wreathed in a yellowy cloud of cigar smoke — with heavy jowls, a balding crown, and reddish-gray tufts of coarse hair that bristled out around his ears. His glasses, thick-lensed, in tortoise-shell frames, had slid down onto the purplish bulb of his nose, and he peered over the tops of them, his eyes glittery, small and moist and mean and dark. His thin lips were pulled tight across the nubs of his gray teeth in what was, for him, a smile. He held a folded newspaper on his knee, and his hand was curled around a glass of bourbon and ice, more ice now than booze. His name was called, and a waiter brought him the phone. Mr. Craig turned, took it, listened for a moment, hung up, put the phone on the floor, and sat back. He picked up his newspaper, and he slapped it against the leg of his chair, hard. The card players all stopped, shielding their hands, and looked up at him, but seeing his face, streaked with tears like a rain-washed rock, they quickly glanced away. He rattled the ice in his glass until the waiter heard him and came and took the phone away and brought him another drink.

*   *   *

Mrs. Craig, waiting for her husband to come home, sat on the flowered cushion of a white wicker chair, in the dark, on the screened porch at the back of her house on Edgewood Road, and she sipped at her second tall glass of cold vodka and tonic and lime. One thin strap of her summer dress had dropped off over her shoulder. Loose skin hung from the backs of her arms. I look like a chicken, she thought, and she hated what she had become. She avoided her reflection; she ducked away from it. Tonight her hair was done up with bobby pins. She'd taken off her shoes and was barefoot; her toenails were polished, and she sat in the chair and swung her leg, admiring the long arch of her foot, wiggling her pretty toes. She rolled the cool glass over her forehead. The ice clinked against her teeth when she drank.

She looked at her watch, trying to make out the time in the darkness, and then looked out through the screen, hoping to catch the gleam of Archie's headlights as he turned into their drive.

When tears welled up, unexpectedly, in Mrs. Craig's eyes, they startled her and made her breathless with surprise. She wiped them away quickly with the back of her hand.

"Dammit," she whispered. "Dammit."

Moths threw themselves at the screen. Outside, on Edge-wood Road, the streetlights flickered on. Mrs. Craig stood up to walk. She moved through her house, from one room to another, looking at her things. There was a picture of Katherine in a frame on the piano. Mrs. Craig caressed it with her fingertips, put it back, moved on.

*　*　*

The night was cool, and the sky overhead was clear of any clouds, bright with stars and the creamy shimmer of a new crescent moon. Bader sat in a chair outside on the porch of the cottage, staring at the woods until he saw Lee. The boy was a bit of brightness that emerged from the dark, climbing up out of the shadowy yard, blooming between the trees, beyond the fence. He was a boy in a cotton T-shirt and blue jeans. He climbed up onto the porch.

He looked at Bader, studying his pale, shocked face, his sunken cheeks and bloodshot eyes and the grizzle of day-old beard that he hadn't bothered to shave.

And Bader told him. He said, "My wife is dead." And he saw Lee's small smile flicker at the news. Bader shook his head, snapped it, wagged it hard, from side to side. Lee reached past him, picked up the bottle of scotch that was standing on the floor near his feet. Bader's shoulders twitched, and he made a move to stop him, but he was slow and clumsy, and Lee pulled away and cradled the bottle close to him, smiling mischievously and shaking his head.

He unscrewed the cap, took a quick swallow, gasping, then handed it over to Bader.

Lee dabbed at his mouth with his fingertips. Bader rolled his head against the back of the chair and closed his eyes and he whispered, without turning to Lee, without looking at him, as if his voice might reach him without having come from him. "I'm sorry, Lee."

He heard the boy shift, the floorboards creaking, the squeak of his shoes.

Bader's head was pounding. Lee leaned against him. He slid his hands up over Bader's shoulders, and he wrapped his arms around his neck, and brought his face forward, toward him, close to his. He pressed his lips to his throat, and Bader could feel his own pulse beating against the soft pressure of the boy's kiss. He held himself perfectly still, frozen, his eyes closed, smelling Lee, drinking him in.

"No, Lee," he whispered, struggling.

Lee had slumped to his knees next to Bader's chair. And his hands were on Bader's legs, moving. His fingers were up inside Bader's shirt, fluttering, his hair was against his belly, tickling, his mouth was moving over him, as Bader strained and rolled his head against the back of the chair, gripped the bottle of scotch in his hand, squeezing it, while the boy's narrow shoulders hunched and shifted and rolled.

*   *   *

Mudd lay in bed, staring at the ceiling, listening to the familiar rasp of Roy's breathing, matching it to her own. She turned on her side, propped her head on her elbow, and watched him. He was on his back, his eyes were closed, he was asleep. She got up, rocking the bed. She went into the bathroom and dampened a washcloth. She swiped her face and the back of her neck with it. Her big hips rolled like boulders under the shiny nylon of her slip as she moved to the window and peered out. She could see a light from the Von Vechten cottage up on the bluff behind her house, twinkling in the trees. A car had pulled up off Bell Road and was passing through the open gate at the edge of her yard, but Mudd could see that it was too big to be Mr. Von Vechten's black convertible. It was ponderous and dark, rocking in the ruts. It was a bad sign, she thought. Mr. Von Vechten's wife must have died. She turned to the bed again, and she sat down at the edge of the mattress. She placed her hand on Roy's belly, laid it flat against its soft rise and fall. She could feel the pounding of his heart, beating deep inside him. He opened his eyes, and when he saw her hovering there above him, he smiled.

* * *

Archie Craig's car crashed up the rugged dirt road, and his headlights splashed light across the face of the cottage and the forms of Bader and the boy beyond the wrought iron railing of the porch. Lee reared away and pressed himself into the shadows against the cottage wall. The big car stopped, rocking on its chassis in the yard, and Mr. Craig climbed out. His hair was mussed; his pant legs were crumpled and creased. He walked slowly toward the porch, dragging his feet heavily up the steps. Lee wiped his mouth with the back of his hand and watched Mr. Craig with narrowed eyes that darkened from gray to black. Bader, looking at his father-in-law, was seeing Katherine there in his face, as if he were carrying her inside of him now, hidden away.

Archie Craig was drunk. He stumbled, then sat down heavily in the chair next to Bader's. He leaned forward with his elbows on his knees and let his head hang between his shoulders for a moment before he straightened and sat back.

"She's dead, Bader," he said. His voice was low, his words elongated and softly slurred.

Lee stood back, in the shadows, tensed and wary, watching.

Bader stared at his own hand, clasped around the neck of the scotch bottle, wondering if it might begin to disintegrate, his flesh dry up, his muscles atrophy, his skin wither down over bones that cracked, shattered, crumbled to powder, dissolved to a fine, gray dust, gathered up into a swirling cloud

that thinned and vanished and was swept entirely away. Mr.
Craig reached over and pulled the bottle away from him. He
threw back his head and took a long swallow, gasping.

"You think maybe you wanna sell this land now, son?" he
growled, swinging his arm wide to take in the sweep of the
yard and the nearby woods. "Hell." He brought his hand
back, slammed the bottle down on the floor beside his chair.
"The Von Vechtens and the Craigs," he said. He laughed,
coughed, choked. "Now this." He turned awkwardly in his
chair, full around to look at Bader's white face. "That what
it was, then, son? A payback, was it? Some kinda fucking
family pride?"

He noticed Lee, then, standing in the shadows behind
Bader. Saw his face shining in the dark. Saw Bader's open
shirt, his hand splayed out over his lap. He shook his head,
as if to clear it, looked at Lee again, and then lunged out of
the chair toward Bader. He grabbed his shirt and pulled him
up to his feet. Bader struggled against him, trying to duck
away and wrench himself free, and Archie brought his fist
back and slammed it into Bader's face. Bader toppled back
away, stooped over, holding his head in his hands.

Lee had slipped sideways into the cottage, and he came
back out again with the shotgun hanging from his hand. He
brought it up to his shoulder and moved up behind Mr. Craig
to hold the muzzle pressed up into the heavy folds of flesh at
the back of the older man's neck. And Mr. Craig brought his
own hands up. His knuckles were bloody. Sweat rolled into
his eyes.

Bader lifted his head, and he saw Lee, he saw Lee's gray
eyes, and he knew what the boy was doing, what he meant
to do, what he would do, and he told him, he said, "No, Lee,
don't, put the gun down, Lee, no."

But Lee looked back at Bader and his eyes were gray,
deep, empty, bottomless; he held him; he drew him in, and

Bader gasped, choking on blood, and reeled, and Lee blinked
once.

"It went like this," he said, and then he squeezed the trigger, and the night brightened as the boy's shoulder was
jerked back, jolted by the sharp kick of the shotgun's thunderous blast.

Lee drew himself up, and he stepped away, out of the
light, into the shadows on the porch again. Mr. Craig's body
had been thrown against the wall; now it was slumped down
on the floor. Most of the head was gone. Bader was splattered
with gore, blood and flesh and bits of bone.

"That's how it was," Lee said again.

He turned and walked slowly down the steps, with Wolfgang's shotgun still hanging from his hand, and he crossed to
the Mustang, and climbed inside. The ignition screamed, the
engine coughed and caught, and the headlights came on,
skimming the grass as Lee rolled the car forward and swung
it around the yard, pulling up close to the porch again.

He leaned out the window, with his elbow on the door,
toward Bader. "Now you can write about it, Bader," he said.
"Now you know."

Bader, trembling, moaned.

He heard Lee's cry then — it was a high, thin keening, a
shrill, rising wail. And he heard the movement inside the car
— it was a jostle, like the frantic flapping of a bird, trapped,
throwing itself against the sides of its cage. Lee had shifted
the Mustang into gear. He'd released the brake, and he
stepped on the gas, and the car shot forward; it bounded over
the lawn, fishtailing and then straightening, skidding at an
angle, tires spinning as it turned to crash through the split-
rail fence and careen toward the opening in the trees. The red
of the taillights was like blood splattered out over the grass.
And then it seemed as if the Mustang had begun to fly; it was
airborne; like a solid black bird it soared upward, off the bluff

and then it banked, leaning, and it rolled, tumbling, in slow motion, gracefully, in a gentle long slow loop. It broke through the brush, and then, in a shower of sparks, the Mustang slammed into a tree, and stopped.

Bader hurdled the fence and ran down the path, slipping on the dirt, slapped by leaves and branches, his hands and his face still sticky and warm and wet with his own blood and Mr. Craig's gore. The Mustang's headlights were skewed, like crazy eyes, pointing up and down. The air was filled with a smell of smoke, burned rubber, and black exhaust.

Bader slumped to his knees in the grass. He pulled Lee toward him, folding himself over the boy, cradling his broken body in his lap. He tugged at the thin cotton fabric of his T-shirt, desperately straightening it. He plucked at the torn flesh of Lee's face, at the hanging flap of his pale, white skin, trying to smooth his features back into place over the tangle of bloody muscle and the sheen of bared bone.

Roy came crashing up the path through the trees. Mr. Craig was a headless dark form huddled on the porch. The moon shape of Mudd's white face rose over the ridge, as she huffed up the road. Darcy trailed along after her, ghostlike and small.

Bader cradled Lee in his lap, hugging him close to his chest. He rocked back on his haunches, and he staggered up to his feet, and as the Mustang exploded into angry flame behind him, he bore the boy's lifeless body in his arms.

THREE

I N THE EXTRA BEDROOM AT THE END OF THE HALL-
way upstairs, the morning sunshine has been enhanced
to a blinding white brightness by the outside world of
snow. It streams in through the window, and bathes
Bader Von Vechten with a wash of light and stinging heat.
He's drawn up from the depths of his feverish sleep by the
steady drip of water as ice melts and snow dribbles, into the
gutters and down the drainpipes, off the tree trunks and the
branches and the twigs, the telephone poles and the electrical
wires, falling like a soft, cold drizzle outside. A large block
of sticky snow slowly separates and, hissing, it slides down
the angle of the porch roof, sags off the edge of the eaves,
slips over the gutter and crashes to the ground with a dull,
soft, solid-sounding *whoomp*.

Bader cracks his eyes open, and the sunlight is a sudden
sharp razor slice of blinding pain. He's been sleeping here like
a baby, curled up on the small single bed, tucked in under the
faded interlocking scraps and shapes of a handmade crazy

quilt, with his knees bent and his feet folded and his hands pressed together flat, tucked under his cheek. When he rolls over onto his back, the metal bedsprings loudly creak, complaining at the awkward shifting of his weight. He squints up at a ceiling that's bright with the dazzle of white sunlight reflected off the snow outside and beamed in through a window in the far wall of the room.

Bader smacks his lips and waits patiently for some memory to come back to him, for the world to fall into position again and settle in place. The air seems filled, abuzz, twinkling with sparks of light, black and red circles that swirl and float before him, bits of dust that drift and spin, like atoms spiraling through space.

He turns his head to see the green string fringe on a lampshade that he doesn't recognize. The wallpaper — a pattern of thin stripes and tiny flowers — is not familiar. His mouth feels mossy, sticky, and dry. His lips are cracked and chapped, and his throat is scorched and raw. The muscles in his neck and shoulders are cramped and sore, and his joints ache. He thinks he can feel the hard, sharp edges of his bones scraping and grinding inside him, rubbing painfully against each other, when he moves. He straightens his legs, and his knees pop and crack. He shakes his head from side to side, rolls his shoulders, flexes his fingers, stretches his hands.

He sees that there is a pair of shoes — his own brown leather loafers — arranged side by side on the floor near the foot of the bed. He wiggles his toes inside the stiffened funk of his socks. A coat — his own tan trench coat — has been thrown over the back of a small upholstered chair. A hat — his own black felt fedora — is sitting on the seat cushion, like a cat curled up. There's a rag rug on the floor; like the quilt that covers him, it's many-colored, handmade, woven together from scraps and leftover pieces of worn cloth.

Bader groans and arches his back. He swings his feet over

to the floor and sits upright. His head swims and throbs. He's dizzy. His pants are rumpled, and one cuff has pulled up over his calf, baring his leg — hairy, white, blue-veined — above the top of his sock. His shirt has come unbuttoned and un-tucked; its tails hang and lap against his legs; its fabric is thin and soggy-feeling, cold and damp with his sweat. He squints at the window on the far side of the room — sheer yellow curtains, ruffled at the edges, and beyond them, brightness, blinding and white.

He begins to move slowly across the room, one step at a time, one foot forward, then the other, like an old man or an invalid. The stillness and the silence of the house seem to be holding him in a sort of a suffocating embrace. He stands at the window, shading his eyes, squinting against the bright white glare, and he looks down at the figure of a boy, with a shovel in his hands, and on his head an odd, old-fashioned, worn leather hat, with its flaps pulled down over his ears. The boy's breath comes out like pale, white puffs of smoke as he works, rhythmically shoveling snow, scooping and scraping and throwing it against the building drift that's piled up at the side of the drive.

Bader pulls his coat off the back of the chair, and, hugging it against him, swaying, he pats it with the flat of his hand, searching its pockets for the flask that he finds, plucks, shakes. He unscrews the top, takes a drink of whiskey, swirls it in his mouth, gargles, swallows, drinks again. He steps backward and slips his feet into his shoes. He unfolds the coat and shrugs it on, pulling the belt together and knotting it at his waist. He picks up his hat, and he's turning toward the door when he sees that Darcy is standing there, and she's been watching him.

"Hi." Her voice is high-pitched and soft, like somebody whistling in his ear.

Holding his hat in one hand and his flask in the other,

Bader looks at her blearily. "Hi." He squints, his eyes burning. He swoons and leans against the chair again, to steady himself.

She's dressed in a pair of faded, torn blue jeans and a white T-shirt under a bottle green V-neck man's sweater. Her arms are folded over her chest and around her body, as if she's trying to hug herself, or to hold herself together. One small foot, delicate-looking in a blue wool knit slipper, is crossed over the other.

"You're up," she says, her face unsmiling, her tone flat, words clipped, so it sounds as if she might be scolding him or cursing him or accusing him of some crime. She unwraps her arms and brushes one hand through her hair.

Bader doesn't know what to say. He tucks his flask back into his coat pocket. He looks over at the window behind him for a moment, desperately, as if it might be something that he can use as an escape — dash back toward it, throw it open and climb out onto the roof, jump off and run away. He's turned to look at Darcy again. And all he can do is shrug. And all he can come up with to say to her now is his name.

"Bader," he says. "Bader Von Vechten."

She wags a hand, dismissing him, and cocks her head, and she flashes a wry, lopsided smile that lifts up one corner of her mouth and draws the other down. A vaguely familiar smile, it stings him. She's moved out of the doorway toward him. She seems to glide into the room, soundlessly, with a minimum of movement, until she's standing right next to him, so close that he can smell her — lavender and burnt toast, he thinks — and she's tipping her head back to look up closer into his face.

"How are you feeling?" she asks. She reaches up and touches his forehead with her fingertips. "Any better?"

He squints at the sunlight that seems to be radiating outward from behind her, so bright now that it's sharply painful, jabbing at his eyes so his head has begun to ache in earnest now. When he coughs into his fist, his chest hurts, and he can feel something thick and sticky and hot come up from his throat into his mouth, so then he's fumbling awkwardly in his coat pocket for a handkerchief, which he finds and pulls out and spits into, embarrassed and disgusted with himself.

Darcy hasn't taken her eyes off him. She watches him, waiting, he thinks, for him to say something, to explain himself. He folds the handkerchief, stuffs it back into his pocket, clears his throat, and looks at her, trying to keep his gaze focused frankly on her face and his trembling hands still.

"What are you doing here, Mr. Von Vechten?" she asks.

"I came back to . . . ," he begins, but he's lost. His gaze has slipped down, he's looking at his feet, his mouth is working, but, no words. What? He's come back to what? To see this place again? To say he's sorry? To tell her that he loved her brother? That he never meant for anything to happen the way that it did? That he was just as much a victim of the circumstances as anybody else? That it wasn't his fault? If Roy hadn't . . . if Katherine had . . . if Lee weren't . . . ? That Bader had never meant for anyone to be hurt?

But none of these words come out. He can only shake his head. "I saw a boy," he says. He shrugs.

Her eyes are hard. "You chased him. You scared him."

"I thought he was Lee."

"He wasn't Lee."

"No, of course not."

"Lee's dead, Mr. Von Vechten."

"I know that."

"The boy you saw is my son. His name is Cort."

Darcy reaches out to put her hand on Bader's arm, and she leads him away from the door, turning him toward the window again. Bader looks down at Cort, who's still shoveling snow in the driveway, but truly all he can make out is the blinding sunlight.

Darcy has moved to the bed, and she's begun to strip the mattress, yanking off the damp sheets and the blanket, snapping off the pillowcases, dumping the quilt onto the floor at her feet in a heap.

"So, I guess you must have got my letter after all, then," she says. She stops and turns to him, her arms loaded up with a rumple of dirty linens.

He's crumpling his hat in his hands, squeezing it hard, trying desperately to hold back the sudden wave of loss and loneliness that's swelled up, unwanted, unbidden, unrestrained in his chest, hitching his breath.

"Yes," he says.

"You didn't have to send us money, you know."

Darcy has shifted the pile of bedding in her arms. She tugs at the corner of a pillowcase that's begun to slip free.

"I know," he says. He feels a movement behind him — the faintest gentle stirring in the air, the softest quiet rustle of fabric sliding over flesh, and when he turns to look, he sees that it's Mudd.

She's a huge, dark shadow looming in the doorway of the little bedroom. Her face is a blank, her look is placid and empty, and Bader wonders whether she knows who he is. He puts out his hand, awkwardly, trembling, and he introduces himself.

"Bader Von Vechten," he says foolishly, feeling ridiculous, and the syllables of his own name seem to catch in his throat, so he coughs.

Mudd is staring at him, her gaze unbroken, and he begins to feel that she isn't seeing him at all, but is looking past him, or through him, at some other person, someone behind him, maybe beyond where he stands. He jerks his head around and sees that there isn't anybody else, only Darcy, with that crooked smile still playing on her face.

And now he can see, too, that a sparkle of tears has come

brimming up into Mudd's eyes. She blinks twice, and they spill over onto her cheeks.

She turns then, and she ducks away. Her steps are shuffling and slow, like someone who is laboring under the weight of a great burden, massive and clumsy and awkward to bear. Her hips move heavily beneath the checked pattern of her housedress. She's wearing a shapeless sweater, its wool matted and pilled, with twines of cabled stitching down the front and the back. A plastic barrette is clamped in her hair; short curls, like dull brown feathers, lie against the folds at the back of her neck.

He listens to the scuff and plod of Mudd's footsteps as she moves away, along the hallway to the stairs and down, deliberately, step by step, slowly, one hand slapping and squeaking against the wooden railing, the fingertips of the other whispering over the surface of the wall.

"I better go," he says, squeezing his hand into the hard ball of a fist and rocking back on his heels. "I'm sorry, Darcy. I shouldn't have come back here."

Darcy's face looks tired. "Have something to eat first, why don't you?" she says. Her eyes are shadowed; parallel lines cross her forehead, long and deep. She reaches for Bader, and her fingers brush his, burning him, as she takes his hat and sets it down on the bed. She steps behind him and pulls off his coat, and he follows her downstairs.

*   *   *

Darcy serves him steaming chicken soup in a white china bowl. There's a straw basket filled with muffins that she's made. There's butter heaped in a custard cup. There's milk and hot black coffee and a jar of Darcy's own homemade raspberry jam.

And there is Darcy herself, seated in the chair across the table from him, watching wordlessly while he eats, her chin in her hand and her gaze fixed on him. He sits hunkered over his meal, awkward, a muffin slathered with butter and jam in one hand and a spoon heaped with broth and bits of meat and vegetables in the other. Slurping and chewing, gulping milk, he eats quickly, ravenous, surprised at how good it all tastes, at how hungry he is, feeling like a bum, some skid row vagrant, a beat-up old drunk in a mission bread line, but too hungry to do anything about it, too grateful to care very much.

"What'll you do now, Bader?" Darcy is asking, when he's finished, when he's dabbing at his lips with the napkin that she's given him, when he's raised his head, finally, to look at her, sheepishly, she thinks, his face boyish, fever-flushed, eyes crystalline, icy blue and bright.

He smiles, shrugs. "I don't know," he answers.

Cort blusters into the kitchen from outside, shaking the snow off his shoulders, and stomping it out of his boots.

"Cort, this is Bader Von Vechten," Darcy says, and Cort looks up at Bader and smiles, mumbles hello.

He takes off his parka and hangs it on the hook behind the door. He pulls off his hat and his gloves, and he drops them near the heat register, on the floor. He opens the refrigerator door and takes out a carton of milk. He pries the top open, tips back his head, and he drinks. His Adam's apple bobs in his throat. There's a Craig Dairy logo printed on the side of the carton.

Cort's upper lip shines with a white milk mustache. He licks at it with his tongue first, and then he takes a swipe at his mouth with the back of his hand.

"Use a napkin, Cort, for heaven's sake," Darcy scolds him.

He looks at Bader and, smiling, shrugs. "So, are you the one that wrote that book?" he asks. He turns to his mother. "Is he?"

Darcy sees the tremor that's begun to shudder through

Bader. His body is trembling, his hands shake. The china on the table rattles as he shivers. His face is slick, drenched in a hot, slimy sweat. Darcy, alarmed, rises from the table and comes around to help him. She puts out her hand and touches him, she skims her fingers across his brow, she leans over and presses her lips, soft as flower petals, against his forehead.

"You're warm," she says.

He closes his eyes. He laughs, coughs, sneezes. He's embarrassed, it seems. His face is hot and red, both with the fever of the flu and with his humiliation and shame.

"I don't know what's wrong with me," he croaks, rubbing his eyes.

But Darcy's taken hold of him. She grasps his arm with both her strong hands. "You aren't well," she says. She helps him up to his feet, and she's leading him out of the kitchen, through the front of the house, into the living room.

And there, in an embossed silver frame, on the spindly-legged table next to the sofa, is a framed photograph of Lee. There's his white face and his blond hair. His gray eyes. That slanted, mocking smile. His head tipped to one side. His back straight, shoulders squared. His hands, long fingers intertwined, folded on one knee. His feet, planted side by side, on the floor.

Bader gasps and reels backward, closing his eyes as if stricken, as if he's been punched, as if he's met with the wildest swing of Roy Kimbel's flailing fist, until Darcy steps quickly past him and scoops the picture up from the table. She opens a drawer and deftly slips the frame inside. Bader's mind is singing *Leland,* it is humming *Leland,* it is buzzing *Lee.* And when he looks again, the picture is, mercifully, gone.

*   *   *

Darcy leads Bader upstairs to the bathroom at the far end of the house. She sets a bundle of clean clothes and a folded towel down on the counter by the sink. She bends over the claw-foot iron tub, turns on the taps, and holds her hand under the faucet, letting the water run hot and steamy over her fingers, testing its temperature. She sprinkles bubble bath from a box and it suds up, a snowy, white, fragrant foam.

She smiles at Bader then, and backs away. She slips out the door, pulling it softly shut, and now he's alone, squinting at the sheen of white ceramic tile and porcelain and polished chrome.

The wallpaper is printed with a red and white and blue design of ships and anchors and ropes. There's a pile of magazines in an old tin milk box — with the Craig Dairy logo printed on the side, its letters chipped and worn away. Bader stands at the sink for a moment, regarding his own reflection in the mirror — the ragged tangle of his hair, the shadowy stubble of his beard, the bleary redness of his eyes. He takes up a tube of toothpaste, and brushes his teeth with his finger. He splashes a handful of cold water on his face.

He turns off the taps and steps out of his damp, soiled clothes. He climbs awkwardly into the bathtub, slipping on its slick bottom, coming down into it with more force than he means to, so that the soapy water laps out over the top and puddles on the tile floor. The tub is too short for the length of his body — to sink his shoulders under, he has to bend his legs. His knees are islands in the foamy water, and his feet seem far away and separated from the rest of him.

He leans his head against the back of the tub, and he listens to the sound of water dripping from the tap, watches the ripples rolling outward, the bubbles bobbing and floating. In the window hangs a pair of white lace curtains and beyond them there is only the thinnest shell of blue, blue, cloudless, clear sky.

*   *   *

When Bader comes into the kitchen, later, Darcy is standing at the sink, washing dishes. She turns when she hears him, and for one frightening moment she sees a man in work pants and a blue cotton shirt. She sees the big paint-spattered boots on his feet. Her heart begins to race, she reels back, as if she's been slapped. She has to grab hold of the counter to steady herself. Oh, she thinks, he isn't dead, after all.

But this isn't her father, brought back. It's only Bader Von Vechten, dressed in Roy's old clothes and smiling at her, sheepishly. She pours two cups of coffee and sets the steaming mugs down on the table.

"I hope you're feeling better," she says.

He picks up his mug, blows on it, and sips it, then peers at her, leaning forward toward her, his eyes probing hers.

"Where's your husband, Darcy?" he asks.

"He left," she answers. "Before Cort was born."

Bader pulls the silver flask out of his back pocket and splashes some whiskey into his mug. "I'm sorry," he says, but she's raised up her hand to stop him.

"It was a long time ago. It's okay." She tosses her head and reaches for her coffee. She takes a sip and it scalds her mouth, so hot that it brings tears to her eyes.

*   *   *

It's twilight on a Sunday night. Bader Von Vechten is sitting in the living room in Roy's chair, wearing Roy's clothes, playing a game of gin rummy with Cort. He's smoking a cigarette and drinking a glass of scotch over ice. Roy never played cards, Darcy thinks, smiling, reassured. And he didn't smoke, and he didn't drink scotch. She tallies up these differences between the two men, as if she were keeping a score.

"Gin!" Cort exclaims, grinning, laying down his cards.

Bader squints at him and frowns. Darcy puts her hand on Cort's shoulder, feeling its warmth and how it twitches at her touch. He turns to her and smiles, and she tangles her fingers in his hair.

"I love you," she wants to tell her son, but she bites her tongue, for now. Later, she thinks. I'll tell him later, when we're alone, when it's quiet, when he's listening, when he'll hear.

She picks up the book that he's left lying out on the table — *Wolfgang's Empire* by Bader Von Vechten. Its cover is glossy and dark — a tangle of trees and bushes and weeds closing in on the outline of a small, dimly lit house. The title page inside has been signed, inscribed "With all best wishes from the author," followed by the lavish signature of Bader Von Vechten's name. On the dedication page a single line reads, "To the Memory of Leland Kimbel." The photo on the back cover is of a younger Bader, posed against the iron porch railing up at the limestone cottage, his face serious, mottled with sunshine and shade.

"You might as well stay over here again tonight, Bader," Darcy says. "Tomorrow, I can take you back out to the Estates to get your car."

He looks up at her, and he nods. "That would be fine," he says, his voice trembling. "Thank you."

*　　*　　*

Night has closed in, dark, moonless, warm with new spring. The branches outside the guest room window are silhouettes, fingering the windless sky. And the sounds of this house rise and fall in Bader's ears, with the clear comfort of water spilling over rocks. Footsteps. A voice. A faucet turned. Water streaming through pipes. The clatter of the dinner dishes being cleared off the table, brought to the sink to be rinsed and washed. Music, and a pounding steady rhythm that thrums from the speakers of the stereo in Cort's bedroom downstairs, traveling through the walls of the house, pulsat-

ing in its posts and beams like the throb of blood against
bones.

Bader lies on his back in this bed, sleepy, dozing, his fever
gone, and his belly full, after a meal of Darcy's meatloaf and
green beans and mashed potatoes and rhubarb pie. A smile of
satisfaction is curled on his face.

He hears the squeak of the floorboards in Darcy's room
across the hall now, so he knows that she's come upstairs.
She walks from the closet to the bed, to the window to the
dresser. She must be getting ready to turn in. Cort has school
in the morning. Tomorrow is another day. She'll have to be
up early to wake him, fix him breakfast, see him off. Her
door creaks open, the bathroom door thunks shut, there's a
whoosh of water, running.

Bader thinks of Darcy in there — first, he remembers her
as she was, a young girl just beginning, that summer, to
bloom, and then he pictures her as he's seen her now. She'll
be scrubbing her face, brushing her teeth, combing the tangles out of her hair. She'll be stopping for a moment to look
into the mirror, her eye caught by the shift of her own reflection; she'll be studying what she sees there, frankly, without
affectation or artifice or pose. He can hear the slap of her bare
feet against the damp tile of the floor.

Her father would have killed him, once.

Bader, in his bed, turns, and drifts. He forgets how nice
these cool sheets feel against his skin. He remembers standing
at the graveside — his shoes wet in the damp grass, his nose
bandaged, his eyes blackened, swollen almost shut — watching while they lowered Leland Kimbel's casket into the
ground.

Everybody thought he'd been a bad influence on the boy.
They blamed him for what had happened, without even
knowing just how much his fault it really was. They believed
that it was his stories about Wolfgang that had turned Lee's

mind to the madness that allowed him to kill Archie Craig and then himself, in the end.

Bader had tried to go back to the cottage again afterward — driving a rented car, silver, with four doors and a hard top and an automatic shift — but he'd found that the gate across the road up to his cottage had been posted with threatening signs — NO TRESPASSING! PRIVATE PROPERTY! KEEP OFF! — and chained and padlocked shut.

He had gone to the Kimbels' then, and Mudd had let him in, she'd brought him through the house to the back, and there was Roy, in the kitchen, into his third whiskey shooter already, down to the last can of his first six-pack of beer. He was a shadow in the darkened room, alone.

"I loved him," Bader had said, and Roy had stared at him, confused at first, and then he'd pushed himself off from the table and Bader, frightened, had staggered up to his feet and backed away — because Roy was a greater threat; he was more real, more serious, more deadly, than Archie Craig had ever been. This man would kill me, Bader thought, and Roy had roared, he'd bellowed, a monster. He'd howled, "What?"

Bader's confession had come boiling up out of him, burning hot and white, and Roy, propelled into motion, had raised his big fist up with a wide, slow, graceful arc and brought it down hard on the table. He'd reeled, and, groaning as if his body were racked by some excruciating pain, Roy had pulled his fist back, whirled, jerked his elbow, and swiftly punched the glass window in the back door, with enough force to shatter it like cracked ice. Bader had stood frozen, paralyzed, unable to move. Roy was swaying from side to side, like a bear. And then he was on Bader, pummeling him with both fists, in the face, the ear, the belly, the chest. Roy rocked and swayed. And Bader fell. He crumpled. He sank to his knees, and then Roy was kicking him, with his steel-toed boots, his arms up in the air, his foot swinging, thunking into Bader, sinking into his side, his stomach, his back, and Bader, curled up on himself, dissolved and disappeared.

"Do you want to press charges against him, Mr. Von Vechten?" they'd asked him later, two men in dark blazers, one with a green and red striped tie, the other in a crumpled pink shirt, the two of them standing together by the side of his hospital bed, one asking him questions, the other one taking notes. But Bader had shaken his head, closed his eyes, winced.

"Of course I don't," he'd answered. "No."

Bader had signed the deed to his land over to Mrs. Craig, then. He'd taken a motel room out by the airport in Cedar Hill, and he'd finished his book there: it had ended with a boy, fifteen years old, who'd murdered a man, and had tried to bury him in the woods. Who had taken a rope and looped one end around the highest crossbeam in the cabin's ceiling and the other end over his own head. He'd climbed up onto the table, and he'd leaped away, hard and high. His neck had snapped. His toes had brushed the floor. His body had turned and swung.

*   *   *

Darcy, leaning on the bathroom sink, bends toward the mirror and traces with her fingertips the lines that have become a part of her face, on her temples and her forehead and at the corners of her mouth. She pokes at the spongy softness of her chin, and she prods the pouches under her eyes.

One Saturday afternoon not very long after James left her, before Cort was born, Darcy went into Cedar Hill to see a movie by herself, and after the lights went out a man came into the theater and took the seat beside hers. In the dark that day, with Cort fluttering in her belly and James disappeared, her loneliness had seemed a big hungry thing that might well up and swallow her whole. She sat there, holding herself perfectly still. She didn't turn to look at him, but she could smell this man who was sitting beside her. She could hear him breathing and feel how warm he was, and large. First, his shoulder innocently and carelessly brushed her arm. She heard him murmur, or clear his throat, and then his hand was covering hers on the armrest. She allowed him to press his knee against the side of her thigh. He brought his arm down around her shoulders, he touched her throat with his fingertips, and then he leaned over her, his breath hot in her face, and he pulled her chin toward him, and he kissed her. He touched her teeth with his tongue; his mouth tasted like popcorn and mints. He reached his hand up under her sweater and cupped his palm around her breast. He grazed his fingers across her stomach, slid his thumb down into the waistband of her jeans. And then, when the movie was over and the house lights had come back up again, he was gone.

Darcy thinks she might go back to her room right now, and she might climb up into her bed. She might turn off the light and lie in the darkness and wait. And maybe Bader Von Vechten will be thinking of her, maybe he'll come to look for her, and maybe he'll find her there. In the dark, she wouldn't have to see his face. In the dark, he wouldn't have to know what she looks like or even be sure of who she is. She could be anybody he wanted her to be, she could be nobody at all, in the dark. And then, in the morning, when the sky began to lighten again, when the sun came up and brightened the windows, then he could go away, he could disappear, burned off like a mist. He might have been a dream, for all she'd be able to remember of him, and she wouldn't ever have to look at him, she wouldn't have to know who he was, she wouldn't have to see his face, to look into his eyes, and she might not even know his name. It just might be as if it had never even happened at all.

*　*　*

At the other end of the hall, in her own bedroom, Mudd is rummaging through her closet. Wire hangers chatter in her hands. The heavy buckles of Roy's belts clang together as she pulls them down and slings them over her arm one by one. Mudd has begun to gather up all of her husband's old clothes — she's dragging out his plaid shirts and his white T-shirts, his overalls and his dungarees, she's bundling them up in her arms, and she's carrying them across the room. She's throwing them out the window, into the yard below. She watches each piece sail away from her, floating downward like a swirl of falling leaves. His heavy shoes thunk against the ground and bounce and roll away. One shirt has drifted, and it's caught on the bony twigs of a bare tree branch, its arms outspread. She lobs the lopsided balls of his rolled-up socks and tosses the crumpled wads of his underwear, the clumps of his sweaters and his sweatshirts, the stiff slabs of his suit jackets and pants. His hats — straw, felt, wool, suede — sail. His ties lap the air like tongues. The pile has begun to build up on the wet ground below Mudd's bedroom window.

And in the far back corner of the closet she's found a small bundle of Roy's old dirty laundry, and she gathers it up into her arms, and she hugs it against her body, she buries her face in it, reviving him in her memory of how he used to smell, rocking on her heels, back and forth.

Mudd Kimbel has become a swamp, she is a bog, she is the mire into which all her memories and all her affections have been submerged and sunk. Roy emptied out Lee's room like this after he died. He hauled off all of her son's things — his furniture, his clothes, his books and magazines, his old toys. He carried his mattress out of the house, and he put it in the back of the truck, and he drove it down to the river, and he shoved it off the embankment into the water. He used a stick to push it out, away from the shore, and it was carried with the current, floating, turning, rolling, spinning away.

Mudd saw it later, in the shallows downstream, snagged on
an old fallen log, half swallowed up by the river's muck, its
flowered pattern spattered and dirtied and blackened with
slimy mud.

* * *

Darcy, asleep, dreams of James Mackin, and in her dream
he's traveling, he's rolling over a long, thin filament of white
roadway, through cornfields and hay fields, pastures and
meadows, over hills and up mountains and into valleys,
crossing streams and creeks and rivers, circling ponds and
lakes, winding, turning, circling back, and James is moving
away from her, forward and forward, and on and on, farther
and farther into the distance until he's smaller and smaller, a
dab, a dot, a speck. And then finally, nothing. Like smoke,
he's gone.

* * *

Mudd is standing in the yard near the high pile of Roy's stuff.
She's spattered it with lighter fluid. She has a box of kitchen
matches tucked down in the pocket of her dress. She takes
pleasure from the sounds — the chirp of the crickets in the
bushes, the pounding of her pulse in her head, the whistle of
her own breathing in her chest, the scrape and snap of a
match head struck against the edge of her thumbnail, the poof
of each small, delicate flame. The crisp scent of leaves burning reminds Mudd of some time when she was a little girl,
working beside her father in the yard. A whisker of smoke
unravels upward, it snakes and twines and swirls.

Small brief flares have flickered into bigger, stronger
flames. They move together, gathering as one great strong
force, building up around the pile of Roy's clothing, leaning
toward the trellised apron of the front porch, sparking against
the brittle thin slats of wood.

In the firelight, shadows turn, wrestling with each other, dancing and writhing, they squirm away from Mudd. The smoke has blackened and thickened; roiling, angrily, it turns and twists. It rises up like a specter resurrected, it surges, the ghost of a past revived. Of Wolfgang Von Vechten or Horace Craig. Of Margot or Katherine or Archie or Lee. Or Naomi LeSage. Or Ridge Hamilton. Or Roy.

As the fire builds, bits of burned cloth are carried off, wafting upward like leaves, they turn and twirl and float away and seem to vanish in the sky. Bright flames are reflected in the clear flat glass of the windows.

They lick the steps and lap the porch railing like water rising. Smoke curls. Flames have leapt onto the bushes, they crackle through the dried branches. They follow a strand of ivy upward toward an open window. Wind ruffles a curtain; the flames touch it and catch it, they grab hold. The fire climbs toward the sky. Smoke billows.

* * *

Cort, on his stomach, twitches in his sleep. He's dreaming of his grandfather, dreaming that he's running from Roy, and then he's running with him, and then he's running while Roy drives the pickup truck alongside him, hanging out the window, urging him on, with a whoop, a grinning face, his hand out, fist waving, horn honking, and people have crowded up to the roadside to see — they hail him and shout out his name and cheer him on.

What draws him forward is the smell of smoke. He follows it. And the sound of his mother, screaming. And the voice of a bonfire that's blazing up from the front yard, rippling the air, shattering the windows with the appalling force of its heat. Cort sinks deeper into his sleep, breathing smoke, and he dreams of fire, of heat, of ashes, of grasses burning, of flames roaring upward to engulf him, his house, the city, the whole planet ablaze, whipped by wind, and an anger that crackles and shimmers and flares.

*   *   *

A film of ash swims in the sweat that coats Bader's skin. The fire's light seems to caper in his eyes and stroke the smudged features of his face. He stumbles in the unfamiliar dark, through the smoke-filled house, down the hallway, down the stairs, around the corner, through the kitchen to the boy's room at the back. He breaks through the door by throwing his shoulder into it. He gropes into the room with his hands outstretched, blind, tripping over clothes, shoes, magazines, and books, until he finds the bed. And the boy is there, unconscious, and Bader reaches for him, he puts his hands on his body and he pulls him close, he lifts and carries him in his arms.

Darcy in her white slip in the yard looks up to see Bader, a huge shadow in the doorway, with the body of a boy in his arms — limp, hands hanging, head thrown back, throat bared, legs dangling, bare feet.

Bader is gasping, gagging; tears are streaming down his smudged face; he bears the boy in his arms, and he stumbles out of the house onto the porch, down the steps, into the yard; sobbing, panting, gasping, he lays Cort on the grass, and he kneels next to him, he hovers above him, his hands move over him, he brings his face down onto him, and he breathes into him, and he brings him back to life.

And, overhead, the sky has exploded with rain.

*   *   *

If a boy of fifteen has time on his hands — nothing to do, nowhere to go, no one to talk to, everybody else too busy or too tired or too lazy or too dull, no one to call on, no one to see, at the short end of a long, dull autumn afternoon, too cold to be summer anymore, too warm still for snow yet,

after lunch, before dinner, not hungry enough to think of
anything good to eat, not tired enough to be dozy, too restless to read, not ambitious enough to want to do any work
— if he has the time he might take a ride on his bicycle, he
might pedal out beyond the easternmost edge of Empire,
toward the flared outskirts of the city of Cedar Hill. He might
search the farthest dark corner of the oldest lost section of the
Cedar Hill Memorial Cemetery, and he may be lucky enough
to find there, amid a snarl of dried weeds, beneath a blanket
of blown leaves, whatever there is that still remains of the
murderer Wolfgang Von Vechten's grave.

A youth — fifteen, too old anymore to want to be thought
of as the child he has been, too young to seriously expect that
anyone might begin to treat him now like the man he will
become — pedals his bicycle along the hump and dip of a
narrow gravel road. His tires churn up a cloud of dust. He
rides standing up, with his butt waggling and his chin jutting
and his elbows angled out. His legs pump with a strength that
seems mechanical, almost, an endurance that he has learned
to expect and take for granted in himself.

The boy's body is gangly with adolescence — he hasn't
finished growing into the length of his feet in their hightop
black sneakers, laces untied and trailing like the streamers that
he once attached for decoration to his handlebars, or the
spread of his hands, rolled fists, thick-knuckled and hard. His
shoulders have begun to broaden and the muscles in his arms
to swell, but his chest is narrow, his belly is flat, his hips are
still fragile-looking and slim. He has a rock in his pocket
that's shaped like a toe, a gleaming silver marble, a stick of
chewing gum, a box of matches, a bent baseball card, thirty-
eight cents, and the lozenge of a lubricated rubber, bought
for a buck from a machine in a gas station bathroom,
wrapped in red and purple and gold foil. There's a film of dirt
on his neck and behind his ears, and an accumulation of grime
squeezed in under his nails. A line of fuzz has begun to darken

the ledge of his upper lip, down has thickened into hair in his armpits and on his belly and his legs, the skin on his forearms retains the last remnant of his summer suntan. There is still a spray of freckles splattered like mud over the bridge of his nose. There is a crack in his voice, and a cluster of pimples has begun to fester on his brow.

It's getting late on a shortened autumn day, and the boy has turned his bicycle toward home. The sun is low and cool in the sky, a chill has begun to creep into the air, and the wind is stirring — it tosses the piles of leaves in the bottoms of the ditches that drop away from the gravel shoulders of the road. It aches in the boy's ears, it yanks at his clothes and tugs at his hair, until, breathless, he's come skidding to a stop in the middle of the bridge that arches up over the creek.

The boy has been told that Wolfgang's ghost still haunts Empire to this day. Why, only last week, the outline of a youth was seen hovering between the trees at the edge of Old Indian Woods; what hunter hasn't claimed to have heard the echo of screams roaring through the underground maze of limestone caves? An apparition has been said to prowl the paths of the Cedar Hill Cemetery after dark or to roam the verges of the parkway or to wander the fields, lost, disoriented, crashing wildly up and down between the rows of ripened corn.

This boy has been warned, what kid hasn't? Everybody says so. Stick together. There's safety in numbers. Don't go down to the river. Stay off the old bridge. Keep out of the woods. Steer clear of the caves. Stick with your friends.

The boy leans forward, with his elbows on the handlebars. He straddles his bike, and he peers out past the rickety railing of the bridge, beyond the rush of water over rocks, toward the shadows that cluster between the trees. Is anybody there? He squints. He's holding his breath now. Does he see a shadow moving, or is that only the turmoil of branches thrown by a panting wind? Does he hear the crunch and crash of footsteps in the brush, or is it only the hard hiss of the water rolling through the rugged bottom of the creek? A furtive rustle in the weeds? Warm breath whispering in his ear?

The boy has turned, and he's begun to run his bike over the arch of the bridge. His shoes churn against its wooden planks. Face flaming, heart lurching, he's running for his life, he thinks.

Every demon that ever disturbed his sleep, every creature that ever concealed itself beneath his bed or at the back of his closet or in the corner of his basement, under the attic stairs, behind the dining room drapes, every misgiving, each self-doubt and bit of self-hatred, all his guilt and all his sins are gathering together in the trees, they're congealing in the shadows, breathing down his neck, roaring in his ears, reaching out to touch him, looming at his back. The bike under him wobbles as he follows the long slow slope toward Empire, pedaling as hard and mighty as he knows how, until he's reached Bell Road, and he's turned. Now he soars, he sails, he flies. And he rides on, without stopping, all the way home, until he skids into the dust of his own driveway, and, dragging one foot, he coasts to a stop. He throws his leg back and lets the bike slide out from under him. It bounces onto the yard; one pedal bites the yellow grass and kicks a divot out of the packed black dirt. He's breathing hard — with effort and with relief — because he's ridden hard, and because now he's home. He's made it. He's seen no ghosts. He's met no psycho killer from the movies, with a chain saw or a hatchet, no armed robber from TV, with a nylon stocking pulled down over his head to distort the rubbery, flat features of his face, no thick, dark shadow of a hitchhiker, with the gleam of a knife blade jutting from the pocket of his palm.

The arch of a spigot pokes out of a hole in the limestone foundation at the side of the house. When he turns its round knob, he hears a moan and a complaining grumble rise up from deep inside the pipes before a stream of water trickles, then pours out, splattering the rubber and canvas of his shoes, kicking up dust and a thin, brown soup of mud. He bends and slurps at the warm water. Its rusty taste aches in his mouth, like blood. He cups his palms under the faucet and splashes his face, rubs the long tangle of his hair with both his hands, shakes his head hard, spattering moisture, like a misty rain.

He wipes his hands on his shirt and stuffs them into his pockets. He kicks at the rocks in the driveway. He leans back against the side of the house, and now, home safe, he's smiling to himself.

Dusk has begun to creep in from the woods, and it rises up from the ground, fingering the shrubs and the bushes, like a thick, dark fog. He shivers; he feels the chill. He's leaning against the clapboard wall of his house — its flank still holds some of the heat of the day, and it's warm and huge behind him, like some gigantic, breathing beast. Soft light spills out from a sunken, leaf-filled window onto the grass near his feet. It flutters with the shadow of someone moving past it — his grandmother, downstairs in the basement, doing the laundry.

He knows there's an old refrigerator down there, too, under the stairs, and that it's filled with bottles and cans of cold beer. He can only hope that she won't have some reason to look inside it, and if she does, that she won't notice that there's one bottle unaccounted for, one bottle gone. She'll think that someone else drank it, anyway. She'll never, he knows, allow herself to be suspicious of him.

She'll never guess that he's had the nerve to do something like that, to sneak down into the basement, after everyone's gone to bed. That he's crept down the stairs in the dark, in the cold, in his pajamas, in his bare feet, holding his breath against his fear — not of what might happen to him if he's caught, but of the dark itself and of what ghosts he can imagine might be lurking there. That he opened the refrigerator and took out a beer and tucked it under his pajama top and held it pressed against his bare skin and carried it that way until he was safe, upstairs again, in his room. That he drank the whole thing down, in a darkness that was a comfort to him then, because it hid his secrets for him, and because it was filled with a warm, sweet buzz, like insects flying in a swarm inside his head.

He pushes off from the wall and turns to look up at this house, his home — he studies its serene face, its stony gaze, its implacable windows. Moving around outside it, toward the back door, he prowls the yard; he becomes a shadow in the shrubbery, crunching in the dry grass, craning to peek in the windows at the life that's being carried on inside. A shed looms behind him. Piles of junk are huddled near a rambling, rusted fence that runs along the edge of the woods, down toward the creek, and then rises up again, toward the cluster of the houses in the Craig Estates that are perched up there on the top of the bluff like great, predatory birds.

He steps around the bicycle that he's left lying on the grass, and, on tiptoe, he peers in through the kitchen window to see that his mother is there, making dinner. She's humming as she works. He can see that she's wearing lipstick, and earrings, and she's let her flowered blouse come unbuttoned and open at her throat. He can smell the food — chicken and onions and steamed vegetables and rice — that she's cooking in the covered pots on top of the stove.

He ducks down into the shadows again and moves along toward the back of the house. Four places have been set at the table in the dining room. The light from the hallway spills out through the doorway into the living room, where Bader Von Vechten leans back against the cushions of the old easy chair and reads the news in the evening edition of the Cedar Hill *Gazette*. He's holding a cigarette between his fingers; there's a tremble in his hand, and a crystal ashtray and a glass of scotch and water on the table nearby.

The boy stretches out his arms, and he feels the strength that's begun to grow into his muscles and the hardness that's beginning to creep over his limbs. He feels sometimes as if he might be about to burst out of his own body, like a cicada that's clinging to a tree and cracking out of the confines of its delicate, brown shell.

When the screen door creaks open, the boy sees his mother framed in the rectangle of the doorway, her shape outlined in its cozy light, her hair framing her head like a delicate web. And she's calling out to him, her son, her voice lilting, singing out the single syllable of his name.

"Cort?" Darcy cries. "Come in for dinner now. Can you hear me? Are you out there, honey? Cort?"

And he answers her quickly, he calls out, "Yes, I'm right here."